KILLER SECRETS

KILLER SECRETS

An
Organized Crime
Cozy Mystery

Jackie Layton

First published by Level Best Books 2025

This novel is entirely a work of fiction. The names, characters and incidents portrayed in it are the work of the author's imagination. Any resemblance to actual persons, living or dead, events or localities is entirely coincidental.

Jackie Layton asserts the moral right to be identified as the author of this work.

Author Photo Credit: Kellianne Layton

First edition

ISBN: 979-8-89820-047-3

Cover art by Level Best Designs

This book was professionally typeset on Reedsy.
Find out more at reedsy.com

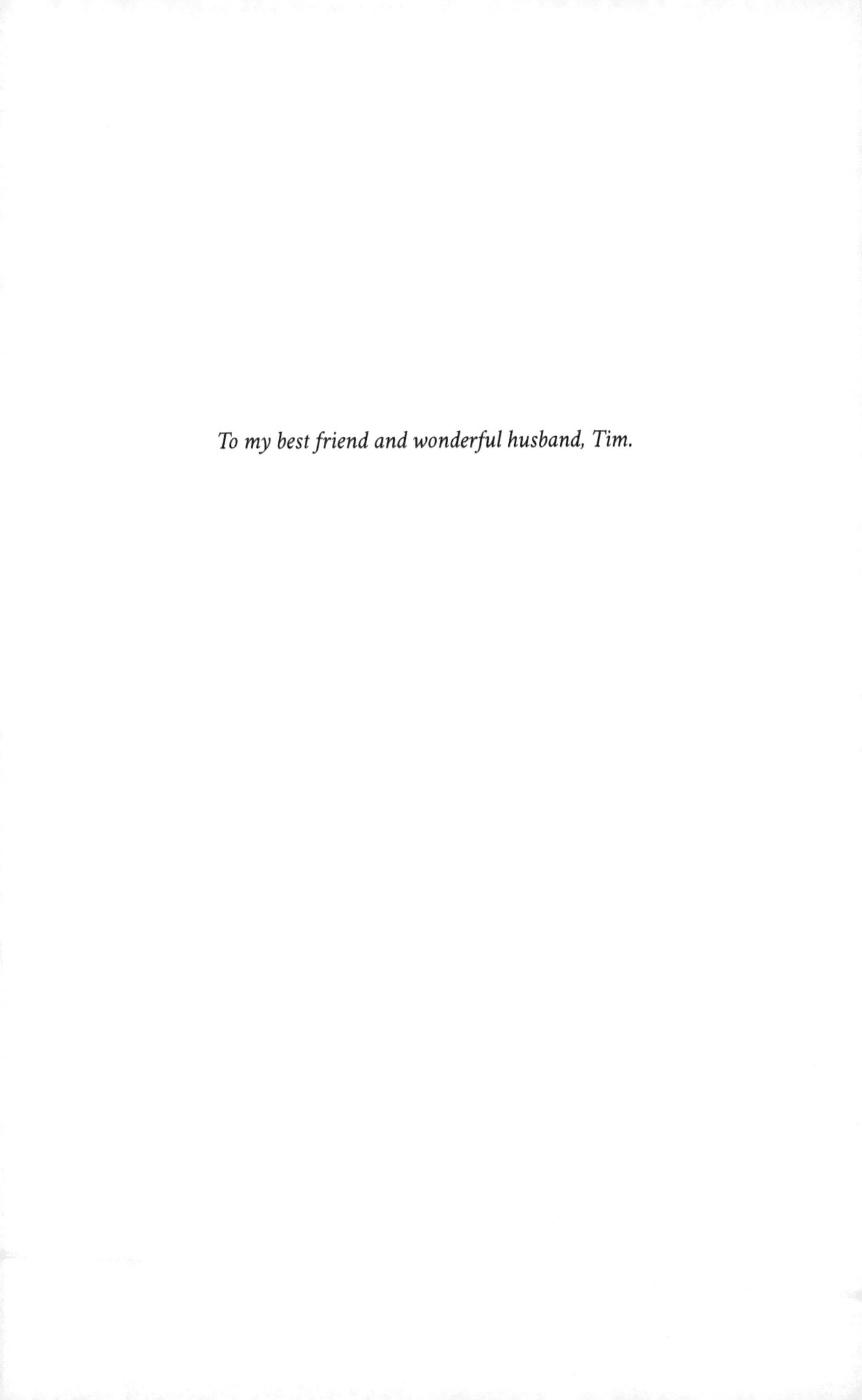

To my best friend and wonderful husband, Tim.

Praise for the Organized Crime Cozy Mysteries

"This is the second in the series and I'm enjoying the adventures of Katie Sloan. I like how she manages herself and when it is best, she's looking for clues to help solve the mystery, especially after having discovered the body. The author did a great job in staging this whodunit with a solid mystery, good clues, and twists to keep me engaged throughout. There is romance in the picture which flows alongside this murder mystery."—Dru Ann Love

"*The Con* starts off with Kate being hired by Ben Hauser the new owner of the historic resort, spa, and golf course. Ben's office is a bit of a mess with stacks of papers and miscellaneous items everywhere. When Kate arrives for their first onsite appointment she overhears Ben in a heated discussion with another man. This is but one of several altercations that Kate witnesses involving Ben all in the same day. These encounters set the stage for why more than one person is tee'd off with Ben and why it is no surprise that Kate finds him dead in a golf cart.

"As with other cozy sleuths, Kate feels like she needs to do something to find the killer or to at least help her brother Paul to narrow down the suspect list. Suspects range from a family member to possible business partner(s) and at least one person with ties to Ben's past. So is the murder a result of a current con or a past transgression? How does the rather expensive coastal guide book figure into this mystery?

"The clues are well organized (Kate is an organizer after all) and the story moves along at a good pace. There are all sorts of cozy aspects from a sweet rescue pet to a sweet romance with high school sweetheart Reid. There are also helpful family members, such as the chief of police, who happens to be her brother, Paul, and it looks like Kate's son, Ethan, has moved to town just in time to try and keep an eye on his mom, or to at least help her with her latest investigation endeavor. This is definitely a page turner with a bit of excitement when you least expect it. I am looking forward to the next Organized Crime Cozy mystery." — Tracie Condie, *Kings River Life* Magazine

"If you enjoy cozy mysteries, you'll want to read *The Con*, book 2 in the Organized Crime mysteries. Kate Sloan is a professional organizer. She's hired to help organize an office at a resort and discovers a body. What can she do but solve the mystery? The setting is lovely and the characters are great. I recommend all of Layton's books. They just get better and better." — Penny Frost McGinnis

Chapter One

My new husband and I stepped out of Shrimp and Grits restaurant and were greeted by a wave of coastal Georgia humidity and the sound of familiar laughter. Down the block was my best friend. "Reid, there's Bess."

"Yeah, but who's that with her?" Reid placed his hand on my lower back. "Should we go say hi?"

"Of course." I swatted at a gnat before walking toward my friend and the unknown man. "Hey, Bess."

Cars were bumper-to-bumper on Ocean Boulevard, and it was only Thursday night. Still, it was tourist season at the beach.

Bess pulled an envelope off a nearby bench and waved it in the air. "Found it."

"Great. What does it say?" The man asked. His sunglasses were attached by a black strap with the University of Georgia football logo on it.

It wasn't like Bess to be rude. Maybe she hadn't heard me. "Bess, hi there."

She turned toward us. "Hi, Kate. Reid. Fancy meeting you here."

Reid gave her a slow, steady smile. "It's a small town."

Her eye twitched, a sure sign she was worried about something.

Reid turned to the gentleman. "Hi, I'm Reid Barrett, and this is my wife Kate Sloan Barrett."

"Nice to meet you. I'm Peter Rodale." A goatee with a mix of gray and black hair framed the tall Black man's big smile. He reached out and shook Reid's hand.

I said, "Welcome to Fox Island. Are you new in town?" I shook his hand next.

He met my gaze. "Bess and I met tonight at a scavenger hunt for couples."

"Oh, that's nice." If Bess fell for this man, I wanted to get to know him better. She was in her early fifties, but she didn't have much experience with men.

Bess held the envelope toward me. "We've been tracking clues, and our prize is in here."

Reid stuck his hands in the pockets of his khaki shorts. "I'm curious to see what you won."

"Me, too." Peter stepped close to Bess. "You do honors."

Bess opened the envelope and held it so Peter could read it, too. "Dinner and drinks at Seaside Hideaway for tonight. Live music by Dwayne Gray. Do you want to go?"

"Of course. It's part of our date. Let's go."

I said, "Bess and I need to catch up. Do you mind if she rides with us? We'll meet you at the resort."

Peter nodded. "I'd never want to get between old friends. See you in a bit, Bess."

"Okay." My friend smiled.

We went to my old Wagoneer, and we were soon seated. Reid turned on the air conditioner.

I twisted around and faced Bess in the back. "When did you decide to start dating? I thought you were interested in Tom Cross."

"I've wasted enough years on him. He's hot. He's cold. He's confident. He's confused. I fall for him, and he backs off. I don't know what his problem is, but I'm tired. My sister suggested I try this event and online dating."

"Oh, brother." Bess's sister had pushed her for years to get married. "There's no rule that says women have to get married."

"I know, but try telling my sister."

Reid pulled onto the street and drove in the direction of Seaside Hideaway.

Bess said, "I'm trying speed dating, websites, and events like this to meet men. Either I'll meet my match, or Ruth will be forced to back off. Tonight hasn't been bad, though."

"What do you know about Peter?" Besides standing too close to Bess, was there a reason for my anxiety? I'd known my first husband for a long time before marrying. It didn't stop him from cheating on me. He'd died years before I moved back to Fox Island, Georgia. One big blessing of returning home was reconnecting with the love of my life. Reid and I had been given a second chance, and I cherished every moment with my husband. "Do not answer that. I have no business judging your relationship with the man."

"Girl, there is no relationship. I only just met him. He seems nice enough, but maybe a little intense." She sighed. "Still, I should give him a fair chance."

Reid said, "Intense how?"

"Peter was determined that we'd find the envelope and beat the others back to the resort. I thought this event was designed to help us get to know each other better and enjoy the experience. He made it more of a competition."

Reid rubbed his chin. "You know what? Katie and I are going to have coffee and dessert at the restaurant by the pool. Might even convince her to join me on the dance floor. If you become uncomfortable with Peter, we'll be around."

My best friend giggled and poked my shoulder. "Your husband treats me like a sister, and I appreciate you all caring. I've got extra tickets for speed dating tomorrow night. It's one of the prizes I won. I'd feel better if you two attended."

"But we're married."

Reid turned into the parking lot. "If Bess needs us, we'll go and pick each other all over again."

"Aw, you say the nicest things." I squeezed his hand and then looked at Bess. "Okay, we'll be here."

"Thanks, guys."

We exited the car, and I studied the full parking lot. "It looks like the Seaside Hideaway is doing well."

Bess said, "It could be due to the dating events. There's an entire weekend of activities."

Peter met us in the lobby. "Oh, there's the most beautiful Bess and her friends."

"Hey. Don't worry. These two aren't going to crash our date." Bess used her best flirty voice with a Southern drawl.

Was she trying too hard, was she attracted to the man, or was she nervous?

"I'm glad to know that." Peter put his arm around Bess's shoulders.

We might not be crashing their date, but I was keeping my eye on them. Bess's inexperience and fragile heart would make her an easy target for a player. With the speed at which Peter was moving, he appeared to be a smooth operator.

Bess raised the envelope. "Are you ready to eat?"

Peter nodded. "I worked up an appetite on the scavenger hunt."

Reid said, "We're going to the back patio to listen to Dwayne Gray and enjoy some dessert. Maybe we'll see you again."

"Sure." Peter turned his attention from Reid to Bess. He pointed out a gray-haired man with a deep tan. "There's Clint. Bess, would you like to show him what we won?"

Bess's eyes widened. "Aren't you going with me?"

"I need to stop by the restroom, but I'll find you at our table for two." He kissed her cheek, and I almost gasped.

Was that a little forward for having just met? What was my problem, other than wanting to protect my best friend? Was Peter legit? Surely the dating company performed background checks. I should give him the benefit of the doubt. "Bess, we can stay with you until he's back."

"That's okay. Clint Speck is the leader, and I should talk to him about my prize. Don't worry about me. My van's here, and I can get myself home."

I hugged her. "We can walk you to your van when you're ready to leave."

Bess laughed. "I know some of Reid's friends call him Bear. Now that you're married, I may start calling you Momma Bear."

Reid nodded. "I like it."

Hmph. "See you later, Bess." I wasn't crazy about the nickname, but I walked with Reid to the hostess station at the outside restaurant. A young lady with a dragon tattoo on her arm led us to a table on the patio where we could listen to music.

We ordered decaf coffee and slices of peach pie with ice cream on top.

I reached for Reid's hand. "Tomorrow morning, I'll need to go for a run and work off the calories I just ordered."

Reid was a contractor and never seemed to have weight issues. He pulled his phone out and checked the work schedule. "I can join you if we get an early start."

"It'll have to be early if I'm going to survive. Getting used to summertime in Georgia is an adjustment." I'd returned to Georgia from Kentucky when I became an empty nester. It was so much hotter than I'd remembered, but it was worth it to live on the island. No matter how much I had enjoyed my time in Kentucky, Fox Island was home.

"Early it is."

A man sat at the keyboard and tinkled the ivories. "I'm glad to see so many happy people here tonight. I'm Dwayne Gray, and this is a love song I wrote in my twenties. Maybe you've heard it."

There was a smattering of applause, and the singer broke into a familiar tune.

Reid pointed to the makeshift dance floor. "It's a shame to see it empty. What do you think, Momma Bear?"

"I've never been good at resisting you, Reid. Yes, to dancing, but please don't call me Momma Bear. Like ever again."

He laughed. "Deal."

We made our way to the designated area, and Reid took me in his arms.

The joy of being married to Reid brought tears to my eyes.

He whispered into my left ear because, thanks to an acoustic neuroma, I was deaf in my right ear. "Dreams do come true."

"That's for sure."

We danced until the waitress tapped Reid on the shoulder and pointed to our table. Coffee and dessert waited for us.

The next couple of hours drifted by with the musician playing rhythm and blues.

One of our favorite pastimes was listening to musicians and bands. There were plenty of venues on the island to indulge in our hobby, without having to drive to Savannah. Living in a tourist town had some nice perks.

At last, Bess appeared. "This singer is amazing."

Reid said, "Yeah, he is. How was your date?"

"He insists on driving me home, and I don't want to hurt his feelings."

I didn't want to nag. "Please, call me when you get home, and Peter is gone."

"Happy to." Bess gave me a quick hug and took off.

Reid stretched. "Looks like we can call it a night."

"Yeah. It's probably a good thing I never had a daughter. I had an easier time raising a son than my friends did with daughters."

"It could be you had a good son."

I smiled. "Ethan has always been a good son."

We paid the waitress, and Reid tipped the musician on our way out of the restaurant area. While walking through the cool, air-conditioned lobby on the way to the parking lot, I saw a distinguished gray-haired man in the shadows. His arms were wrapped around a much younger woman with curly blond hair in what seemed like a friendly hug.

Another man stalked through the lobby and stopped in front of the couple. The first man looked familiar, and I shifted to get a better view.

The woman walked away, but the two men had words.

"Kate, that is none of your business. Let's go home." Reid sounded like a man who'd been dragged into two murder investigations by his wife. "Please."

Oh! "The older man is the dating events leader this weekend."

"Still, none of our business." One side of his mouth shot up in a smile.

He made a good point. I should not be concerned. "You're right. I'm just being nosey. Let's go home."

"Finally."

Soon, we were back in the heat of the night. We walked past Bess's van on the way to my vehicle, and I paused. "Why on earth did she agree to a ride when her van is right here?"

"Relax. She was probably being polite to Peter, and you made her promise to call."

I nodded. "You're right again. There's no reason to worry."

"Unless she doesn't call."

"Oh, you." I gave him a soft punch on the arm.

Chapter Two

Friday had been a busy day working at Let's Get Organized. I'd been too busy to quiz Bess about her date with Peter, but I did confirm she still wanted us to join her for speed dating at the resort.

After work, I took a cool shower and styled my hair into a low, twisted ponytail. It was too humid to try anything else. I slipped into a simple yellow dress and white sandals before joining Reid in the great room of our home. Lady whined when Reid picked up the car keys, so I gave her a treat before we left to make the short drive to the resort.

Hand-in-hand, my new husband and I stepped into Seaside Hideaway to attend the speed dating event with my best friend.

Reid said, "Where are we meeting Bess?"

"I thought she'd be here. The receptionist can probably tell us where to go." I headed for the thin blond at the front desk.

She looked up and smiled. "Good evening. Are you checking in?"

A glance at her name tag reminded me of who I was speaking to. "Hi, Gloria. I'm not sure if you remember me—"

"Yes. You're the professional organizer. It would be hard to forget you." She pointed to Reid. "And you remodeled one of the suites. You're Reid Barrett."

"That's right. It's one of the fastest projects I've ever done." He flashed a smile at her.

She smiled back and appeared to relax. "The new owner is focused on making this place profitable as soon as possible, but I'm sure you've heard all about his goals."

Reid nodded. "Craig Hauser is determined, that's for sure. Say, we're supposed to meet a friend for speed dating. Can you give us directions?"

"There was supposed to be a sign in the lobby." Gloria sighed and leaned toward the man working next to her. "I'm going to help them, and then I'll be right back."

"No prob." The younger guy never took his eyes off his computer monitor.

Gloria did a double-take before focusing on us. "Follow me. I need to discuss the signage with Clint. Um, Mr. Speck runs the dating events."

I scanned the area, trying to see what caught her attention. In the shadows were two people in an embrace, and one resembled Clint. The other had blond hair, but I couldn't see much more. The embrace seemed more like a hug than the display of affection we'd witnessed the night before.

The two people pulled apart, and the man placed his hands on the woman's shoulders. He looked down at her, but I still couldn't see her face.

Gloria shook her head and then took off at a fast clip. She muttered, "If he'd focus on work and not pretty young things, I wouldn't be forced to pitch in."

I struggled to keep up with her in my sandals. "I'm sorry, Gloria. What did you say?"

"Nothing important. Oh, look. There's Diane. She's in charge of registration. She'll take care of you, and I'm going to find Mr. Speck." Off she went.

A beautiful lady with sassy short gray hair stood. "Welcome to speed dating. My name is Diane Field, and I'm one of the leaders."

"Nice to meet you." I shook her hand. "We're meeting a friend of ours, Bess Walker. Has she checked in?"

"Yes. So far, Miss Walker and Peter Rodale are the only two here. But don't you worry, we've got a lot of people planning to attend. Tell me your names."

"Kate Sloan, and this is Reid Barrett." Once the words left my mouth, I felt uncomfortable. Reid and I both wanted to make sure Bess was safe, so we were playing along. But it was still a lie.

"Here we go." Diane handed us magnetic name tags. "I'll explain the rules when it's time to begin. You can go through these doors for happy hour, and the doors to the main room will open at seven. Have fun."

"Thanks." Reid moved to open the door for me.

"Remember to give all the ladies a fair chance, Reid." She shook her finger at my husband.

"If Kate's the best woman for me, you can't stop me from leaving with her." The tone of his voice dared her to disagree, but his expression remained neutral.

Diane cleared her throat. "True, but the purpose of the event is to help singles meet and hopefully form a lasting relationship."

"I understand." Reid waved me into the small room designated for the pre-event.

I gasped. There were dirty tablecloths on the standing cocktail tables. Garbage overflowed in the trash cans. Plates, napkins, and cups littered most of the tables. "Oh, this is a mess."

"I've seen worse, although you'd expect better from this place." He shook his head. "It'd be interesting to know who's responsible. The resort? Or the people leading the event?

"Somebody dropped the ball."

In one corner of the room, my best friend was talking to Peter. I waved to them. "Hey, y'all."

"Hi." Bess met my gaze, but her expression was flat. They joined us in the middle of the room.

Reid shook Peter's hand. "How's it going?"

"If I'm with Bess, it's going good."

He was a smooth one, for sure. "Hi, Peter."

He said, "It's good to see you two again, but aren't you all—"

Bess said, "Shh. It's complicated. Just don't ruin the secret."

"Of course. Anything for you, Bess." He ran his fingers over her shoulder.

A waiter appeared with a platter of sandwiches cut in heart shapes. He looked unsure where to place them.

I pointed to a table with a clean tablecloth. "Maybe that will work."

"Yes, ma'am." He placed the tray on one end and then high-tailed it out of there.

"This room needs a touch of organization. Bess, do you want to help me pull it together?"

Reid frowned, probably realizing he was about to get stuck with Peter.

Bess nodded. "You're exactly right. I'll work on the appetizer table."

"Perfect. I will gather the trash left from the last group." I looked behind a hostess stand and found a white garbage bag.

Four women entered the room, but huddled together near the door. They were probably in their thirties. The shortest lady did most of the talking and looked more confident than the others.

I picked up paper dishes left on standing tables in the back corner.

Had the leaders peeked into the room and only seen what was in front of them? Diane, or Clint, or whoever was in charge, never investigated the condition of the area behind the door. It seemed like an amateur mistake.

Two men walked through the doorway and paused. They looked around the space and headed for the food.

A few minutes later, a bartender joined us, and I walked to his station. "Where can I take the garbage?"

"Do you work here?" He placed two cocktail shakers on the counter.

"No, but I can't stand a mess and decided to lend a hand."

"Thanks. We are short-handed tonight." He pointed to a side door. "Go through there and down the hall. You'll see big garbage cans to your right."

"Thank you." I followed his directions down the passageway.

Voices came from another room, and I glanced in to see if it was in better condition.

The room was arranged with rows of chairs, and two men stood arguing. One was older. He was thin, with gray hair, and slightly stooped shoulders. Oh, it was Clint. The younger man had dark hair and a clean-shaven face. He was taller than Clint but not as tall as Reid.

I continued down the back hallway to the big gray garbage can on rollers. After dumping my white plastic bag, I retraced my steps.

The men continued to argue. Because of hearing loss, it was impossible to distinguish all of the words. But, I was curious and paused near the doorway.

Scam and *proof* were the only two words that reached me.

Oh, well. Unless it affected Bess, it was none of my business. I dashed away. Back in the room for happy hour, I bumped into a person while opening the door. "Oh, excuse me. So sorry."

It was Peter. "No need to apologize. I should know better than to stand by a door." He walked away.

I surveyed the space from where he'd stood. Why wasn't he with Bess? There was a line at the bar, and the room was crowded. People talked, but I couldn't decipher the words. I spotted my husband.

Reid shot me a pained look, standing alone amongst groups of singles.

I headed straight to him. "I'd give you a kiss, but we might get kicked out."

"I get that. It'd be a shame for Diane to lecture me again." He looked past me. "You're not going to believe who just walked in here."

I turned and spotted my twenty-seven-year-old son. He was handsome and kind. I'd never known him to struggle to find a date.

Ethan crossed the room and gave me a one-armed hug. "Guys, this is a singles event."

"We know, but Bess asked us to attend. She's nervous."

"Then, why is she here?"

Reid whispered, "To get her sister off her back. She thinks Bess should be married by now."

"Makes me glad I'm an only child." Ethan shrugged. "It seems like if you're in your early fifties and single, you must be comfortable in your own skin."

Reid nodded. "Exactly. I was content being single until your mother reentered my life. Why are you here?"

"Please, don't start. I'm researching to see if I can pick up tips for working at the rec center. Not here to pick up women. The leader, Clint Speck, only agreed to talk to me if I'd attend. So, here I am. For work." He cut his eyes to me. "Don't try to set me up, Mom."

I raised my hands in defense. "You got it."

Bess joined us. "The table looks much better, and you did a good job of tidying up the place."

Diane entered the room. "People, we'll start in ten minutes. If you need to go to the restroom, now's the time. Again, in ten minutes, we'll move as a group into the official speed dating room."

Bess looked around with a frown. "I invited Allie, but I don't see her."

Ethan said, "I saw her around the pool area. It never occurred to me that she'd attend this."

Bess sighed. "I twisted her arm. I should find her, but I don't want to miss out."

It didn't matter to me if I was late. "I'll look for her."

Reid's eyes widened. "You're not leaving me alone again. We'll go together."

Bess said, "Don't take too long."

We left the group and made our way to the patio area behind the hotel. There was a restaurant, a bar, two swimming pools, and a path to the beach. Dwayne Gray played a rhythm and blues song on the piano, and Allie stood by herself, swaying to the tempo. She didn't look uncomfortable like Reid had in the room. Instead, she appeared content.

"Hey, Allie. Speed dating is about to start."

"Do you know who that is playing? It's Dwayne Gray. Isn't he awesome?" Her focus remained fixed on the musician.

"Yes, he is good, and it's a beautiful night. In fact, Reid and I listened to him play last night. So, I bet he'll still be performing after speed dating."

"You're right, and I don't want to waste the ticket Bess gave me." She brushed her thick, dark hair back. "Plus, the longer I stand here, the frizzier my hair will get. Not that I'm interested in meeting a man tonight. Although I'm not getting any younger."

I blew a raspberry. "Twenty-four? Give me a break."

"Come on, ladies." Reid motioned for us to follow him. "Allie, I didn't peg you for liking Dwayne's jazz."

"My dad taught me to appreciate jazz and blues."

"You don't say. Do you like working for Kate and Bess?" Reid asked.

"Oh, yes. It's been the emotional break I needed from working as an EMT." Allie had taken part in responding to a multi-car crash. There'd been victims of all ages, and the stress had taken a toll on the twenty-four-year-old.

"We're blessed to have you work at Let's Get Organized." I patted her shoulder.

Reid held open the door, and soon we were back at the check-in table.

"Oh, dear. Allison, you're late. There won't be time for you to mingle and have refreshments. Clint is almost ready to begin." The thin woman looked at her watch. "I hate that for you. Maybe you can wet your whistle, but no drinks in the speed dating room."

Allie nodded. "Yes, ma'am. It's my fault for being late, and I'm sorry."

Diane handed her a nametag. "Hurry on in. Have fun, Allison."

We entered the room and walked to Bess, but before we could speak, a hush fell over the place.

"Welcome to Speed Dating. I'm Clint Speck, your host for the evening." The man smiled at the small crowd. "Here's how it will work. Ladies, enter the room behind me first. You'll sit at tables but choose the side with a heart. After you're situated, the gentlemen will enter. You've got five minutes to get to know each other. There are pens and cards, and you can keep notes on your favorite people. At the end of the evening, we'll tally up results and exchange phone numbers of people who are interested in a second date with you." He made air quotes with his fingers around the word second.

Diane appeared beside Clint. "Ladies, please join me in the next room."

I squeezed Reid's hand and then walked with Bess and Allie. This was for the greater good, but I would not flirt. I had no interest in any man other than my husband. My mission was to find a good candidate for Bess. I took a seat beside my best friend. "Relax. I'm going to take notes on guys who might be a good fit for you."

"Thank you. I'm so nervous that my hands are shaking." She placed them on her stomach.

"What about Peter? Are you interested in him?"

She whispered, "He seems nice enough, but I don't see a future with the man. He's kinda obsessed with jewelry. Nice pieces compared to junk. He says I deserve to wear the finest diamonds available. As if I can afford that kind of thing."

Diane clapped her hands. "Okay, ladies. Here come the men."

Allie sat on the other side of Bess. "Shh, you girls are going to get us in trouble."

We laughed at the younger woman, and the set of Bess's shoulders seemed to relax a bit.

Clint led the guys into the room, and they paraded past us before taking seats as directed by Diane.

Reid's face was red, and he looked down at the table.

My heart pinched at the sight of his misery.

Peter was placed in front of Bess. Maybe one of these men would be a good fit for her, but I wasn't sure it'd be Peter.

"Hello, my name is Hank Ingram."

I turned my focus from Reid to the man across from me. He had my full attention because he was the person who had argued with Clint earlier. "Hi, Hank. I'm Kate."

"Good to meet you. We don't have much time. Believe me, I know from experience. Do you enjoy music? I'm a musician, but I pay for my habit by dabbling in the stock market."

"I love music, especially jazz. What's your genre?"

"I lean toward rock. What do you do, Kate?"

"I'm a professional organizer, but tell me more about your music." Something about Hank made me uneasy. This seemed to be a good opportunity to help Bess weed through the riffraff. "Would I recognize your songs?"

"Probably not. Truth be told, I'm better in the stock market. It pays for my lifestyle. Some might even say music is my hobby, and day trading is my real job. You know what I mean? The money maker?" He leaned closer. "I'd be happy to help you make good investments."

Clint played a riff on a saxophone, and we all looked at him. "Time. Gentlemen, move to your right, ladies keep your seats."

Hank grinned. "We'll chat later."

I swallowed hard. Did Clint suspect that Hank would try to help women invest their money? Had that been part of their argument? I sure hoped Bess didn't fall for him.

Peter took Hank's place. "You were lucky to get the worst man in the room over with. You can enjoy your evening now."

That was a shocking start to the conversation. "You know Hank?"

He chuckled. "We've crossed paths a few times. Let's talk about more pleasant things."

"Sounds like a good idea. You know Bess and I work together at Let's Get Organized. What do you do?"

"I own some jewelry stores. Diamonds are my specialty." Peter reached out and took my hand.

My heart raced, and I jerked my hand from his grasp. Had anybody noticed Peter's action? "What do you think you're doing?"

My best friend was listening to the man across from her with a bored expression.

Peter said, "My apologies. It's a professional hazard to notice jewelry, especially diamonds. For instance, your earrings are cute. Not serious."

Oh, my. Bess hadn't been kidding about Peter's focus on jewelry. "They're supposed to be cute. Not that it's any of your business, but I am finished with serious jewelry. You probably would've appreciated the diamond ring my deceased husband gave me." Peter's snobby attitude flew all over me. I placed my hands in my lap and rotated the diamond so only the band showed. My first husband had been flashy, but he hadn't been faithful. Reid might not buy me the most expensive jewelry, but he'd never cheat. I didn't want Peter, or anyone else, to judge Reid's character by the jewelry I wore. Plus, it was a beautiful ring. I loved it, but more importantly, I loved Reid.

His eyes lit. "Can I see your ring?"

"No." Man, he was pushy.

"If you're not wearing the first diamond, perhaps you want to sell it. I offer good prices for—"

"Let me stop you there. This event is for meeting people."

He narrowed his eyes. "Yet, you're married. What's your angle, Kate?"

"Time. You know the drill." Clint brought our uncomfortable conversation to an end and played a bit of a love song on the sax.

Bess and I made eye contact. She said, "Sorry."

I leaned close. "I'm glad you're not alone. He's a real jerk. Oh, look. That's a handsome guy."

Ethan sat across from Bess. "Talk about awkward. Miss Bess, do you mind if we discuss sports?"

She laughed. "College football? What do you think Georgia's chances are this fall?"

I faced the boring man who'd just been with Bess. Oh, boy. But in five minutes, I'd get to talk to my son. Ethan and Reid would be the highlights of my evening.

Out of the corner of my eye, I noticed Peter and Hank exchange cross words and angry looks.

Was Hank a rascal with everybody, or just men? Peter's disdain for Hank was obvious.

Clint played a romantic song until Diane managed to separate the two guys.

My new 'date' cleared his throat, and we began to discuss his fascination with snakes found around coastal Georgia.

I forced myself to smile and tried to appear interested until it was time to switch partners. Never had I been so happy to hear a saxophone.

"Hi, Mom. This is even weirder than talking to Bess." Ethan rolled his shoulders.

"Are you getting any good ideas?"

"I don't think this will work for me unless it's a New Year's Eve event or something around Valentine's Day. Plus, the age differences here are awkward. You're old enough to be my mother."

I snickered. "Very funny."

He grinned. "Seriously, I can't believe you and Reid are participating."

"We're supporting Bess. When we have a break, can you talk to Hank?" I pointed him out. "He was arguing with Clint before this started, and there's something strange between him and Peter. I don't want Bess to get tangled up with Hank if he's bad news. Peter's not anything to write home about either."

"Bad news?" Ethan laughed. "I'll see what I can find out, but it might look suspicious if I'm talking to men and not women at the break."

"Do the best you can, honey. So, have you met any interesting women?"

"Look around the room. This is not my age demographic. Most of the women are closer to your age."

I surveyed the women in attendance. There were the thirty-somethings, but they didn't look like Ethan's type. "Point taken. Allie is here to support Bess, not find men."

He nodded. "Bess has a good support system. That's one thing I like about living in this small town. Is Allison dating anyone?"

"Not that I'm aware of. Are you interested?" I leaned forward to catch every word.

"Mom, please stop. I was thinking about how to attract younger people to dating events. So many people work from home, and the opportunities to meet others are limited. At least we have nice weather in Fox Island to encourage us to get outside. But it can still be challenging for Millennials and Gen Zers."

"Change." Clint ended the conversation and played a jazzy song.

"See you at the break, Mom." He walked to the next spot.

The break came after we'd met all the participants. It felt good to stand, and I lingered behind while others left the room.

Reid waited for me at the doorway. "Hey there. You look like my kind of woman. Would you like to exchange numbers?"

"Ah-hem." Diane tapped Reid's shoulder. "It's too soon to swap phone numbers. This is the time to mingle casually."

"Yes, ma'am." Reid sighed and motioned with his hands. "After you."

I said, "Diane, how long is the break?"

"Twenty minutes." The tall, thin woman's eyes narrowed. "Don't be late."

"Thanks. It seems like a good opportunity to check out the restroom." I left Reid with Diane, but I sent him a text. **I'll meet you outside by the musician.**

Great.

In less than five minutes, Reid and I were swaying to music on the little dance floor.

I said, "I'm so blessed to be with you, Reid. Can you imagine speed dating in the hopes of meeting someone?"

"Nope, and it's hard to believe we're doing it. Some of the women are desperate, and some must have started drinking well before the event." He held me tight. "You can see why I waited all these years for you. Nobody else compares."

My heart swelled with love for Reid. "Thanks for waiting, and I'll never agree to anything like this again. Even for Bess."

"That makes me very happy." He kissed me.

After the kiss, I asked, "How angry would Diane be if we disappeared?"

"You're not going to desert Bess. Are you?"

"No."

The music ended. Dwayne stood at the microphone, "Ladies and gentlemen, I'm going to take a break, but don't go away. I'll be back."

I sighed. "That must be our signal to return before they start looking for us."

Reid nodded. "We're going to come back one night and enjoy listening to Dwayne Gray for as long as we like."

A deep voice said, "I like the sound of that. If I'm not mistaken, you two were here last night."

Reid said, "Yes. We're Reid and Kate Barrett. We'll return when we have more time. Tonight, we've got to meet some friends at speed dating."

The man's mouth fell open. "I would've guessed you two were married."

I smiled. "Can you keep a secret?"

"As long as you didn't commit a crime, I can keep your secret."

I whispered, "We are married."

"Then why?" He turned his hands, palms facing up.

Reid said, "We're watching out for a friend."

"Aw, well now, that makes sense. You can't be too careful at these things. People think I'm on stage, lost in my music, but I observe stuff. Yeah, yeah, yeah. Your friend needs to be careful." He shook his head. "I best let you get back to it. Have a nice night."

"It was good to meet you, Dwayne." Reid shook the man's hand.

"You, too."

We parted ways and rejoined the others in the dating room. Of course, we were the last two, and Diane gave us an exasperated look.

She closed the door and said, "Clint isn't feeling well, so I will finish us out tonight. I don't play the saxophone, but I have a buzzer from a board game. Let's begin."

Bess leaned toward me and whispered, "Clint pulled me to the side during the break. He told me to be careful."

"Did he say more?"

"Not really. He was carrying a glass of ginger ale and sipping on it."

"How do you know it was ginger ale?"

"He told me."

"Why—"

"Shh. We can talk about it later. Diane is frowning at us."

"She's something else." I bit back a smile and faced the man across from me.

It seemed like hours before Hank returned to me, signaling an end to this session. This round had been focused on hobbies.

Hank pointed to my paper. "I hope you put my name on there."

"I'm sorry, Hank. Somebody else caught my eye."

"You know it's best to turn in multiple names. Hedge your bets."

Diane gathered our notes and suggested we return to the mixer room for more refreshments.

Before I could speak to Bess, Peter hurried her to the other room. I looked at Allie. "What's that all about?"

"He asked her for a ride home because his car broke down."

I gasped. "And she agreed?"

"Seems that way." Allie stood. "Should I worry?"

"No, worry isn't good, but I am a tad concerned. The man's basically a stranger to us." Yet, he'd given Bess a ride the night before.

Reid and Ethan joined us, and we left the event.

In the lobby, Allie faced us. "I'm going to try to catch another set of Dwayne Gray's music. I'll see all y'all later."

Ethan said, "Mind if I join you?"

"Oh, that would be nice. But you should know, I didn't put your name on my card."

My son laughed. "I didn't list you on my card either. In fact, I didn't write down any names."

Her eyes glowed. "Me, either."

In my opinion, there were sparks between my son and Allie, but I held my tongue. "Have a good time."

Reid and I walked outside, and a summer breeze caressed my skin. "I should never complain about the Georgia heat. I love it here."

"Do you want to go for another run in the morning?"

"I've got an appointment to get my eyes checked tomorrow."

"It's about time." He opened the door for me but paused for a kiss.

"I sure do enjoy this honeymoon phase of life."

"Hey, we waited too long not to enjoy our life together. I'm going to love you with your new glasses and one day if you need dentures, I'll keep on loving you. The honeymoon will be more than a simple phase."

"No need to worry about me wearing dentures." One of my brothers was a local dentist. "Bobby will never let that happen, even if he tortures me with a mouth full of implants."

"Did you notice that Peter's teeth looked too perfect? There's something off about his teeth."

"There's something off about the man in general. Would you mind—"

"Mind if we track Bess? Call her first. If she doesn't answer, we'll track her."

Chapter Three

"Hello?" Bess answered her phone.

"Hey. Where are you?" Relief poured through me. I hadn't realized how uptight I was about her and Peter being together. She just didn't have much experience with men, and Peter was a stranger. Although, they'd been together for the scavenger hunt before I met him. I was probably overreacting.

"I just dropped Peter off at his vacation rental."

"Are you going home?" At least she hadn't gone into the place with him.

"Yes, so there's no need to worry. Do you remember the TV announcements in the old days when the announcer asked parents if they knew where their children were?"

"Hmm, yes." I glanced at Reid. "She's okay. Sassy, but good."

"I heard that. You've been gone for a lot of years, and I didn't have to answer to anyone concerning my whereabouts."

"True, and I bet you missed me."

"Honey child, I did miss you. Now, leave me alone so I can drive without getting stopped for talking on my phone while behind the wheel."

"Wait, what did Clint say to you during the break?"

"He said that Peter is a player and not to give him money, my heart, or anything else." She yawned. "I'm not used to having an active social life. It's exhausting. See you tomorrow."

"I'm sorry for not trusting your instincts, Bess."

"Friends look out for each other. I understand." Bess sounded upbeat.

"Good night." On the short ride home, I told Reid what Bess had said.

When he pulled in front of the house, happiness settled over me. "I'm so glad you found this place. It would be hard to imagine a better home."

"And the location can't be beat. How do you feel about a moonlight stroll on the beach?" Reid opened his door but waited for my answer.

"It's not even ten yet, so let's go."

"Yes." His smile made me especially happy I'd said yes.

We changed clothes and then walked the short path to the beach. The full moon shone, and the waves gently lapped the shore.

"Low tide. Nice." Reid took my hand in his. "Which way?"

I pointed in the direction of the resort. "Maybe the music will drift down to us. Wouldn't it be cool if we saw baby sea turtles leaving their nests and going into the water?"

"Yeah. I've witnessed it a few times, and we're in the middle of August. So, it could happen."

We talked about nothing and everything as we strolled and dodged waves washing up the sand.

A jogger came our way. He wore black shorts, a black shirt, and a black ball cap.

He waved as he ran past us, but he was gone before we could speak.

Reid said, "I'm not sure I could run barefoot on the beach."

"You probably need tough feet in case you step on shells. That's not for me."

The evening was humid, but we enjoyed our walk.

The jogger returned. "Guys. Sorry to bother you. Have you seen a man with white hair? I can't find my dad."

I shook my head. "You're the only person we've seen."

"Thanks. My dad is Clint Speck, in case you see him. But you probably don't know him. I can't imagine where he is."

"We were at the resort earlier and met your dad. What's your name?"

"Kyle. Kyle Speck." He ran a hand through his hair and looked in both directions. "If you see him, please ask him to go back to the resort."

"Sure, but maybe he's lying down in his room. Diane said he didn't feel well." And Bess had mentioned he'd been drinking ginger ale. I shifted into mother gear. The poor kid seemed distraught. He was probably around Ethan's age, so technically, he was a man. "I'm sure he's okay."

He stopped moving and closed his eyes. "Yeah. Diane told me the same thing, but I thought he may have come outside for fresh air. My gut tells me he's in trouble. It might seem silly, but I gotta keep moving."

Reid propped his hands on his hips and looked right, then left. "We'll keep our eyes open. I'd say we last saw him around eight."

"Okay. Thanks." He ran off in the direction of the resort.

"So much for our romantic stroll." Reid's eyes met mine in the moonlight.

I glanced at the foaming waves as they crashed and rolled up the beach. "Don't you think we should help? Clint wasn't feeling well. What if he passed out and needs assistance?"

"You're right." Reid looked toward the resort. "Let's keep going this way, but we should walk closer to the homes where there are more shadows. It'll be easier to see him if he's in distress."

"I agree. His son was focused on the area by the water." I walked from the firm, hard-packed sand to the fluffier area. It was more challenging to walk in the dry sand, and there were more shadows. "Can I turn on my flashlight? I don't want the turtle patrol to get mad at me."

"They're more concerned with house lights that stay on. The baby turtles get confused and head to the lights instead of going to the sea."

I had forgotten the reason visitors were told to turn off porch lights. "I can't believe it took me so long to come back home to Fox Island."

"It didn't really surprise me. You dug your heels in and continued your life with—"

I rounded on Reid. "Shh. Let's don't talk about my old life. I want to focus on you."

He took a deep breath. "Sorry. I don't know why my mind went there. Let's find Clint, and then we'll get back to you and me."

I kissed Reid before we resumed our search. I shone my light around the dunes without walking on them. We checked the steps and walkways that led to beach houses. We crept closer to the resort, but there was no sign of the man.

Music floated down to us.

Reid said, "We should probably find out if there's a formal search party."

"That's a good idea." We walked past the closed rental stand where guests could get electric bikes, surfboards, and other fun items to use at the beach. We climbed the steps, and I found myself breathing harder. At the top, I looked at Reid. "I've been so happy with you these last couple of months, but I'm gaining weight. It's time to get back in shape."

"We ran this morning, and we're walking tonight."

"Nice point."

A hair-raising scream ended our conversation.

The music stopped.

Chatter ceased at the bar and restaurant.

I looked at my husband. "That can't be good."

"You should call your brother."

One of my brothers was the chief of police. "Maybe it's nothing. We're only thinking murder because of our past experience here."

"True, but that scream was alarming, and Clint Speck is missing."

I called my policeman brother.

"Sis, it's Friday night, and I'm on a date with my wife."

"Sorry to bother you, but there may be a problem at Seaside Hideaway." I paused. "Never mind. I'm probably blowing the situation out of proportion. You and Susie go back to your date."

There was another scream, and Gloria Hardee ran onto the terrace from the lobby. "Is there a doctor? Nurse? We need help."

A sweet voice with a distinct southern drawl piped up. "Maybe I can help."

I groaned. "No. Not Allie."

Reid said, "Maybe you should go with her for moral support."

"Of course." I handed the phone to him. "Can you talk to Paul?"

"Yes. Go." Reid took the phone. "Hey, Paul. We're not sure what's happening."

The conversation faded as I ran to Allie. Once again, my mothering instincts kicked in. "I'll come with you."

"Thanks, Kate." She squeezed my hand.

Gloria said, "Follow me."

Allie and I raced behind her. We ran around a pretty fountain and through the open lobby doors. We continued down a hall past the reception area and into a room.

Clint Speck was sprawled on the floor.

Allie stalled.

"You don't have to do anything, Allie." I rubbed her shoulder and then knelt beside the man. "Gloria, have you called for an ambulance?"

"Yes, there's one on the way."

I placed my fingers on the man's wrist. No pulse. "I don't feel anything."

Allie squatted on the other side of Clint's body. She felt his neck. Her hand moved to his other wrist.

I squinted. His neck looked bruised. Or were the marks only images from bad lighting?

Allie rubbed Clint's sternum.

Time seemed to slow down.

Allie straightened Clint's arms and legs and pressed his shoulders back. "Do you see his chest moving?"

I stared at him. "No."

Allie leaned toward his mouth and nose.

Gloria said, "Where's his saxophone strap?"

Her question didn't seem to fit the situation, but I studied the man. It wasn't around his neck, and it wasn't in his hands. "Maybe it's in one of his pockets, but I'm not going to look. The police could accuse me of tampering with evidence."

"He's okay. He's got to be." Gloria nudged me out of the way. "Clint, this isn't funny. Quit fooling around."

"Move. I need to perform CPR." Allie's voice shook.

We scooted out of the way and watched. At last, Allie fell back on her rump. "He's gone."

"Gone? But he only had an upset stomach. Queasy, he said. I told him to come back here, where it was cool. He can't be dead." Gloria stuck her hands in his pockets and tossed out keys, a wallet, change, and a cell phone.

"I should've checked on him sooner, but we were so busy with new guests."

What was she looking for?

"When did he come back here?"

"After the first round of speed dating. He said that Diane wasn't happy with him, but he felt too bad to lead the second session. That's when I suggested he lie down."

Two firemen ran into the room, and I moved to Allie. "We need to get some fresh air."

She nodded but didn't speak.

"Allie, we're going to walk to the patio. You need fresh air and something to drink. Have you eaten anything today?" I used my stern mother-voice.

Her eyes widened, and she rose to her feet. "Not much."

I glanced at Gloria. "Do you want to come outside with us for fresh air? Maybe a snack? My treat."

Her always neat hair had morphed into an unrecognizable mess. "Um, no. I should get back to work."

"We'll be outside if you change your mind." I held Allie's arm and chatted with her until we reached the outdoor restaurant.

Reid and Ethan were sitting in chairs by a fire pit. They were deep in conversation and didn't see us approach.

"Guys, we need to get something for Allie to eat and drink."

Ethan rose. "Yes, ma'am. You all find a table, and I'll order appetizers."

Sirens wailed, and soon the back of the resort was crawling with police officers.

The four of us sat at a table in the shadows and nibbled on spicy guacamole and chips, pimento cheese and pita slices, and mini BLTs. We didn't discuss anything important, and nobody spoke Clint's name.

After a good amount of time, my brother walked to our table. He pointed at Allie and me. "I heard you two have seen the body."

"Yes. I'm afraid so." I reached over and held Allie's hand.

She said, "He didn't make it, did he?"

"I'm afraid not. If it's okay, I'd like to take all your statements. One at a time. Over there." Paul pointed to an empty table.

Allie stood. "May I go first? I'd like to get it over with."

Paul motioned for her to follow him. "Let's talk."

I said, "Can y'all believe there's been another murder?"

Ethan shook his head. "I thought Dallas was dangerous, but it seems worse here."

"Hold up." Reid lifted his hands. "We didn't have murders until a few months ago, but I'm sure Paul can handle this. He'll catch the killer with the help of our capable police force."

Ethan chuckled. "Mom, I don't think your husband wants you to investigate Clint's murder."

Reid shrugged but remained quiet.

"I think I'm a little offended. There's no need to worry about me butting into this murder investigation. I've got plenty of other things to keep me busy."

Chapter Four

Saturday morning, I exited the eye doctor's office, wearing a new pair of bifocals. I wore a pair of glasses to help my far vision. In my purse was a pair of readers. I felt so deflated. The deafness in my right ear had nothing to do with age. The glasses made me feel old. So very old.

I got into the Wagoneer and cranked the engine. I sat there while cool air replaced the stifling heat.

My phone vibrated, and Reid's face appeared. The man made me so happy. With a smile, I swiped the screen to answer. "Congratulations. Feel free to gloat. My vision is worse." I fought against an urge to cry. This was so silly. Everyone got older.

"Babe, you know I didn't want to be right, don't ya?"

I nodded. "Yes." My voice sounded mousey.

"Meet me at Marsh View Brew."

Coffee was a weakness of mine, and Reid Barrett knew it. "Thanks. I'll leave now."

I drove to Fox Island's newest coffee shop, and my heart lifted at the sight of Reid leaning against his pickup truck. He wore khaki shorts and an Atlanta Braves' T-shirt.

I parked, and he was at my door before I reached for the handle.

"Your glasses look nice."

I stood beside him. Oh no. My bottom lip started to quiver. "Thanks."

"Oh, honey." Reid took me in his arms. "What's wrong?"

Tears spilled down my face, and I felt ridiculous. "I don't know. Can we chalk it up to hormones? You deserve better than this."

He rubbed my back and kissed the top of my head. "I feel blessed to be your husband."

My glasses went cattycorner as I wrapped my arms around him. Stupid glasses.

"Kate, is there something else going on? This is not like you." He sounded concerned.

"You're right." I needed to pull myself together. I had faced worse situations than this. I stepped back and straightened my glasses. "Sorry. Let's get that coffee you promised me."

"You sure?"

"Yes, but I'm going to need iced coffee. It's already hot."

"Iced coffee it is."

We entered the new coffee shop, and I headed to the restroom to see how much damage the crying had done to my makeup. The door was locked, so I studied the community bulletin board. One paper listed a kayak for sale.

A woman came out, and I entered the restroom. "Oh, dear." I pulled a tissue out of my purse and began tackling the damage from my silly cry. I removed my glasses during the process. As much as I didn't like the things, I put them back on and walked out with my head high.

My vision was beyond my control, but I could certainly get in better shape. Reid smiled when I joined him at a booth. "How do you feel about kayaking?"

"I haven't been out in years, but I'm willing to give it a try." He pushed a mug of black coffee toward me. "After whatever just happened, I was afraid to add cream and sugar."

"Aw, poor thing. I'm sorry. Be right back." At the station, I added stevia and a splash of almond milk. Back at the table, I smiled at Reid. "Again, I'm sorry."

"Is there something upsetting you besides the change in your eyesight?"

"Clint Speck. Maybe." I sipped my coffee. "You know I saw him arguing with Hank Ingram before speed dating."

"Yes, but you didn't tell me what the disagreement was about."

"Something about a scam." I shrugged. "You know I don't hear so well, but I thought I heard one of them say proof."

Reid propped his left foot on his right knee and leaned back in his chair. "I'm beginning to think somebody needs a new journal. It's a good thing I have a spiral-bound polka dot journal waiting for a special occasion to give it to you. Not that Clint's murder is a special occasion, but I know how you like pretty, little notebooks to keep organized."

He knew how much I loved polka dots. "I didn't think you wanted me looking into the murder."

"Ethan's words. Not mine. Did I mention the journal is teal? At least I think it's a shade of teal. That color always confuses me."

I leaned close and then backed away, trying to get him in the best focus so I could read his expression. "There are different shades of teal. How would you feel if I wanted to investigate the murder?"

"We've survived two investigations and managed to get married. Why do you want to do it again?"

"Hmm. Good question. You and I were at the resort, specifically, we were at the event. Clint was fine. He argued with Hank, but he turned around and led speed dating. During intermission, he warned Bess about Peter. After the break, Clint felt bad. Then he was murdered. What if we subconsciously know a clue?"

"We answered Paul's questions." Reid's tone was calm.

"True." My heart beat faster.

"But you still want to investigate?"

"Yeah. Between you and me, we interacted with every person attending the event. You met all the women, and I met all the men."

"Don't forget Diane and Clint." He uncrossed his legs. "It's Saturday, and I didn't schedule any jobs today. What do you think about us driving to the resort?"

"Can we stop by the house and take Lady out for a few minutes?"

"Of course. Then I'll have time to give you the new journal before we go to Seaside Hideaway."

"Thanks. You're the best."

On the drive home, I replayed the previous night in my mind. The most obvious person to put on my list of suspects was Hank Ingram. I needed to find out more about his argument with Clint. Hank had attended speed dating, so had they worked out their differences?

I pulled into my driveway and parked beside Reid's truck.

There would be time to decide after we walked my goldendoodle.

Chapter Five

"You should get you some of those clip-on sunglasses," Reid commented as we walked into the resort.

"Actually, I ordered a pair of prescription sunglasses. The office sends off for those instead of making them on site." I clutched my new journal as we entered the lobby.

Gloria stood behind the reception desk and nodded at us.

I said, "Looks like she'll be the first person I question."

"I'd suggest asking to buy her lunch or something on her break. Then she won't hurry through her answers."

"Great idea. You should come with me, because she might be sweet on you." I hurried to Gloria before an onslaught of people appeared. "Hi."

"Hi, Kate. Reid. How can I help you this morning?" She spoke the appropriate words, but her tone was flat as if her heart wasn't in her job.

"Can we treat you to lunch? Maybe at the restaurant here. That way you won't feel rushed to return to work."

"Why?" She narrowed her eyes.

"Last night was a shock. It would help me to discuss it with you."

"What about the medic? Should we include her?"

"Allie? I'll text her. What time is your lunch break?"

"Let me take a quick look." She tapped computer keys. "Today, my break is at noon. Can we eat on the patio? I know it's humid, but I think fresh air will do me good."

"Noon on the patio, and I'll text Allie."

We walked to the back patio and stood in the shade near the fountain. I sent a message to Allie.

Reid looked at his watch. "It's eleven now. So, we've got an hour to kill. Have you talked to Bess this morning?"

My heart dropped. "No, I was preoccupied about my eye exam. I'll call her."

"No need. She's over there with Peter."

Sure enough, the two of them were leaving the restaurant. My heart sank. "I thought his car broke down. How did he get here?"

"You can ask him yourself."

Bess and Peter walked up to us. "Girl, did you get glasses? It's about time." Bess hugged me.

"Reid said pretty much the same thing. Have y'all been conspiring behind my back?"

She laughed. "You spend most of your time with us, so it makes sense that we're both aware of your vision problems."

"Ouch." I frowned at her. "What are you doing here?"

"Peter needed a ride back to the resort, and he called me."

"Yes. The car dealer is sending a tow truck and a loaner vehicle. Not just anyone can work on a Jag." His condescending tone irritated me.

Reid said, "I imagine that's right."

Peter's gaze bounced around our small group. "Bess, thanks for the lift. I'm going to the parking lot. Do you want to go with me?"

"I'll stay and visit with my friends." She inched closer to me.

He ran a hand over his bald head. "Maybe we can meet up later."

"Give me a call."

Peter walked into the lobby, which would allow him to exit on the other side and get to the parking lot.

Bess pointed to chairs circled around a fire pit. "Can we sit over there?"

"Yeah." I checked my phone, but there was no reply from Allie.

We scooted three chairs close together, and Bess said, "Peter told me that Clint was murdered last night."

"Yes. I'm afraid it's true." The sun was too strong for my eyes, so I removed my glasses and put on sunglasses.

Reid said, "You and Peter left together. How did he find out about the murder?"

"I don't rightly know." She crossed her legs and swung the top one.

"Bess, when did he tell you the news?" I angled my head to hear better.

"Not until after we got here. We went to the resort's breakfast buffet. He spoke to another participant from last night's event." Her voice trailed off.

"And?"

"Clint was hosting multiple events. Thursday night's scavenger hunt kicked off the singles' weekend. Speed dating was last night, and today is game day. There are events scheduled for the afternoon. Participants are encouraged to go on dates tonight, and tomorrow is the weekend finale."

Should I let her ramble? Was her long answer helping her process Clint's death?

Bess said, "I didn't sign up for today and tomorrow."

I patted her hand. "Are you okay?"

She nodded. "Yeah."

"Which participant told Peter about Clint?" I needed to find out who knew about Clint's death and when they knew.

"Hank. Um, Hank Ingram. He seems nice, don't you think?"

"I don't know, Bess. He argued with Clint early last night. Plus, he and Peter got into a disagreement."

"Really? He showed enough interest in me to give me his phone number." She pressed her lips together. "Besides, he wasn't the one Clint warned me about. That was Peter."

"Yeah, so why do you keep hanging out with him?"

She shrugged. "He seems to like me."

"I'm not surprised." Reid rested his forearms on his thighs. "I would think all the men would've wanted to give you their number, but that doesn't mean you should agree. Your sister pushed you to meet men, but you're a grown woman. You can decide for yourself."

Bess tilted her head. "Yesterday, it seemed like you didn't trust Peter. Now, it seems like you don't trust Hank. Is there any man you trust me to date? Don't y'all want me to be happy?"

I gripped her hand. "Of course, we want you to be happy. The way Tom Cross treated you was cruel, especially for a pastor."

Reid said, "Stop right there. Tom has dealt with a lot of pain in his life. I don't know why he couldn't commit to a relationship, but we might want to cut him some slack. In the meantime, if there's a man you're seriously interested in, let us do a background check."

"Reid's right. I couldn't live with myself if one of these guys hurt you."

Bess shook her head. "No way would Peter or Hank hurt me."

Peter was a charismatic man, and it was easy to see how women fell for him. "Who paid for breakfast?" I hated to be so hard, but my best friend was innocent about scam artists and conmen.

"Peter offered, but he forgot his wallet." She recrossed her legs.

Enough said.

My phone vibrated with a text from Allie.

Thank you. I would like to join. See you soon.

I looked at Reid and Bess. "Allie is coming. Bess, I know you just ate breakfast, but we're going to meet Allie and Gloria Hardee for lunch and kinda decompress from last night. Do you want to join us?"

"I've got a hair appointment. Maybe we can talk later."

I said, "I'd like that."

We hugged, and Bess walked away.

"I'll be right back." Reid sauntered off.

I hadn't learned much, but I started a page of suspects. Peter Rodale and Hank Ingram were the first two men I listed.

"Do you mind if we find a shady table?" Gloria surprised me.

How was it already noon? "Shade sounds good. Allie is on her way. Do you mind if we include Reid?"

"Your hunky husband can most certainly be part of our group. I don't know how you get anything done besides looking at him."

I stood and laughed. "It can be challenging."

We walked to the hostess stand, and the lady at the station led us to a table in the shade. The sea breeze added another element of coolness on this hot August day.

Reid and Allie appeared, and we all ordered cold drinks.

Allie said, "Look, there's Dwayne Gray. He's eating like a normal person. Gloria, does he always perform here? You are so lucky to know him."

She said, "He's a little old for you, dear. Dwayne and the new owner of the resort are friends. Craig asked him to spend the month of August here performing."

Craig Hauser had taken ownership of the resort earlier in the summer after his brother died. "It seems like Craig is doing a good job, but how could he afford to pay Dwayne?"

"Like I said, they are friends. Dwayne had planned to spend August through October writing new music. Craig asked him to perform. He's getting paid, plus free room and board, and to top it off, he can play golf for free." She closed the menu. "Although, I think he did it because of their relationship and not for golf perks."

Allie folded her hands together. "It sounds like he's as nice as I had imagined. My high school music teacher always played his music, and so did my dad. They were both big fans."

"It sounds like you are, too." She signaled our waitress. "We should order."

After we placed our orders, I looked at Gloria. "Last night was terrible. How are you doing?"

"Not great." She pressed her lips together.

"I'm curious if you had a relationship with Clint."

She took a drink of her iced tea. "I gave Clint and Diane advice on the logistics of hosting the events for the single people. You might say the three of us became friends."

"So, you two were not romantically connected?"

"Why would you ask such a question?" She wiped the sweating glass with a paper napkin.

She had seemed jealous when she mentioned Clint and a younger woman. "Did he have a girlfriend?"

"How would I know?"

Oh, brother. I wouldn't get anywhere if she answered every question with a question. I refused to give up. "Who do you think murdered Clint?"

"I thought this lunch was about grieving together. If I'd suspected you wanted to grill me, I would've refused your invitation."

My face warmed. "I'm sorry, Gloria. You're right. Clint's death was a shock. I'm impressed you're back at work today."

Her shoulders sank. "I couldn't sleep last night. Plus, I need the money."

Allie leaned forward. "I didn't sleep a wink either. If you have flashbacks, that's normal. There's no shame in going to a therapist. They can be super helpful. If you don't feel like people understand, call us. The three of us went through this together."

"I'm a stranger to you two, Allie. Why would you offer to help me through this?"

Maybe Gloria always answered questions with her own questions. I said, "We care about you. Earlier, I wasn't accusing you of anything. I'm a thinker, and asking questions helps me process situations."

Allie nodded. "That's right. Besides being a professional organizer, Kate is a real-life amateur sleuth. She has helped the police solve two local murders."

"Two? I knew you worked on Ben Hauser's murder."

The waitress appeared with our food, and the conversation turned to more pleasant topics.

When Gloria finished, she looked at her watch. "I need to go back to work."

Reid said, "We're treating you to lunch. You too, Allie. Gloria, have a good rest of your day."

"Thanks. If you're intent on solving Clint's murder, I'm sure I'll see you around."

"Yes, you will. Take care." I waved as she walked away.

Allie said, "I need to scoot and meet Ethan. He wanted to hear my impressions of speed dating to get a woman's perspective. We're going to play disc golf and discuss it at the same time."

"Have fun." I squashed down any excitement trying to rise up in me. Ethan didn't want me to butt into his love life, and I wouldn't.

Reid said, "I've been sitting too long. What about renting kayaks and taking them out in the ocean?"

"The ocean? I'd rather try the creek or bay. I'm probably not strong enough to tackle the ocean, especially during high tide."

"I know the perfect place." He waved to our waitress and paid the bill.

"Do you think we learned much today about the murder case?" I stood and picked up my belongings.

"Your luck may be turning. Didn't you say Clint was in a lip lock before speed dating started?"

"Yes." I wanted to ask him why, but I didn't want to be as annoying as Gloria.

"It's possible that she's sitting over there with an older blond woman." He pointed to a table under an umbrella.

I looked at the two women. The younger one didn't look like the woman I'd seen entwined with Clint on Friday night. I stepped toward them to get a better look. The problem was I hadn't gotten a good view the night before.

"Trust me. You don't want to interrupt them." A deep voice stopped me from taking another step.

I looked into Dwayne's eyes and nodded. He blocked my view of the mother-daughter duo.

Dwayne somewhat resembled Peter. Both were tall Black men, and both were bald. I'd recently met each man. But for some reason, I trusted Dwayne much more than Peter.

Reid said, "Suppose we find a quiet place to talk. I have a hunch you know more than anybody suspects."

He chuckled. "Your hunch may prove to be true. Come with me."

We followed Dwayne into the resort. I didn't know what he'd tell us, but my hopes rose.

Chapter Six

Dwayne opened the door to a suite on the top floor. "Come in. Can I offer you a drink?"

"No, but thanks." I walked to the sliding glass doors. "The view is beautiful."

"This is a beautiful place. It inspires me to write new music."

Reid walked to the seating area. On the coffee table was a guitar. There was a keyboard and two more guitars. Sheet music lay spread out on the table, and some pages had been crumpled into balls.

I resisted the urge to tidy the place, and I moved to the loveseat.

"Remind me why you are hanging out at dating events."

Reid sat next to me. "We're keeping an eye on our friend. Trying to make sure she's safe."

"Is it the young woman you had lunch with?" He sat opposite us and propped his feet on the coffee table.

"No. It's my best friend. She's our age—"

Reid interrupted. "Dwayne, for the record, Kate is older than me. Continue, honey."

Dwayne laughed. "She looks younger than you, man."

I elbowed my husband. "Thank you, Dwayne."

Reid shook his head. "I deserved that."

I said, "My friend has focused on other things in life, and she never dated much. We're concerned some man may try to scam her."

"I see a lot while playing my songs, and you have a valid concern."

Reid said, "Why did you stop us from approaching those women?"

Dwayne changed his position and leaned forward. "The young one was in an interesting relationship with Clint Speck."

"Romantic?"

"I don't believe so. They spent time together, but I never saw any romantic gestures. But there was something." Dwayne's gaze bounced from me to Reid. "Her mother arrived a few days ago, and they've talked a lot. Lots of arguing between the two of them. Meanwhile, Clint and Gloria have been seen canoodling."

"Ah ha. I thought something was off." I opened my polka dot journal. "Do you mind if I take notes?"

"That's cool. The young woman's name is Jennifer Fraser. Her mom, Erica, is a sloppy drunk. She's the reason I know so much. She's here to talk sense into her daughter, because she's afraid they could fall in love."

Reid said, "Erica confided her concerns to you?"

He shook his head. "Nah, man. I went to the bar between sets. Normally, I drink water or electrolytes. The other night I felt weak, and I ordered a smoothie. I'd gotten so wrapped up writing a new song that I forgot to eat. If Craig hadn't called me, I would've missed the first set. But you don't want to hear about me getting lost in music. While I stood at the bar waiting for my smoothie, Erica came up and ordered a whiskey. Neat. She looked at me and began to flirt."

I laughed. "I imagine a lot of women flirt with you."

Dwayne shrugged. "It's part of being a musician. So, I let her ramble, and before I know it, she's telling me about her daughter and Clint. It's true that there was, like, forty years between their ages, give or take, but Erica was furious. Seemed like there was more to the anger than the age difference. But what do I know? I'm just a singer."

I made bullet points of what he was revealing. "I'd say you're more than a singer, and I bet you probably hear a lot working at the resort."

"You have no idea. I stand up every night and talk and sing, and people feel like they know me. They don't, but they feel like it. So they tell me things as if we're friends. It's okay by me, but I know better than to confide in them. It's too easy to find yourself in the news."

Reid rubbed his hands together. "Why do you trust us? You already know we lied to enter the speed dating event."

"You were looking out for your friend. Bess, right?"

"Yeah, that's her. Kate and I've known Bess since we were kids."

"See there? That is exactly why I trust you two. You're loyal to your friend and don't want anything bad to happen to her." He stood and walked to the window. "When I'm on stage, I notice things. For instance, I saw your friend with that dude who favors the actor in the basketball commercials. Samuel L. Jackson, I think."

My heart beat faster. "His name is Peter Rodale. He says he owns jewelry stores."

"Hmm. He drives a Jag, so that tracks."

Reid stood, too. "Do you doubt he's legit?"

"I know the dude eats with different women, and he pulls the same I-forgot-my-wallet act. I've yet to see him pay for a meal." He turned and faced us. "More power to him if he never pays, but it seems suspicious. Legit people pay their way."

I added this information to my journal. "Do you think Peter killed Clint?"

Dwayne raised his hands in surrender. "No way I'm fingering anybody for the murder. I know stuff, but I don't know who offed Clint."

"Okay. Can we go back to Erica Fraser? Was she angry enough to harm Clint?"

"When she was drunk, I'd say yes to mad enough. She wasn't steady. More like loosey goosey. You know what I mean? It's hard to imagine her committing murder in her condition."

Reid said, "Unfortunately, I do. Can you think of anything else?"

"Not right now, but if I notice something, I'll let you know." He stuffed his hands in the pockets of his black shorts.

I stood. "I was one of the first to see Clint's body, but please don't think I want to stop you from telling the police anything important."

Dwayne snapped his fingers. "Important. That's the key word. I just told y'all my impressions and observations. If I'd seen something incriminating, I would've reported it to the police."

"Thanks for sharing all this." I pointed to my journal.

We took turns shaking hands, and then Dwayne opened the door for us. "Tell your friend to be careful with Peter."

I smiled at him. "Thanks, I will. Bye, Dwayne."

Once we were on the elevator, and the doors had closed, Reid took me in his arms. "I'm so thankful we found our way back to each other. I couldn't deal with all the shenanigans with these dating events."

"I know what you mean." I kissed my husband until the doors opened.

A family got onto the elevator. They were all excited to spend the day on the beach.

I was excited to spend the day with Reid, even if we were going to dig for clues.

Chapter Seven

After buying groceries and taking Lady for a short walk around my neighborhood, Reid and I drove my goldendoodle to the house for veterans that he'd built on the river. He parked in the shade of a big oak tree.

Three men were currently living at the home. Two had been homeless for years, and the third man had been shuffled from one family member to the next. When he got fed up, he hit the streets. Lucky for him, somebody told him about Reid's place.

We leashed Lady and stepped out of the truck. It was still humid, but the shade helped lessen the effect of the blazing sun.

Reid said, "Let me go inside first and make sure everyone is presentable and ready for company. I'll let you know when the coast is clear. If the men seem receptive to spending time with Lady, we'll give them some privacy."

"Do you have something up your sleeve?" I passed the leash to my husband.

"Yep, but it's a surprise."

"In that case, hurry up." I smiled at him.

"Patience, woman." He laughed and jogged to the front porch with my dog.

I leaned against the truck and stared at the house. Reid had flipped it with plans to provide a safe shelter for veterans. His dad had been a homeless veteran, and only recently had Sam Barrett returned to the island. He dropped into the lives of Reid and his mother, Joy.

Life had dealt me some unpleasant surprises, but after getting together with Reid, I had begun to enjoy surprises. The man truly spoiled me, and I hope he believed I also spoiled him.

Reid appeared on the front porch and waved his arms for me to come to the house.

I gathered the groceries and walked toward Reid.

He met me halfway and took two bags from my hands. "Sorry. I don't know how I forgot about the food. The men are bonding with Lady."

I adjusted the remaining two bags. "I never doubted her ability to win them over."

We entered the house and carried the food to the kitchen. We had bought staples and some special foods. Crab dip, chicken, and orzo, and a breakfast casserole. I wasn't sure if the men were good cooks, so it could be a nice change of pace.

After we put the food away, I looked at my husband. "What's the surprise?"

"Follow me." He led the way to his office. So far, he managed the home, but he hoped to find an intern to step in. There were still some legal issues to conquer before a staff person could be hired, so Reid was footing the bill. Even better would be if somebody took the place off Reid's hands.

He removed a tube of sunscreen from his desk drawer and passed it to me. "The sporting goods store donated four kayaks to this place. It's time to see how serious you are."

I laughed and began applying the lotion to my skin. "You sound doubtful."

"Hmm, maybe because you backed down from your Memorial Day triathlon challenge." He opened the top file cabinet drawer and rummaged around.

"You're right, but I really do want to kayak." I took off my glasses. "Maybe I should've gotten contacts."

"You can try them." Reid pulled two ball caps out. "Want one?"

"Yes, please." One was a sweat-stained Braves cap. The other was a red-and-black Georgia hat. "I can, um, I'll take the Braves cap." I'd almost offered to wash the hat, but I didn't want to hurt his feelings.

Reid handed the hat to me with a grin. "Betcha want to wash it."

My face warmed, but I put the hat on my head and pulled my ponytail through the back. "What else?"

"The kayaks are already on the dock, so we're good to go." He took my hand in his, and we walked toward the river. "I think we should each use one boat instead of sharing."

"Wait. What?" Maybe this was a foolish idea, and I didn't like to do foolish things. I stopped moving.

Reid turned and looked at me. "Whoa. There is nothing to worry about. You'll wear a life jacket, and we'll stick close to each other. I want you to feel confident by the time we get off the water."

I considered the possible outcomes, and then met Reid's gaze. He'd always watched out for me, even when we were gawky teenagers. "I trust you."

"That's my girl." He kissed me before we finished walking to the dock. Once there, Reid and I put on life vests and got into the kayaks.

They were both a pretty shade of blue, and we drifted away from the shore. I adjusted my sunglasses and looked at Reid. "I'm ready."

"Okay. It's pretty basic." He circled around so he was on the side of my good ear. He showed me how to hold the paddle so the blades were angled for the most efficiency. "Now, hands on the shaft, knuckles up. Elbows at a ninety-degree angle. Relax your grip. There are three phases to paddling. We'll work on them first. After you're comfortable, I'll teach you the reverse stroke."

"Is that like three steps forward, one step back? Kinda like my murder investigations."

"Oh, Katie. Quit thinking about Clint's death."

"Sorry. You're right. I'm paying attention to you." I listened and followed Reid's directions, and soon we were kayaking.

A fish jumped out of the water so high that it splashed me. I squealed then laughed. "Oh, honey. This is exactly what I needed."

"It was your idea. I'm only following through." He pointed to a shady area. "We should turn around there and then head back. I don't want to wear you out on your first day."

I followed his suggestion, and we finished our adventure in a comfortable silence.

My thoughts jumped all over the place. I wasn't too old to try new things.

Yes, I had gained weight, but we were in the happy honeymoon phase of life. I could lose it. I would get used to wearing glasses. Maybe I'd get a cute necklace to keep my new readers handy.

My mind leapt back to the murder scene. Clint had a saxophone strap around his neck the last time I'd seen him at the speed dating event. What happened to it?

I quit paddling and texted my brother. Paul, was there a saxophone strap in Clint's pockets? He played a sax during the event.

"Hey, now. No texting on the river."

"Oops. Sorry."

"This is supposed to be relaxing." Reid pointed. "Check out that dolphin."

I quit paddling and looked in the direction he pointed. "Oh, it looks like a bottlenosed dolphin. I've never been this close to one."

"Sometimes they come up the river a ways. I guess all creatures need a change of pace from time to time."

As I drifted in my kayak, watching the dolphin jump, I allowed thoughts of Clint's murder to drift away. "Thanks, Reid. This was exactly what I needed."

At last, the dolphin swam away from us.

"We should head back and check on Lady and the men."

"Sounds good." My strokes were stronger and more confident than when we'd begun. It didn't take long to return and put everything away.

My phone vibrated, and Paul's name flashed.

Reid looked over my shoulder. "You should take that. What if I grab your dog and meet you at the truck?"

"Our dog." I grinned at my husband.

He chuckled. "Right. She's our goldendoodle."

"I'll see you at the truck." I broke off and walked along a shady path to the front of the house. "Hi, Paul."

"Sis, there is not a saxophone strap, but that explains something."

"What?" My heart beat faster.

"Clint was strangled, and it's possible that's the murder weapon. I've got to go, but keep this to yourself. Well, you and Reid. Nobody else."

"Yes, sir."

Paul said, "Wait. One last question. Do you have any thoughts on who may have emptied Clint's pockets?"

"Gloria Hardee removed his wallet, keys, and maybe his cell phone."

"Good to know. Thanks."

"Be careful, Paul." A glance at my phone showed he'd already hung up. I opened the truck doors to allow the hot air to escape. I sat in the grass and let my focus drift to the murder. No matter what I did, my mind kept turning back to Clint's death.

Why had the killer used the saxophone strap to strangle Clint? Was the murder in the heat of the moment? Or had it been planned? If planned, it seemed like the killer would've brought the murder weapon. If the saxophone strap really was the murder weapon, where in the world was it?

Chapter Eight

Saturday night, I took Reid upstairs to the art studio. I placed an art pad on an easel. "There hasn't been time for me to get back to painting, so let's use this as a murder board."

"Great."

I frowned. Maybe he had grown tired of this murder investigation.

He coughed. "I mean, great idea."

"Are you sure? I can investigate on my own. You don't have to help."

"No, ma'am. This is one of our hobbies, right? Solving crimes."

"Not sure it's a hobby, but maybe you're right. Let's begin with suspects." I blew him a kiss, and then reached for a marker. "Peter and Hank are the only two on my list, so far."

"Don't forget the Fraser woman whose daughter was in a relationship with Clint." He sat in the recliner and kicked up his feet. The room had good light during the day and plenty of lights and lamps for the night. There was enough room for Reid's drafting table, a desk, and my art easel. We also had lots of storage space.

"Right. Erica Fraser." I added her name. "You know what? We may as well add Jennifer Fraser."

"Mother and daughter, but why include Jennifer?"

"Because Dwayne said that Clint and Gloria Hardee had something going on."

"I'll add this to your notes because you can't drag your murder board all over the island." He got my new journal and a pen from the desk. After he resettled into the chair, he clicked the pen. "Proceed."

"Thank you. Oh, we may as well include Gloria. She seemed jealous of Jennifer even though Dwayne doesn't believe Clint was interested in a romance with Jennifer."

"Anybody else?" Reid lifted his eyebrows.

"Possibly his assistant, Diane Field. She may have had a crush on Clint, too."

"Six suspects. Nice round number. Interesting that most of them are women. What is our next move?"

"I want to talk to Bess." Lady climbed the steps and entered the art studio. "Hey, girl. If it wasn't so stinking hot, I'd let you outside."

She stretched out beside Reid's feet.

He said, "You two should get together. If Bess agrees to come here, I'll take Lady and visit my parents."

I moved over and sat on the arm of the chair. "You don't need to leave."

"Yeah, I know, but Bess may just want to talk to her best friend without interference from me."

"I'll call and see if she's available." I tapped my friend's number into my phone.

"Hello." Bess's tone sounded happy. "What's up?"

"Are you free tonight?"

"I've taken the night off from dating. I'm in my pajamas and trying to pick a movie to watch."

"Would you like some company? I'll bring popcorn."

"What's Reid doing? I don't want him to see me in my pajamas." Her upbeat tone made me feel good.

"He's going to visit his mom."

"Then come on over, girlfriend."

"See you soon." I ended the call and looked at Reid. "I'm going over there. Do you want me to take Lady?"

Reid said, "I think Bess is more of a cat person. Lady and I will be good together, and we'll go see Mom and Pop."

I reached for the journal. "Thanks for letting me go see Bess, honey. I don't mean allowing me, but, I mean—"

"Kate." He intertwined our fingers together. "You can have as many friends as you want. We're married, but I don't own you, and I won't stop you from spending time with your family and friends."

I reflected on his words. We had become absorbed in each other and our relationship. "I never want to stop you from seeing your family and friends either."

"We waited so long to get married, it's probably natural that we've gotten lost in each other. We should have a cookout or something and invite friends over."

"That is a spectacular idea. We can plan one for next weekend."

He kissed me. "Sounds like a plan."

We left the house at the same time. Reid opened the door of my Wagoneer for me. "Call me when you start driving home. Wait a minute. Where are your glasses?"

"Um, in my purse."

"No, ma'am. They won't help if you don't wear them."

I stared at Reid. He made a good point. I didn't want to put myself or anyone else at risk. Hearing loss had been an adjustment, and I'd adapt to wearing glasses. I pulled my glasses out and put them on. "Thanks for the reminder."

"I'm happy to know you'll be driving safely." He shut the door, but the window was down. "Tell Bess hi for me."

"And tell your parents the same for me. You're going to be okay if your dad is there?"

"I'm working on my issues with Pop."

I paused and met his gaze through my new glasses. "I love you, Reid. Thanks for caring about me."

"Always."

I drove to Bess's place, and she opened the door before I rang the bell.

"Get in here. You won't believe what happened."

"What?" I put down my big bag on the kitchen counter. Bess lived in a nice condo. The main room included the kitchen, dining area, and living room. It was comfortable and spacious. She had decorated it in blues and greens. The place was beachy without being over the top.

Bess said, "Dwayne called me. You know who I mean? He's the musician at the resort."

"Yeah, I've met him. He seems pretty dreamy and a good match for you. Did he ask you out?"

"He didn't come straight out and ask, but he hinted. I can't date him right now, even if he officially asks." Her eye twitched.

"Why not?"

"He's not in our dating group thingy. Those who are participating in the events for singles are supposed to date other participants."

"Bess, we live in a free country. You can date anybody you want. What did you tell Dwayne?"

"Same thing I told you." She crossed her arms. "I'm obligated to date Peter and Hank. Plus, two more men asked for my phone number. Can you believe I wasted so many years pining for Tom? He dealt my ego a blow. No, it's more than that. I cared about him, and he made me feel unworthy."

I hugged my friend. Tom had broken her heart. "I'm so sorry. Nobody should treat another person that way, especially a woman as spectacular as you."

"You are off your rocker, my friend, but I appreciate the sentiment." She stepped back. "I wish you had moved here years ago."

"Me, too, but I'm here now." I pointed to the blue couch, and we sat on each end. "I didn't think you were especially comfortable with Peter. Plus, Clint warned you to be careful. And to be honest, somebody who works at the resort suggested Peter might be up to no good. I'm not accusing him of murder, but please don't waste your time dating him."

"Un hunh. You think he's interested in my money. The joke's on him. All my money is invested in our business and my home." She circled her hand to indicate the space where we were standing.

"He probably doesn't know that. He sees a beautiful, independent businesswoman—"

"Please stop. You're embarrassing me." She picked the TV remote off the coffee table. "I don't want to talk about it anymore."

"Fine, but consider going on one date with Dwayne. We can even make it a double date." If she didn't agree, I would make sure we invited both of them over.

"I didn't say I'd never date Dwayne. Just not yet." She turned on the TV. "What would you like to watch?"

"A comedy or romance. Nothing related to murder. I'll fix the popcorn."

"The air popper is in the pantry."

I walked over to Bess's organized kitchen. "Girl, I thought my space was organized, but yours puts me to shame. We should take pictures and show customers a sample of your talent for organizing."

"Aw, thanks. I appreciate you thinking it's worthy of showing clients. It takes work to stay organized, but it's worth the effort. Sometimes it's hardest to organize our own space, and I enjoy helping people work on their spaces."

"There is a sense of satisfaction after we finish a job." I pulled out a big bowl and everything I needed to prepare popcorn. We chatted back and forth, and soon we were watching one of our favorite romantic comedies, *While You Were Sleeping*. Bess had often hoped some drastic event would open Tom's eyes. He'd realize how much he cared for her, and then he'd propose.

When it was over, I helped Bess clean the kitchen. "Do you have any thoughts on who killed Clint?"

Bess shook her head. "No. Clint was one of those people you either like or hate. He was also a big flirt. I heard some of the other women say that the more Clint had to drink, the flirtier he became."

"Do you think Diane had romantic feelings for Clint?"

Bess tossed paper napkins into the garbage can. "Probably. She looked at him the way I imagine people said I looked at Tom."

"Explain." I put soap in the big bowl and washed it.

"I'd say she was starry-eyed and believed Clint could do no wrong." Bess frowned. "Yeah, that's probably what people said about me. Fool for love. Yep. I feel bad for Diane."

Her words made me sad. "Why?"

"She lost the man she loved and her job just like that." Bess snapped her fingers.

"Are you sure she lost her job? I figured she'd take over the weekend events and maybe the business."

Bess gasped. "Kate, are you suggesting that Diane murdered Clint?"

I had the woman's name on my murder board. "It's possible. What if she gets the business? Or maybe she was jealous of other women. That would mean she had two possible motives. Plus, I heard Clint was in a relationship with a much younger woman."

"There's a rumor it was Jennifer Fraser, but he was interested in other women, too."

"Dwayne doesn't think Clint was interested in romance with Jennifer. Maybe they were only friends. We should put her on the back burner. You say other women. Besides Diane and Gloria Hardee, the lady who works at the front desk? There were others?"

Bess grimaced. "Have you met Lauren Lee? She runs the spa at the resort."

"I met her once, but are you saying Lauren and Clint hooked up?" I put the bowl in the drain rack.

"According to the rumor mill. Once I saw him go into the spa after closing hours. The place was dark, but the door opened for him. It could've been perfectly innocent, though."

"Hmm. You know what? We've worked very hard since we opened Let's Get Organized. I'm going to schedule massages for us. Allie can handle the business for a few hours without us."

"I know this isn't a reward for our hard work, but count me in."

"Perfect. Do you want to try going to a different church in the morning? It can't be easy to listen to Tom preach."

Her shoulders slumped. "It hasn't been easy, but what will people say?"

"Who cares? That's my new motto."

"I don't believe you, but I shouldn't worry about what others think. Where do you want to go?"

"There's another non-denominational church near the marsh. Reid and I will pick you up in the morning."

"Thanks. See you then."

I walked outside. Humidity clung to my skin, and I jumped into the Wagoneer. After the air conditioner started, I texted Reid. **Heading home.**

I couldn't wait to tell him about Lauren Lee and Clint. One more person to add to our list.

Chapter Nine

Sunday afternoon, Lauren Lee had an opening for a couples massage. It'd be a perfect way for Bess and me to quiz her about Clint. So, I booked it, and after church, Bess rode to the resort with me.

When we arrived, Lauren took care of me, and a new lady gave Bess her massage. It felt so wonderful, and I hated to ruin it by asking questions about Clint's death.

With some reluctance, I dove in. "I heard there was another murder at the resort."

Lauren's finger stilled. "Shh. You need to relax."

"Did you know the victim? Clint Speck." I'd be more relaxed when the killer was behind bars.

Lauren returned to working on my lower back. "Yes. The poor man. He had been in a recurring argument with his son, and he was distraught. He begged for a massage after closing time. He said he needed positive energy before leading the singles weekend."

Bess said, "I would've never guessed Clint had been arguing with his son. He was always so happy and upbeat. Was it a serious argument?"

Lauren said, "I didn't ask many questions. If you want to know, ask Kyle."

I lifted my head. "Do you know Kyle, too?"

"We have met." Lauren tapped my head, and I lowered it. "He's a good-looking man, but his dad spoiled him."

"But Kyle is the one who alerted us to Clint's disappearance. He seemed worried." It was hard to imagine the man I'd met on the beach could have murdered his dad.

"Maybe he's a good actor. We need to quit talking about the murder, or you'll feel worse than before you came to me for this massage."

I lifted a finger. "One last question for you, Lauren. Who do you believe murdered Clint?"

"If the motive was unrequited love, my money would be on Diane. She's his assistant."

"Can you think of another motive?" I tried to relax.

"Not really. Clint was a guest of the resort, and I didn't know him very well."

Bess said, "Do you know that some of the weekend participants believe you and Clint were fooling around?"

"Hmm. I try not to listen to gossip. Now, are you two here for a massage or to grill me?" There was no disguising her angry tone.

I said, "Sorry. Massage, please."

Bess turned her head toward Lauren and me. "I'm also sorry. It's so hard to believe Clint was murdered. He seemed like the nicest man. He looked out for the participants. You know what I mean?"

Lauren paused. "No. What are you insinuating?"

"Clint advised me not to date one of the men. He didn't want the guy to take advantage of me financially. Lauren, do you know who I'm talking about?"

"I met a few of the guests, mostly the women, because they often like to get facials before big events. But I have no idea who you're talking about."

I said, "Does that happen often? Men preying on innocent women?"

"Most people don't carry on a conversation when they come here. Your session is almost over."

I held the sheet over my body and sat up. "Lauren, thank you so much for the massage and for answering my questions."

"Please, don't leave a review that you left her more stressed than when you arrived. I did the best I could, considering you are so focused on Clint's murder."

I shrugged. "I won't leave a bad review."

It didn't take long for us to go to the dressing rooms and get dressed. Bess pointed to the outside patio. "How about a fruity drink? My treat."

"Is this about a drink, or are you interested in connecting with one of the men?"

She smiled. "I might take your advice about Dwayne, and it'll be less awkward if we meet casually than if I call him."

"Very smooth, my friend." I was proud of Bess. She'd had a crush on Tom for years, and meeting new men was not in her comfort zone. She and I were taking chances with our lives, both professionally and personally. "Let's get that drink."

We walked to the colorful outdoor bar.

"Ladies, what can I get you this beautiful afternoon?" The bartender had black hair, a thick beard, and a mustache, but it was neat. He was taller and heavier than my son, but he wasn't overweight.

"I'd like to try a raspberry spritzer."

Bess ordered the golden tonic. The bartender stepped back and began mixing.

I looked at my friend, "What's a golden tonic?"

"Who knows? One of the ladies said it makes her feel healthier, and she can dance longer if she drinks it."

Mason East was on the bartender's nametag, and he shook his head. "I wouldn't go that far, unless she drinks it regularly. It's healthy with ginger and turmeric, and if she believes it allows her to dance longer, then it probably does."

Bess said, "I'll keep your secret."

The bartender focused on our drinks.

I tapped Bess's shoulder. "Don't look now, but I think Dwayne is headed our way."

Mason placed the drinks in front of us. Mine was a cheerful red with raspberries on top and a sprig of mint. Bess's was gold. "Ladies, have you met Dwayne Gray? He's the best musician around, and he's playing here for a few weeks."

I smiled at Dwayne. "Hi, there. It's nice to see you again. This is my friend, Bess Walker."

"Kate. Good to see you, and I know who Bess is." His attention shifted to my friend, and they struck up a conversation.

I took a sip of my drink. "Oh, Mason, this is delicious. Um, sorry. I probably shouldn't call you by your name without your permission."

"No, ma'am. No need to apologize. It's why we wear nametags at Seaside Hideaway."

"I'm Kate, and this is Bess." I thumb pointed to my friend, who was deep in conversation with Dwanye. "Were you here the night of the murder?"

"Yes, this place was packed with vacationers and singles attending the dating event."

"Did you know Clint Speck?"

"Yes, he was a nice enough guy, but a terrible tipper. Excuse me." He moved to a young couple and took their orders.

I looked toward the swimming pool area. There were comfortable places to sit, but I wanted to ask Mason more about Clint. I sipped my drink.

Before the bartender returned, Dwayne said, "I've got two sets tonight, and I came down to pick up my order. Ladies, it was nice to bump into you. If you're free tonight, y'all should come out."

I nodded. "I'll talk to Reid, but tomorrow is a workday. He usually starts early, before it gets hot. If you don't see us, that'll be the reason. Will you be performing next weekend?"

"Yes, ma'am."

We said our goodbyes, and he walked to the end of the bar and picked up a bag from the restaurant. He waved to us and walked to the lobby of the resort.

Bess raised her hand to get Mason's attention, and she pulled out her credit card.

"Ladies, is there anything else I can get you?"

Bess handed the card to him. "I'll let you know if it works as fast as the other lady promised."

He chuckled.

I said, "Mason, did you notice anything suspicious Friday night?"

"You mean concerning the murder?" He swiped the credit card.

"Well, yes. Let's start there."

"Clint came over before the first round of speed dating. He said his stomach had been queasy, and he asked for a ginger ale. I fixed him one, and his coloring was off. Kinda grayish. He came back at his break for more."

"Oh." That would make sense if he'd been poisoned, but Paul confirmed Clint had been strangled. "Anything else?"

He handed the receipt and card to Bess. "Not that I can think of, but we were busy. Are you two cops?"

Bess sniffed. "No, but my friend here has helped the police solve a couple cases."

"Cool. You two have a good day, and holler if you need another drink." He turned to the people on the other side of Bess and talked to them.

Bess said, "Do you want to walk around while we finish our drinks?"

"Definitely. If you spot people from the dating events, will you point them out to me?"

"Yeah, but you met most of them Friday." She headed in the direction of the adult pool.

"Were there people at the scavenger hunt that didn't go to speed dating?"

She sipped her drink. "Yes, if I see any of them, I'll let you know."

"Thanks." I kept my eyes open as we strolled.

"Bess, hold up."

I turned to see who was calling out to my friend. It was the man I'd seen arguing with Clint before speed dating. Hank Ingram. Chills zipped up my spine despite the hot August day.

Chapter Ten

"Hank, how are you? Have you met Kate Sloan?" Bess pointed to me.

"Yes, we met at speed dating." The ocean breeze caused his dark hair to flap.

I nodded to the man. "Hi, Hank. Good to see you."

"Do you mind if I steal Bess away for a few minutes?" He flashed his white teeth at me, probably thinking he'd dazzle me into submission.

"Honestly, I'd rather you not. We don't get a lot of time to hang out, just the two of us. Can you talk to her another time?"

His smile disappeared. "I was trying to be polite, but Bess can decide for herself."

Sunglasses hid Bess's eyes. "I'm sorry, but Kate's right. This is supposed to be our day. Let's get together later."

"Sure. In fact, if you give me your address, I'll bring you breakfast tomorrow."

Bess's mouth dropped open.

I said, "Tomorrow is Monday, and there's a work breakfast."

Bess met my gaze. "Um, yeah. Why don't I call you, after I look at my calendar?"

His eyebrows rose. "Do you have that many dates? These events must have gone well for you."

Bess lifted one hand, palm up. "I'm also a businesswoman, and there's not much free time. That's why it's important not to neglect my friend today. We can talk another time, Hank."

I said, "You mentioned the other night that you're a musician. Are you going to perform in our area any time soon?"

"There's—"

Bess interrupted him, "Oh, there's a competition at the lighthouse starting Thursday. Will you be in it?"

He gave a slight shake of his head. "I don't know anything about it."

Bess elbowed me. "Do you think there's still time to enter? We could go cheer for Hank."

"I bet it's not too late, but who's in charge?" I sipped my raspberry spritzer. The ice had started melting, and I stirred the drink with my straw.

Hank waved his hands in front of us. "Ladies, I appreciate your support, but—"

I said, "Didn't you tell me you're a musician?"

"Well, yeah, but I support myself by day trading. I'm way more comfortable talking to you two about ways to invest your money than my almost non-existent music career."

Ah ha. Was that the cause of his argument with Clint? "I already have a guy who helps me with my investments."

"They can't make you as much as I can." He turned to Bess. "Why don't you take a chance on me? You can help me prove to your friend that I'm good at investments."

Bess stepped back. "I'm sorry, Hank. Everything I have is already invested in—"

I fake coughed. Bess was smart, but she wasn't necessarily street-smart. She might tell him her money was invested in her home and our business.

"Girl, hold your arm up." Bess took my drink and raised my arm.

"I'm outta here." Hank walked away.

I coughed a couple more times until he was out of sight. I reached for my glass. "Thanks."

"I hope you have a good reason for that little scene."

I stood close. "Hank is the man I saw arguing with Clint before Friday night's event. There's something shady about him."

"Is that why you interrupted? I know better than to tell a stranger where I live." She drained her drink and tossed the plastic cup in a nearby trash can.

"You're right, and I'm sorry. Neither one of us has much experience dating. I fell in love with Reid, but I left for college. I met David and married him. We both know that was a terrible decision. After his death, I focused on taking care of Ethan and surviving. I didn't date during those years."

"Yes, but you reconnected with Reid and married him."

"True, but we didn't really date. That's my point. Neither of us has experienced the boy-meets-girl and asks her out for a date."

She looked at the ground. "I see your point. I wasted so much time pining for Tom."

"I'm also sorry for interrupting the investment conversation. I was afraid you might tell him we own our business. What if he mentioned taking a second mortgage or something? You don't need that kind of pressure."

"You're right again. I'd like to think I'm smart enough to see through a plan like that."

I touched her arm. "You're sweet and trusting and the perfect kind of person for a conman to target." Plus, Bess's family had always been protective of her. I'd never completely understood why. I had two younger brothers, and they'd watched out for me, but they'd also taught me to be tough.

Bess sighed. "Let's get out of here."

It was a quiet drive back to Bess's home. I pulled onto her street, and a familiar red car did the same. I breezed past the condo entrance.

"Kate, what are you doing?" Bess leaned toward me.

"It's probably an overactive imagination, but do you know what Hank drives?" I tightened my grip on the steering wheel.

"It's some kind of red car."

I glanced in my rearview mirror. The vehicle was a red Camry. "That's what I was afraid of. Will you call my brother and tell him that we're being followed?"

"I assume you mean your cop brother and not the dentist." She swiped her phone.

"Yes. Paul will be way more helpful than Bobby. In fact, Bobby would probably give me a lecture on making good decisions."

She tisk tisked. "I can imagine it now."

"Yep. If Paul asks, it's a Camry." I turned onto Ocean Boulevard. It was the main road on the island, and you could get anywhere from it.

"Paul, it's Bess. We're on the Boulevard, and a red Camry is following us. The driver could be one of your suspects in Clint Speck's murder." She paused. "Yes, Kate's driving the Wagoneer. Right. Right. Okay. Bye."

"What does he want me to do?" I leaned in her direction to hear better.

"Drive slow and head for the pier. He plans to catch Hank there."

My pulse raced. "What if I'm wrong?"

"Is he still behind you?"

I glanced in the mirror again. "Yes." My voice squeaked.

"Trust your instincts and drive to the pier."

I'd been in worse situations, but this still made me uncomfortable. I slowed and signaled my intention to turn. The crosswalk was full of people going in both directions, but at last it cleared, and I turned.

I cruised down the street toward the pier. "Do you see Paul?"

"Not yet." She leaned forward and looked in both directions. "Oh, there he is."

Sure enough, my brother stood by an empty parking space and motioned for me to pull in.

I did as directed and rolled down the window.

"I don't see a red car of any sort following you."

"That's impossible." My heart dropped. I shut off the SUV and jumped out.

Bess joined us. "I don't understand. He was right behind us."

"Is it possible he wasn't really following y'all?"

Bess and I looked at each other. In unison, we said, "No."

"Let's grab a cup of coffee at Island Perk, and you can tell me everything that happened." He pointed at the coffee shop. "Kate, something tells me you're investigating Clint Speck's murder. There's no good reason for you to butt into my investigation."

I didn't relish upsetting my brother, but I wasn't ready to quit. My suspect list was made up of single people who had traveled to Fox Island for dating events. Despite the fact I'd crashed speed dating, I was a familiar face to the participants and people who'd landed on my list. It was possible they'd open up to me, and I had no intention of backing off.

Chapter Eleven

Monday morning, I was late for work because of Reid. He had to leave town to meet with a potential investor for the veteran's home in Atlanta. The investor knew about laws, tax regulations, and things that made my eyes roll back in my head. I was glad Reid understood more than I did.

I'd made him a hearty breakfast to hold him until he reached Atlanta. It was the first time we'd really been apart since we'd gotten married, and I felt unsettled. I would miss him, but it was more than that.

My first husband's affair had scarred me, but Reid was not David. I couldn't give in to negative thinking. Reid was trustworthy. We loved each other, and we hadn't waited this long to screw up our relationship with secrets or affairs.

I picked up drinks and muffins at Island Perk Coffee Shop and set a white chocolate latte on Bess's desk when I arrived at work. "Where's Allie?"

"She insisted on loading my van, so she's in the back." She reached for her drink. "Thanks."

"You're welcome. Allie's the nicest thing." I placed an iced matcha latte on the young woman's desk. "What's on the agenda today? Be sure to get a muffin because I said something about a breakfast meeting when we talked to Hank yesterday. I don't want to be a liar, even if he is a suspect."

Bess opened the small box and picked out a blueberry muffin. "Yum. I'm going to work on a closet for a woman who moved into my building. Afterward, I need to draw up some plans for a family with a newborn baby. According to the schedule, you're giving a talk to school teachers about the best way to organize their classrooms. Allie wrapped prizes, and I think it will be a fun event. Allie is going to make a list of calls and contacts we received on the website over the weekend. Do you mind reviewing them when you get back?"

"Sure." I sat down and sipped my coffee.

"What's wrong?" Bess sat on the side of my desk and swung her skinny legs.

"Reid's going to be out of town for a couple of days." I explained about the potential investor.

"That's awesome. Reid had the vision and created the place, but running it isn't exactly in his wheelhouse."

I nodded. "You're right. The veterans are adults who can probably cook and take care of their laundry, but it's like they need one person to be in charge. The person should be able to cook, buy groceries, and take care of the place. Reid's passion is transforming old houses into livable homes. He can do the paperwork for the veterans' place, but he'd rather be renovating."

"I understand. The administrator may need to drive the veterans to appointments, help them find work, or what have you. Actually, when Reid gets back, I may know a person interested in the job."

"They'll want to get paid, and I guess that's where this person in Atlanta fits in. Wouldn't it be great if the person knew how to go about everything needed to run a veteran's home?"

The back door slammed, and Allie entered from the storage room. "Sorry about that. The wind got hold of the door and ripped it out of my hand."

"No worries. Grab a muffin, and I brought you a drink."

She looked over. "Matcha tea? Y'all are the best. Let me wash my hands real quick like."

She walked to the restroom.

"Something's going on with you, and I guess it has to do with your husband. You know Reid has always loved you. Hear that? Always. He's not gonna step out on you or do anything dumb."

I swiped at a stray tear. "I know. He's the best, and I know he loves me. Otherwise, I wouldn't have married him. It's stupid to be afraid."

"Maybe, but it's probably natural after what David put you through. If your mother hadn't pushed you to marry him, well, we'll never know."

"I wouldn't have Ethan."

"What about Ethan?" Allie returned. "He's super nice, Kate. You did a good job raising him. He's got good manners, and he's fun." Her southern twang made me smile.

"Thanks."

She took a chocolate chip muffin and sat at her desk. "The website got a lot of traffic this weekend. You know I don't mind working on the weekends if it will help the other days go smoother."

Bess stood. "We all need the weekends off because we have some very long days. It's not all nine-to-five around here."

"You're right about that, but it's better than my EMT schedule."

I turned my attention from Reid to Clint's murder. "Allie, did you see anything suspicious at the dating event?"

"Um, Friday was so weird. When my therapist heard what happened, she called. She even met with me." Allie took a deep breath.

"I'm glad she reached out. I'm not a therapist, but if you ever need to talk, I'll be available." Allie's ordeal with Clint had probably set back her recovery from a multi-car accident. It'd been so traumatic that she'd taken a break from her career and come to work with us.

"Thanks."

"If you think of anything, please let me know. I feel like I owe it to Clint to help solve the mystery."

The front door opened, and Paul walked in. "How's everyone this morning?"

"Good." I went and hugged my brother. "What's new with your case?"

He raised one eyebrow in the irritating way only a brother can get to you. "None of your business."

I sighed. Arguing wouldn't get me far this morning. "Would you like a muffin from Island Perk?"

"Afraid not. I'm here on official business."

"Okay. Do you have more questions for me?"

"Not you." He shook his head. "Bess."

We both turned and looked at my best friend.

Her eyes widened. "Me?"

"Yes. You were the last person seen with Clint, and I have a few questions. We can talk here or at the station."

The work phone rang, and Allie answered it with a quiet voice.

Bess crossed her arms, but it looked more like a protective shield than a defiant move. "Is it only a couple questions? Or a long conversation? I've got an appointment, and this is our place of business. Anybody could walk in on us."

I said, "Do you want me to work on the client's closet?"

"No. We're friends, and she's expecting me."

Paul pointed to the storage room. "If you're comfortable with me, we can talk in there. It shouldn't take long."

Two women entered the store.

"Fine." Bess's shoulders slumped, and she followed Paul to the back room, where they could have a private conversation.

I went to greet the women who'd walked in the front door. "Good morning. How can I help you?"

The older woman said, "My daughter's getting married, and I'd like to hire you to organize the primary bathroom. It's small, and I think if they have an efficient system, it'll lead to less conflict. It's my wedding gift to them."

The young woman rubbed her earlobe. "I appreciate it, Momma, but I think we need more help in the pantry."

"Trust me, when you two are running late for work and sharing a bathroom, you'll be happy with my gift. Newlyweds do not need to start their marriage, and their mornings, in conflict."

The storage room door clunked shut behind me.

I smiled at the ladies. "I'm a newlywed myself, and your mother makes a good point. However, if you need help with the pantry, maybe we can work out a special deal for you."

The young woman's eyes sparkled. "Yes, please."

"First, I need to come to your home and see each of the spaces for myself.

Then I can give you a quote."

The mother of the bride said, "Do you have a wedding registry? For supplies?"

"Um, no, but that is a wonderful idea." I turned to Allie, who was off the phone and looking at the computer screen. "Allie, do you think we can create wedding registries?"

She crossed the room and joined us with a notepad and pen. "Are you thinking for services or products? Or both?"

"Both." Our services weren't exorbitant, but they weren't cheap either.

The daughter clapped her hands. "Yay! I love that idea. If you figure it out in time, I'd like to be your first guinea pig."

Allie and I got their information and scheduled a time to inspect the home to design a plan. Allie said, "There's a questionnaire online. It's helpful if you fill it out because it gives us a better idea of your tastes. Knowing your preferences allows us to make good choices with the materials we present to you. For example, do we think you'll prefer wicker baskets, plastic bins, or modern metal options?"

We continued the conversation and arranged an appointment.

Bess entered the room, grabbed her purse and latte, and then returned to the storage room.

The women left, but Paul reentered. "Muffins, you say?"

I met him at the box. "Yes. Help yourself. What happened to Bess?"

"She left to meet a client." He grabbed a peach muffin with streusel on top. "Thanks."

I walked outside with him. "Is Bess in trouble?"

"I didn't arrest her. Gotta roll. See you later, sis."

I tapped my foot and watched him drive away. It didn't feel right. Bess took off without a word, and Paul didn't deny that she was in trouble.

I had a bad feeling, and the urge to solve Clint's murder was stronger than ever.

Chapter Twelve

My speech at the local school had gone well despite my distractions over Bess and Reid. On the way back to the office, I stopped by the house to take Lady for a stroll. She seemed lonely, so I took her to work with me.

Allie looked up when we entered the store. "How'd it go?"

"They were very nice. There were questions at the end, and people picked up brochures and business cards."

"Sounds like a success to me." Her dark hair was pulled into a messy bun. Has Bess returned?"

"Not yet. I wasn't sure if I should be worried or not." Allie crossed the room and loved on my goldendoodle. "Hey, girl. It's good to see you."

Lady wagged her tail.

I smiled. My dog could be a fierce protector, but also the most loving thing ever, depending on the circumstances. "Did you make a list of contacts for me to review?"

"Yes, ma'am. They're on your desk. Since you're here, why don't I inventory our supplies?"

"Good idea. I'll holler if I need you." I sat at my desk, and Lady settled at my feet. I got lost in contacting potential clients and scheduling appointments.

Allie returned and handed me a piece of paper. "We're running low on these items. Have you ever organized pet supplies? I didn't see anything related to animals."

"Hold your horses. We need to perfect the systems for humans, first. Why don't you add animals to our list of future goals? We can discuss it down the road."

"Okay, but humans take care of their pets." She shrugged. "Just saying."

"I'll keep it in mind, and I appreciate your suggestions and all of your hard work."

"Thanks, Kate. What else can I do?" Her thick, dark ponytail was lopsided, and she adjusted it.

"Hmm, I'm not sure. I hope we hear from Bess soon."

"I'll call her."

"Thanks." I quickly finished and saved the revised work schedule.

"No answer. Would you like me to walk Lady?"

At the sound of her name, my dog jumped up.

I laughed. "You can't say that word and not expect her to understand. If you walk her around the block, I'll get ready to close. It's almost five."

"I got the better end of this deal. Be right back." She attached the leash to Lady's collar, and they walked out the front door.

I texted Bess. **We're about to close, and I'm worried about you. Let me know you're okay. Please.**

I shut down the computers and got the place ready to close.

Allie and Lady returned. "There's a red car parked around the corner. It was there earlier today."

"Is anyone sitting in it?"

"There was a glare on the windshield, and I can't say for sure."

"Okay, I parked beside you in back. Let's set the alarm and skedaddle. If the driver doesn't follow me, I plan to go to Bess's place and check on her."

"I can take Lady with me and meet you later."

"Thanks, Allie." I set the alarm, and we left the store. Sure enough, there was a red Camry parallel-parked on the street. "I'll be in touch."

"Be careful." She and Lady got into her Highlander.

I hopped into my SUV and followed her out of the parking lot. Once I was comfortable that the red car wasn't following me, I drove to Bess's condo. She was assigned two parking spots in the garage, and I knew the code to enter. Once inside, I parked beside her minivan.

She still hadn't replied to my text, so I called Paul.

"Hey, sis. What's up?"

"There was a red Camry parked near the store today. I didn't approach it, though. I'm at Bess's condo and wanted somebody to know where I was."

"Is there a reason for me to worry?"

"I don't think so, but Bess hasn't been in contact since she left for her meeting. You know the one. It was right after you talked to her. What'd you say?"

"Well, multiple witnesses told us that the last person they saw talking to Clint was Bess. I can't rule her out just because she's a friend."

I clenched my keys. "I understand."

"Do you want me to come over there?"

"Not yet. Give me an hour. If you don't hear from me before then, I might be in trouble."

"You've got thirty minutes."

My heart warmed at his reply. "Thanks, Paul."

"You got it."

I walked to Bess's unit and knocked on the door.

No answer.

I rang the doorbell.

Still, no answer.

I called her phone.

No answer on it either.

I had a key for emergencies.

Did this constitute an emergency? Wait, she'd been working on another condo today. I used my phone to log into the work calendar. There it was. Angie Cornish. Her address was included. I jogged from Bess's home to the client's place and rang the doorbell.

"Just a minute," a feminine voice called out.

Anxiety built as I waited.

The door opened, and a woman on the small side with big red hair smiled. "Hi."

"Hi. I'm Kate Sloan, um Kate Barrett. I recently got married. Anyhow, I work at Let's Get Organized. I'm looking for Bess. Is she here?"

"No, she left hours ago. Probably a little after one o'clock. She's delightful to work with."

"Yeah, she is. Well, I'm sorry to have bothered you."

"It's no problem. Maybe her phone ran out of juice. She got a text right before she left, and I figured it's why she took off so abruptly. Say, my closet looks terrific. Do you want to see it?" Her country twang relaxed me.

"I'd love to see it. Where are you from, Angie?"

"Oklahoma. Tulsa, specifically. I came to Georgia for love, but that was a mistake." She motioned for me to enter her unit, and she locked the door behind me. "Follow me."

"You have the same layout as Bess." The interior colors were neutral instead of blues like in Bess's home.

"Check it out." She opened the closet door.

I stepped inside. Bess had areas for tops, skirts, shorts, pants, and scrubs. "Are you a doctor?"

"Pharmacist. I used to dress up, but then my boss decided to change us all to scrubs. It saved him from constantly changing the dress code, and it's easy. What do you think of this?"

"It's fabulous. Bess did a great job." I walked out and headed to the front door. "I'm sorry to have bothered you."

"You're no bother. I'm looking forward to becoming better friends with Bess. Maybe one day we can all do something together."

"Sounds good. I hope to see you soon."

"If I run into Bess, I'll tell her to call you."

"Thanks." I walked back to Bess's condo with a sense of urgency. I sure hoped somebody would look for me if I went missing. Where could Bess be? The clock was ticking, and Paul would head over in ten minutes if I didn't find Bess. If this didn't constitute an emergency, I didn't know what did.

I inserted the key into Bess's lock and walked into her condo. "Bess. It's Kate. I'm inside."

I strained my one good ear, and it seemed as if there was a sound coming from the bedroom.

With shaky legs, I walked to the room.

My friend stood at the end of the bed, staring at a suitcase.

"Bess, are you okay?"

"I'm leaving town, and nobody's going to stop me."

My heart dropped.

Chapter Thirteen

From Bess's kitchen, I called Paul. "False alarm. Bess is fine."

"Good to know. I checked for the red Camry, but it was gone."

"That figures. Thanks, Paul."

"See you later."

I slid the phone into my pocket and poured Cokes for Bess and me. She was still in the bedroom, and I walked in there. "You nearly scared me to death. What are you doing? You can't leave town."

"I've got to go. My sister needs me, and it might be wise to get off the island until Paul catches the killer." She paused. "Has he said anything to you? I'm a suspect."

I handed one drink to her. "First, Paul knows you didn't commit the murder. He's got to conduct a thorough investigation and prove he questioned more than one person. Tell me about Ruth. Why does she need you?"

"Not so fast, sister." Bess took a drink of her Coke. "You didn't hear the way Paul questioned me. People have been telling the police that I was the last person to be seen with Clint. So, if the last person is the killer, then it looks like I am the killer." She guzzled her drink.

"Nobody believes you murdered Clint. Even if you'd stood over his dead body with the murder weapon, I'd know you were innocent. Let's sit down and reconstruct Friday night's timeline." I nudged her to go into the other room and sit at the kitchen table. I refilled her drink and pulled my polka dot journal from my purse.

"Okay. Friday night. Speed dating. You and I cleaned up the outer room.

I overheard Clint arguing with Hank." I wrote this in my notes along with the time.

"I remember you said that." Bess rubbed her hands together. "By the time you returned from taking out the trash, people began filling the room."

"Yes. Do you remember anything weird before we entered the dating room?"

She sipped her drink. "Despite all the people, it was a little tense. Maybe it was my nerves. Who knows? Anyway, Clint said he wanted to talk to me."

"Okay. That's good. What else?"

"I met him in the hall between the two sessions while others mingled over refreshments or visited the restrooms. That's when he warned me to be careful with Peter."

"But he didn't mention Hank?" How bad was Peter if Clint had argued with Hank but warned Bess to be careful with Peter?

"Correct."

"That's strange. They couldn't possibly both be conmen. Right? But I heard the word scam."

"And proof."

"Right. I'll investigate Hank and Peter and figure it out."

Bess grabbed my arm. "No. It's too dangerous. What if one of the men murdered Clint? Let Paul handle it."

"I have other suspects on my list, but the more I know about these people, the easier it'll be to catch the killer. Many women were infatuated with Clint. Unrequited love or jealousy could be a motive."

"Promise me you'll question the women first." Bess stared at me.

"We should question them together. Try not to worry. Paul knows you're innocent. The department has been under scrutiny this year, and I believe he's taking all the necessary precautions to prove he knows how to run a murder investigation. He must look at all the potential suspects. If there's an inquiry, he'll be able to prove he performed a thorough investigation." I stopped trying to convince her. She knew the more I rattled, the more nervous I was.

"Do you think he can run a murder investigation without your interference?"

"Yes. Absolutely." I hoped my brother could crack the case. Fox Island was a small town at heart, but Paul had helped solve other murders.

"Shush, now. I'm sorry, Kate. If I wasn't so scared, I wouldn't have asked the question." She gasped. "Oh, no."

"What?"

Bess leapt to her feet and turned off all the lights.

I looked out the window.

It wasn't dark outside, but hopefully her actions would make it hard for anyone to see us. My heart raced. "You're scaring me, Bess."

"I think I spotted the red car from last night." She growled.

I rubbed her shoulders. "Where is it?"

We crept to the window, but stayed behind the curtain. She pointed to a vehicle parked across the street. "There."

I squinted. "Wait a second. I need my glasses."

I moved to my bag and rooted through it until I found the case. I put on my new glasses and joined Bess at the window. Relief swept through me. "That's not a Camry. It's a Honda Civic. You can breathe now."

Her posture sagged. "Maybe I should've let Tom continue stomping on my heart. At least I wasn't in danger or being accused of murder."

"You deserve better than Tom. This too shall pass."

"Kate, I really do need to leave town."

"Oh, Bess. Won't it be better to surround yourself with friends?"

"You don't understand. There's more."

"I met Angie, and she loves her closet redesign." I chatted about what a great job she'd done in hopes of breaking her out of the melancholy.

"Thanks." She picked up my bag and handed it to me. "Seriously, I should probably go to Atlanta and help Ruth."

"Why?"

"She was in a car accident and needs my help." Bess shrugged. "What else can I do?"

"What about her husband? Can't he take care of her?"

"He's in the middle of a big merger." Her tone was flat.

I hugged my friend. "Don't worry about the murder investigation. I'm going to continue trying to solve the case. Diane is next on my list. Please don't leave until we have some answers."

"I don't know if I can do that. If my sister insists, I'll need to leave."

"Give it one more day. Please. One more day."

Bess shrugged. "You're the best friend a person could hope for. We'll talk tomorrow."

I drove to the resort with my windows down because the air conditioner was blowing hot air. This was one more thing I needed to tackle this week because August was too hot to drive without cool air.

I parked at the resort and entered the main entrance.

Gloria was working at the registration desk, and I waited until she was free.

When the guests had been taken care of, I approached. "Hi, there."

"Kate. How can I help you?" She held up a finger. "Let me guess. You're here to discuss Clint's murder. I didn't do it."

"I'm actually looking for Diane. Do you know if she's in town, or did she leave?"

"The police asked her to stay a few more days, and the boss comped her room." Gloria didn't sound happy about it.

"Okay. I guess it's best for the resort if the police solve the case quickly. So, any idea where I can find Diane?"

"But you're not the police."

"True, but I want to help."

Gloria tapped the computer keys and studied the screen. "Best guess? The pool bar. But, you didn't hear it from me."

"Thanks. See you later." I walked to the back of the resort. Canned music played over the speakers. Children squealed and laughed at the family pool. Men and women huddled in the corners of the adult pool. I turned my focus to the bar.

Sitting on a stool surrounded by men was Diane. If she'd been in love with Clint, she'd moved on fast enough, given the way she flirted with the men.

I took a deep breath and walked to the opposite end of the bar.

Lucky for me, Mason East was the bartender. The sight of him eased my nerves. It was time to plan my questions and make my move.

Chapter Fourteen

I nursed my raspberry spritzer until Diane walked away from the bar. I followed her to some lounge chairs situated away from the pools. "Hi, Diane. How are you doing?"

She set her bag on the ground and turned to me. "Oh, Kate. It wasn't nice of you and your husband to pretend to be single for speed dating." She spread a towel on the chair and sat on it, stretching out her legs.

"It was for the greater good." I sat on the closest chair and faced her.

"Not really. If people don't believe it's safe to attend dating events, then we'll be out of business."

"Sorry, but Bess is my friend." I adjusted my sunglasses. "How are you doing?"

"I'm as well as can be expected, considering."

"You and Clint must have been very close. Did you travel together for the events?"

"We did, but we concentrated on the states in the southeast. Florida, Georgia, well, you must know geography. Florida is popular for senior singles. The group that attended on Friday was typical, with ages ranging from thirty to seventy. Forties and fifties make up the largest age range."

"There must have been problems from time to time."

"Drinking too much was the biggest problem we faced. In fact, we began to serve less alcohol at the events. It helped the participants to make better decisions about who to date later."

"Makes sense. Friday night, I overheard Clint arguing with Hank Ingram before speed dating."

Diane's expression froze.

I decided to push. "Um, I think it was about a scam. Did you have problems with people more focused on swindling the attendees than finding love?"

"We did run into a few fraudsters over the years, but once Clint realized their intentions, he kicked them out."

Did that track with what I knew? "Um, why did he allow Hank to participate?"

"I don't know." She sat up, pulled sunscreen from her bag, and applied it to her feet and legs.

The sun was setting, and I wondered if she was nervous about our conversation. Why else apply sunscreen this late in the day? "What do you know about the jewelry shop man? Pete?"

"Peter Rodale. Don't call him Pete." She returned the tube of sunscreen to her bag and pulled out a floppy white hat.

"Did you know that Clint told one of the ladies not to fall for Peter? If he felt that way, why let him participate?"

"Some of the shysters change their names."

"How does that work?"

"Let's say Mr. X attends a dating event in Atlanta. He cons a woman, or a few women, out of their life savings. It takes a few months for the women to catch on, but by that time, Mr. X has disappeared. However, he was successful. It makes sense that Mr. X wants to try again. So, he changes his name and applies to attend another dating event. When he arrives, he steers clear of Clint. Mr. X may even change his appearance to throw off Clint because eventually they'll cross paths."

On Thursday, Peter had asked Bess to turn in the winning envelope to collect their prize from the scavenger hunt. Had he avoided Clint on purpose? "Clint was suspicious of Peter, so why didn't he prevent him from participating?"

"It can get complicated. One man sued Clint for something like defamation of character. They settled, but after that, Clint wanted proof before he stopped a participant." She adjusted her hat, and then took it off. "You should know that it's not only men who pull scams."

"I believe you." I looked at Diane. "Will you continue to run the business?"

"I guess it depends on Clint's will."

"Oh. I met his son, Kyle. Does he have other children?"

"Not that I know of."

Interesting answer for someone who'd worked with Clint. "Did Kyle and his father get along?"

"That's a question for Kyle." She waved to a waiter who was working the deck area.

The young man appeared. "Yes, ma'am."

"I'd like to order a Caesar salad and sparkling water." She gave him her name and room number.

The waiter looked at me. "Can I bring you anything?"

"No, but thanks."

He trotted toward the bar.

"Diane, who do you believe murdered Clint?"

She wadded up the hat and stuffed it in her bag. "He was a modern-day Casanova, and he joked about writing a memoir. It's possible he wasn't joking. If that's the case, the book could be motive for his death."

"How so?"

"Clint was a wonderful person, but sometimes his love life was chaotic. He left a trail of brokenhearted women, and I am sure they didn't want to read about it in a book."

"Were you ever romantically involved with Clint?"

She sighed. "We never hooked up."

"You two cared for each other. Why not get together?"

"It wouldn't be good for the business. I was crazy about Clint, but he would've broken my heart. I'm smarter than that. Besides, I have enough self-respect not to be one of his groupies."

"Good for you. I agree that Clint was nice, and it appeared that he wanted to protect your participants. Very respectable." I looked toward the ocean and breathed in the breeze. "Besides the possible memoir, can you think of a reason to murder Clint?"

"I'm sure it's related to his romantic relationships. My guess is one of them was jealous, and he pushed her too far." She looked toward the ocean. "Gloria Hardee is the first person I'd consider."

"I've talked to her, and she didn't appear to be heartbroken."

"She's a good actress. Don't let her slip off your radar."

"I'll keep that in mind." I took a deep breath. "Diane, where were you after speed dating? Do you have a witness for the time frame when Clint was murdered?"

Her face turned red. "It's none of your business, but something tells me you're not going to back off. I don't need a witness, because I didn't kill him."

"Okay. Thanks for your time, Diane." I left her alone and walked through the lobby.

For once, Gloria wasn't working at the desk.

It'd been a long day, and time for me to go home. I texted Allie. I'm ready to pick up Lady. Where are you?

By the time I'd walked to my vehicle, she'd replied. At your house with Ethan.

Interesting. Ethan and Allie were together. I shot off a reply and headed home. When I pulled into the driveway, Ethan was drying off my goldendoodle.

"Hey, Mom. We thought Lady might like to walk on the beach, and I just gave her a quick shower."

Allie sat on the wooden steps, holding a bottle of dog shampoo. "I hope you don't mind. It seemed like such a nice evening for a walk."

"It's all good. Have you two had supper?" I was hungry and needed to eat before I got cranky.

Ethan said, "I ordered pizza and salad. It should be here any minute. Why were you driving with the windows down?"

"The AC's not working." I was perspiring like crazy, but I couldn't ignore the hunger pangs. "Am I interrupting a date?"

Allie laughed. "We're at your house. You're not intruding."

"There's plenty of food coming. You should join us. Where's Reid?" Ethan released Lady, and she ran to me.

"Hey, girl." I rubbed her damp head. "He's in Atlanta hoping to get support for the house for veterans."

"Cool. Cool. Cool."

"I'm going to change clothes, and I can set the table."

Lady followed me inside, and after taking a quick shower, I put on shorts and a T-shirt. While waiting for the pizza, I set the table. There were still a lot of vacationers on the island, and the pizza place was probably slammed. I snuggled up with Lady on the couch and added Diane's notes to my journal.

Ethan and Allie entered the house, carrying our food. "Supper's ready."

"I'll be right there." I flipped back to my notes from the conversation with Gloria. Yep. It was like I remembered. She denied having a fling with Clint.

Tomorrow, I'd talk to somebody different. "Did y'all meet Clint's son, Kyle?"

Ethan poured drinks. "Yeah, he's around our age and a decent-looking dude. I doubt he ever attended his dad's events to get a date."

Allie said, "I agree. Kyle didn't participate in speed dating, but he did hang around the resort and dating areas."

Ethan said, "I wondered how Kyle convinced his dad to leave him alone. I'm surprised Clint didn't push him to participate. It seems like the son would be a draw to get single women to sign up. I know that when I asked Clint for pointers, he insisted I join the event." Ethan's gaze shifted from Allie to me. "Not that I'd do anything underhanded if I throw a similar event at the parks department."

I patted his hand. "I know you'd never pull a stunt like that."

I divided the salad onto our plates. "Did either one of you have anyone talk to you about investing money?"

"No, ma'am." Ethan dug into his food.

Allie focused on me. "Yes. The jewelry man. He commented on my necklace. He said he could sell me antique ruby earrings that would go perfectly with it. Peter claimed it originally came as a set, and he just so happened to have the exact matching earrings. He went on and on about how beautiful they'd look on me, and he'd give me a good deal."

I leaned forward. "You didn't believe him?"

"No. My granddaddy went mining and found the ruby. He had the necklace made for my grandmother, and there were no earrings. So, I knew he was lying, but I just smiled and changed the topic."

Ethan looked at Allie. "You should tell Uncle Paul."

Allie shrugged. "It never occurred to me to report the issue. Is it even a crime?"

"Good question." I said, "We should all be careful when it comes to Peter. Clint warned Bess to steer clear."

"And now Clint's gone." Ethan pointed at the pizza box. "Good to know about Peter, but our pizza is getting cold."

"You're right." All conversation ceased related to Clint's death. We enjoyed our food and discussed the upcoming college football season.

After they left, I reviewed my murder notes while Lady snoozed at my feet. Had Clint felt like the walls were closing in on him? Hank and Peter had both joined the dating events, and he didn't appear to trust either man. Hank wanted to invest women's money. Peter wanted to sell them jewelry. Had the stress caused Clint's stomach problems?

Anxiety hadn't killed Clint. He'd been strangled. That's where I needed to stay focused.

Chapter Fifteen

Tuesday morning, I was late for work. Again. Bess wasn't going to be happy, but I had a good excuse. Reid had called to discuss the man in Atlanta. I'd wanted to give him my full attention because this could turn out to be a huge deal for Reid, the veterans, and Fox Island.

I was so late, I figured even a latte wouldn't get me out of hot water with Bess. I entered the store empty-handed.

Allie sat at her desk and wore our company polo in a shade of green. "Good morning."

"Hi, where's Bess?"

"She left a message that she won't be at work for a couple of days."

I gasped. "I thought there was more time to convince her to stay, but it sounds like she may be on her way to Atlanta. I should've asked more details."

"What happened?"

"Ruth was in a car accident and asked Bess to take care of her. I don't know if she's at home, rehab, or the hospital."

Allie's eyes widened, but she didn't speak. Instead, she moved to the coffee station.

I called Bess to make sure she'd arrived in Atlanta safely.

No answer, but it rolled to voicemail. "Bess, please call me." I pushed the end button on my phone. Had she left town? Or what if Hank had gotten to her? Or Peter? I needed to know for sure that my friend was safe.

Allie placed a cup of coffee on my desk. "I fixed it the way you like. What do you need me to do?"

"Thanks." I sipped my coffee and reflected on the investigation.

"Kate, I don't believe you're focused on work. What's your main concern?"

"Clint was murdered. He warned Bess to stay away from Peter. You said Peter lied to you. So, something's going on with that guy." I drummed my fingers on the desk. "Plus, Hank Ingram followed us the other day."

"Do you think Bess is in danger?"

"She could be the next target, depending on the killer's motive."

"Tell me more."

"We don't know why Clint was murdered. What if the killer believes Clint told Bess something incriminating? She could be next on the hit list."

Allie gripped my arm. "If that's the case, we've got a serial killer. What are we doing sitting around? Let's go find Bess. I'll drive."

"But she might be on her way to Atlanta."

"She's not answering her phone."

"True."

"I'll reschedule our appointments, and then we'll drive around the island. You keep trying to reach Bess."

I dialed again. "Last night, she didn't answer my calls either. I wonder if she lost her phone."

"It's possible." Allie grabbed her purse and keys. "I sent out a generic text to our clients. Are you ready?"

"Almost." I transferred my coffee to a travel mug, we closed the store, and we hurried to Allie's SUV. Once she pulled out of the parking lot, she glanced at me. "To the condo first?"

"Yes. I've got a key for emergencies." I sipped my coffee during the short journey. "Thanks for driving."

"It's too hot for us to ride without air conditioning. You need to get your Wagoneer fixed if you hope to survive the rest of August. Or get a newer vehicle."

"You're not the first person to suggest trading. I feel safe in it, though."

"The thing is older than me." She turned onto Bess's street.

"Have you noticed anybody tailing us?"

"No, I wasn't paying attention. I'll drive around the block and see if I notice a car following us." She drove past the condos.

I watched out the side mirror but didn't see a red Camry or anything else suspicious. "I think we're safe."

"Okey-doke." She turned off the main drag, up Bess's street, and pulled into the parking garage. There was a security box with a mechanical arm down. "I need a code to get in."

"One, nine, seven, three. Bess has two parking spots around the corner."

Allie punched in the numbers and backed into the empty parking space I pointed out. "Are you worried that Bess's van isn't here?"

"It could be good or bad. Hopefully, it means she's driving to her sister's place, but I thought she would call me first." I pulled the key from my purse. "I don't want to be paranoid, but let's see what we can find."

It didn't take long for us to reach Bess's place. There was an ecru white envelope propped up against the door. Allie picked it up and then stepped back.

I unlocked the door and entered the condo. "Bess, are you here?"

Nobody answered.

I waved Allie in and locked the door behind us. "Last night she was packing a suitcase. I'm going to see if it's still here."

"What should I do?"

"Look around for anything unusual." I walked to the bedroom. There was no sign of the suitcase, and a pillow was missing. Bess always took her pillow if she was traveling.

Allie appeared, carrying a yellow sheet of paper. "She left a note for you. It was on the refrigerator door, and the fridge is empty except for mustard, mayo, a water pitcher, and a box of baking soda."

"She's gone. What does the note say?"

"She left at o-dark-thirty to drive to Atlanta. She doesn't want us to contact her because she wants to focus on her family."

"That makes sense. What's in the envelope?"

"Is it legal for me to open it?"

"I think that law applies to the United States Post Office. I'm not afraid to open it." I held out my hand.

She passed it to me.

Except for the hum of the air conditioner, the place was quiet. The flap wasn't glued, and the envelope opened easily.

A piece of paper floated into my hand. It matched the envelope, and there was a blue border on the piece of stationery.

Allie looked over my shoulder.

If you know what's good for you, you'll forget about Clint Speck. Mind your own business.

I shivered.

"It's a threat." Allie gasped. "Honestly, I imagined it was going to be a note from the HOA."

"I need to text Paul." I took a picture of the note and sent it to my brother. **Can you meet me at Bess's place? Somebody left this note. Bess is gone.**

A reply popped up. **OTW**

I looked at Allie. "He's on the way."

"Are we going to get in trouble?"

"You'll be fine. However, I may receive a stern lecture. Let's take pictures of the place before Paul kicks us out."

"Why don't you take pictures in here, and I'll start making a video in the main room?

"Why?"

"What if Bess knew something about the murder and didn't realize it? The killer must think she has information."

"Good point. You may take over my job as Fox Island's amateur detective." I got busy snapping pictures with my phone.

"As an EMT, I noticed how the police recorded a scene." Allie gave me a sad smile before she moved to the front room. Nothing jumped out at me, but I continued to take pictures until there was a pounding on the door.

"Kate, let me in." Paul yelled loud enough that I could hear him clearly, even with my deaf ear.

I opened the door. "Come in."

"For the record, do you have permission to be in here?"

"Yes. Bess gave me a spare key for emergencies, and she left me a note." Oh, man. Why hadn't I taken a picture of Bess's note? I had no doubt my brother would keep it for evidence.

Allie joined us. "Hi, Chief Wright."

He nodded. "Allie. Which one of you is going to explain what's going on?"

We both started talking at the same time.

Paul whistled. "One at a time. I assume you cleared the place."

My heart skipped a beat. "What do you mean? I haven't taken anything. Well, I did read the note Bess left me, and we opened the threatening letter."

He ran a hand over his face. "Did you touch it?"

"Well, yeah. I never dreamed it was connected to Clint's murder."

Allie said, "It's my fault."

"Hold up, you two. Right now, we need to confirm that Bess is safe. It's doubtful Clint's killer left a note and harmed her, but we need to know for sure. Kate, write down a list of Bess's contacts. Family and friends."

"No need. She's gone to Atlanta to take care of Ruth, who was in a car wreck." I found Ruth's information in my phone and texted it to my brother. "I know where she keeps all her family contact information if you think it'll help." I crossed the room and reached for the desk drawer handle.

"Don't." Paul put on gloves and joined me at the desk.

"Hey, I was here last night. My fingerprints will be all over the place."

Allie said, "Mine probably are, too."

Paul pulled out the address book. "Anything else you need to tell me?"

I crossed my arms. "It might not be a bad idea to talk to Tom Cross."

"Why? You don't believe she confessed to murdering Clint. Do you?"

"Of course not, but she's in the habit of talking to Tom. Maybe she's talking to him on the phone this very minute."

Paul studied the note and the letter. "It seems straightforward. Bess is driving to Atlanta. I'll look through the unit and make sure we're not missing anything. Why don't you two leave?"

Allie said, "You don't have to tell me twice. Bye, Chief Wright."

"Be careful, y'all." Paul grimaced.

I followed Allie to the garage, and we got into her Highlander.

She looked at me. "Where to, boss?"

I laughed. "Oh, Allie, I always knew I liked you. Let's drive around the island and see if we can spot Bess's van."

"Hey Kate, why is everyone so worried about Bess? I mean, she's a grown woman. Isn't she allowed to leave town for a few days?"

"Of course, she can. There are a few reasons I'm more concerned than normal. Clint was murdered. Plus, Hank followed us in his red Camry. What if she was forced to write the note and somebody kidnapped her?"

"That would be terrible." She pulled out of the parking garage.

"Or maybe she confided in Tom. Or maybe she's hiding on the island. Or—" I couldn't utter the words. What if she had been attacked and needed to be rescued?

I watched for Bess while Allie drove us to the church and prayed we'd get good answers from Tom.

Chapter Sixteen

Allie pulled into Fox Island Community Church's parking lot and parked under a big oak tree with Spanish moss dangling from the branches. "I don't see Bess's van."

"Me either."

"This morning is flying by." Allie dug her phone out of her purse. "I was planning to meet Ethan for lunch. Do you want to join us?"

"Thanks for offering. I'd enjoy having lunch with you two. We can update him on Bess. If you don't mind, I'm going to walk around the church campus real quick."

"Go for it."

I got out of the SUV and made my way around the main building.

Tom's white sedan was parked near the church offices. There was also a familiar black Ram pickup truck. If I wasn't mistaken, it was Reid's dad's truck.

I froze.

Why? My mind raced with possibilities. The church was a sponsor of drug and alcohol addiction classes, and this was the day they usually met. Was Sam Barrett struggling to stay sober? Had he fallen off the wagon?

No. I was panicking. Possibly overreacting. There weren't enough cars on site for a class to be meeting at this very moment, but Tuesdays were the day they met. Had Sam come for one-on-one counseling with Tom? Maybe it wasn't connected to his sobriety. I sure hoped he wasn't struggling. Reid would be brokenhearted. But if Sam was dealing with temptations, nobody would understand better than Tom. When his wife had been alive, she'd struggled. Tom's son was an adult who also dealt with addictions. Yeah, Tom understood substance abuse. Still, I hoped Sam was okay.

Think, Kate. There must be a logical reason.

The church door opened.

I darted behind a crepe myrtle.

"What are you doing?" Allie surprised me.

I yanked her closer to me. "Shh. Somebody's coming out of the building."

Allie whispered, "They're going to see you."

A familiar laugh reached us. Joy Barrett walked out, and Tom and Sam followed her.

Allie elbowed me. "It sounds like Reid's parents."

"Yeah. I can't imagine why they're here together."

"I think Joy sees us."

"Kate. Allie. What are you doing at the church on a Tuesday morning?" Joy wore bright blue leggings, an orange floral-patterned top, and strappy brown sandals. A chunky gold necklace and hoop gold earrings completed the outfit.

I stepped up to my mother-in-law and hugged her. "I was about to ask you the same thing."

Sam gave me an awkward hug. "Good to see you, Katie." His voice was warm and only a little deeper than Reid's.

I loved that Sam called me Katie. Reid was the only other person who called me that. "Hi, Sam."

At last, Joy returned to her original question, "What are you doing here, hon?"

"I'm looking for Bess, and we thought she might be here." I fixed my gaze on Tom. "Have you seen her?"

The pastor shrugged. "Not recently. Is she okay?"

"Probably." I turned back to Joy. "Why are you two here?"

Joy flashed me a big smile. "Sam proposed. We were going to tell you and Reid when he got back from Atlanta. Please, keep our secret until he gets home."

"Oh, Joy. I'm so happy for you both." I hugged my mother-in-law. "Y'all should call him soon. It'll lessen the chance I spill your secret."

Sam said, "We'll call today."

I gave Sam a good, long hug. "Reid will be happy to hear the news straight from you."

Sam nodded. "Reckon we best shove off. We'll study Georgia's football schedule, and then we'll send you one of those save-the-date cards. Nobody will come to our wedding if the Bulldogs are playing." Sam reached for Joy's hand, and they walked to his truck.

Tom said, "That's the truth. Go Dawgs."

Once they left, an awkward silence descended. I wasn't sure how to proceed because of Tom's past relationship, or non-relationship, with Bess.

Tom stuffed his hands into the pockets of his khakis. "What's going on with Bess?"

I took a deep breath to calm myself.

Allie said, "She invited me to a speed dating event at Seaside Hideaway. The man in charge was murdered, and it's safe to say that she's really upset."

Tom frowned. "Was she dating the man?"

Allie smiled at the pastor. "No, but he was a nice guy. We got to know him before he died."

I said, "We're all upset. I thought maybe Bess came here to pray."

"Feel free to look around, but to the best of my knowledge, she's not here."

"Thanks, Tom. I think we will peek in the sanctuary." I turned to Allie. "You with me?"

"Of course. Lead the way."

I started walking.

Tom cleared his throat. "I'll look, too."

We made our way to the sanctuary and entered. It was cool, peaceful, and empty. I began to think clearly. Bess's note indicated she was on the way to Atlanta. Hopefully, the message was legit. If so, she was probably there by now. If only she'd answer her phone, then I'd feel better. "Tom, I'm sorry to have bothered you."

"If she shows up, I'll ask her to call you."

"Thanks." I walked away first, and Allie followed me to the parking lot.

I got in the passenger seat. Tom had taken advantage of Bess's feelings for years. Maybe he'd been conflicted about being a widowed pastor and dating, but he should've realized how much my friend had cared for him.

Allie started the engine. "Were Bess and Tom in a relationship?"

"They worked together for years, and they grew close. There was some hanging out together and a date or two, but they never officially dated."

Allie drove out of the parking lot. "It's been an interesting morning. Ethan is going to meet us at Dairy Barn. Are you in the mood for a burger?"

"Sounds good to me. Do you mind if I write some notes while you drive?"

"Go ahead while it's all fresh on your mind." She stopped at a light.

I got lost in recording my thoughts and observations until Allie parked.

Ethan opened my door. "Hi, Mom. Something tells me you're not staying out of trouble, and you've dragged Allie into your investigation."

I stepped out. "Dragged may be a strong word."

Allie met us at the front of the SUV. "There was no dragging involved. I am fully committed to helping your mom solve Clint's murder. When Gloria screamed for help, we were the ones who went with her. We saw Clint's body."

Ethan touched her shoulder. "I know, and I'm sorry you two had to deal with it."

Allie nodded. "Me, too. But it seems logical for me to help Kate solve the murder."

Ethan ran a hand over his face. "Now, I'm going to be worried about both of you."

Allie said, "At least we'll be together. Wouldn't it be worse if we were off in different directions, trying to solve the murder?"

Ethan opened the restaurant's door and held it for both of us. "I don't know how to answer, but I need to eat before you two completely gang up on me."

The place was crowded, and I handed Ethan my credit card. "Lunch is on me. I'd like a cheeseburger and unsweetened iced tea. I'll grab a table for us."

"Thanks, Mom."

"Thanks, Kate."

There was one table available, but it hadn't been bussed. There wasn't a line for the spot, so I stopped a waitress. "Is it okay for me to clean that table?"

She looked at me. "Kate. It's good to see you. Cash told me you were back in town, and yes. If you bus it, you can eat there. Sorry, but two people called off work today."

I studied my old high school friend. "Naomi, we need to catch up sometime. I'll take care of this table."

"Thanks." She pointed to a cart. "There are towels and spray cleaner on it."

"Great." I cleared the table and placed my purse on a chair, so nobody would think it was available. I carried the dirty dishes to the cart and traded them for a white cloth and a bottle of cleaner. Ethan and Allie joined me by the time I finished. "The table might be damp."

Ethan placed the drinks on the table along with a sign indicating our order number. "Mom, the waitress looks familiar. Who is it?"

"Naomi Tucker. Her husband runs the lighthouse." I sat on one side of the booth, and they took the other. "When I was growing up, Cash was the high school quarterback, and Naomi was a cheerleader."

"That's it. He approached me about starting a football program for young kids." He put a straw in his Coke. "I looked him up and saw her in one of the photos. There are rules in place to help prevent child predators working in my programs, and I try to be extra vigilant. Uncle Paul has given me some tips to keep the bad people from slipping through the cracks, but I know nothing is foolproof."

Naomi arrived with our food. "Kate, is this your family?"

"This is my son, Ethan. Allison Cameron works with me."

"Nice to meet you two. Enjoy your lunch." She turned and walked back to the counter.

I smiled at Ethan and Allie. "I'm not going to butt into your relationship or assume anything. If you two start to date, will you let me know?"

Ethan's face reddened. "Yes, ma'am."

Allie's eyes sparkled. "Oh, Ethan. Guess who's going to get married? It's a secret until they announce it to their family."

"How do you know the secret, and why are you telling me if it is a secret?" Ethan's eyebrows rose.

"Good point. I won't tell you." Allie glanced at me. "Kate, do you assume Pastor Cross is performing the ceremony? Or did they meet with him for pre-marital counseling?"

I shrugged. "I don't know."

Ethan said, "I give up. Who's getting married?"

Allie beamed at Ethan. She whispered, "Sam and Joy Barrett."

His mouth dropped open. "Are you kidding me?"

"No. They seemed happy."

I wasn't thrilled that Allie had shared the secret. "Ethan, they promised to tell Reid today, but they're not ready to go public. Sam was always the love of Joy's life, even though he took off after returning home from war. Although, he was active in some military missions besides the Vietnam War. Reid doesn't like to talk about it, so I don't push. Anyhow, Joy tried marrying other men, three to be exact, but none of them were Sam. All the other marriages failed."

Ethan picked up a french fry. "Sounds a little bit like you and your love for Reid."

I speared my son with a look. Did he know his dad had been unfaithful? "Yeah, but—"

"Don't worry about it, Mom. The main thing is that you're happy."

"Thanks, honey." I swallowed the lump in my throat. "Let's eat before our food gets cold."

All these years, I had imagined I was protecting Ethan. I never revealed the secret about his dad and the other woman. Had Ethan known? Did he think I was a liar because I hid the truth?

The sooner we talked about his dad, the better it'd be.

Unless he didn't know the truth. What if he blamed me for David's indiscretions? I'd never told my friends in Lexington about David's affair, but I feared they'd known.

Paul was the person I had spilled my heart to. My brother was always a good listener. If it hadn't been for his support, I'm not sure I would've survived the sorrow. Reid and Bess also knew the ugly truth.

"Mom, you're not eating."

My face warmed. "My mind started wandering."

Allie finished her last fry. "What will we do next?"

I reviewed the list of suspects in my mind. "Did you meet Jennifer Fraser?"

"Yeah, she was the girl with the beautiful blond hair." She held her hands out by her head. "I mean big hair. Curly. Not like the styles in the eighties, but natural."

I laughed. "That's the one. Why don't we try to find her and keep our eyes open for Bess at the same time?"

"I'll look for her on Instagram." Allie smiled at me before turning to Ethan.

They talked softly, while I ate my burger. I sent Bess one more text. **Are you with Ruth?**

I finished eating while staring at my phone, hoping for a reply. Assuming Bess was safe with her sister, my priority was to help solve Clint's murder. It'd be a whole lot easier once I knew my best friend was safe.

Chapter Seventeen

I searched some of the key players on social media. Jennifer Fraser had posted that she and her mother, Erica, were going kayaking on the marsh with a local company. They looked happy in the photo, so maybe they'd made up. Good.

It was time to have a conversation with them about the murder. After lunch, Allie and I changed clothes and headed to the beach at the estuary, where we waited for the kayak group to return.

"It sure is a scorcher today. I'm glad we brought drinks with us." I took a gulp of ice-cold water.

"Kate, we should sit on one of the logs. Or we can find Jennifer another time. No need for us to have a heat stroke."

"Let's give it a few more minutes, but I will take your suggestion to sit." I walked through the sand to a log that may have once been a crepe myrtle. The wood was beautiful and smooth, and I sat on the trunk.

Allie came with me. "Do you plan to talk to Jennifer with her mother watching, or do you want me to try to distract Erica?"

"Oh, I'd love to question Jennifer without her mother hovering." I took another drink. "Suppose there was a romantic relationship. Why do you suppose Erica was so opposed to Jennifer dating Clint? Was it only the age thing?"

"Probably. My parents would flip out if I dated a man more than forty years older than me." Allie sat near me on the log. "I'd like to believe they'd agree to meet him and respect me if I loved the man."

"I don't know how I'd handle Ethan dating a much older woman. A big age gap might prevent her from having babies. Ethan is wonderful with children, and I believe he'll be a terrific dad one day. If he gets together with a woman who doesn't want to have children, or isn't able to have children, I'll have to juggle my selfish desires with trusting Ethan's choices. It won't be easy."

"I see what you mean, but Jennifer would still be able to have babies if she were with an older man." She looked away. "I see a kayaker."

"Great. If anyone questions us, what is our story?" The heat was zapping me.

"Out for an afternoon walk? Slow day at the office?"

"Both are true since we canceled our appointments for this interview." I stood and fought off a wave of dizziness. Once I felt steady, we looked for shells until the first kayak landed on the beach. Diane hopped out of her boat. "Hi, ladies. Our event is over. Sorry if you had planned to go with us."

I glanced at Allie and nodded. "I must've misunderstood."

"How'd you find out we were here? It wasn't an official matchmaking event."

"I came across a post on Instagram."

A man eased out of his kayak while still in the water and helped steady a woman getting out of her boat.

I squinted, wishing I'd worn my new glasses. "Is Dwayne Gray with you?"

"Yes. He came down for breakfast at the resort about the time we decided on this impromptu adventure. I talked him into joining us, and he said something about it inspiring a new song."

Allie said, "He's a wonderful musician. I almost missed speed dating because I was listening to him."

Jennifer stopped paddling and pulled her boat to the beach.

A truck honked.

Diane looked over her shoulder. "They're with the tour company. Jennifer, you can relax. The fellows will collect our kayaks."

She dropped the boat and joined us. "That was fun, Diane. Thanks for letting my mother join."

"Hey, she's single, and she paid." Diane removed her life jacket.

I said, "Jennifer, do you have a minute to chat?"

Diane frowned. "Don't grill her about Friday night."

Of all the nerve. It was none of Diane's business, but instead of telling her as much, I pasted a smile on my face. "Jennifer, I just have a couple of questions for you."

Jennifer nodded. "Okay."

We walked toward the log I'd been sitting on earlier. "I confess to being curious about Clint's death. Have you seen or heard anything that might indicate who did it?"

She unfastened the buckles on her life jacket but didn't remove it. "Nothing comes to mind."

"Anything weird in general among the participants in Clint's events? Or people you've seen staying at the resort?"

"Besides Hank and Peter hitting on my mom?" Jennifer hung her head. "Now, that's strange to me. The way those two flirt with women, it doesn't seem like they have a type. You know how some guys go after busty women, or athletic women, or curvy blondes. But those guys focused on my mother."

Not what I was expecting, but I'd go with the flow. "Diane said that your mom is single."

"Yeah."

"Are you comfortable seeing her date?" I took another drink.

"I've never seen her go out, but I'm twenty-six. Who knows what she's been doing since I graduated from high school?" Jennifer shuffled away from the crowd.

I followed her. It sounded like she had never returned home. "What do you do, Jennifer? Like, careerwise."

"I work in the tech industry. The company is based in Atlanta, but I can work from anywhere with a good Wi-Fi signal."

"Oh, my husband is in Atlanta for meetings this week." And Bess was hopefully there with Ruth.

Jennifer gasped. "Your husband? The man you were with the other night? You were both at speed dating. What kind of con are you pulling? Did one of you murder Clint?"

"No!" I stepped closer to the young woman. "We were there to support my friend. She was nervous, and Reid and I are newlyweds. Why would you think we were pulling a con?"

She looked over her shoulder before turning back to face me. "Clint confided in me about some con artists. He believed in his matchmaking business, and it killed him to think about people taking advantage of single people. Oh, I didn't mean killed."

"I understand. It's hard to believe. We were all together one minute, and then he was gone." I paused and watched a ghost crab dart out of a hole and back into it. "Did Clint mention anyone specifically?"

"No. If he hadn't been so frustrated, I doubt he would've told me." Jennifer pointed to Allie. "What about her? Is she legit?"

"She's single. I didn't mean to upset you."

Jennifer turned her back on me.

"Are you okay?" I moved around her.

Tears streamed down her face, and she yanked off the life vest. "I can't believe he's gone."

"Me, either." I took a deep breath. "Jennifer, were you in love with Clint?"

"Like romantic love? No. But something drew me to the man. I cared about him."

"But your mother thought he was too old for you?"

"Yes. Clint and I spent a lot of time together, but we never got physical. He never held my hand or kissed me. It's hard to explain." She walked aimlessly. "He was more like a dad or big brother."

I patted her shoulder and matched her pace. "Not all relationships need to be explained. It sounds like you two became good friends."

"We did. This wasn't the first event I joined. We first met in Atlanta a while back. Clint wanted to help me find a great man to date and maybe marry. He suggested I attend more events so I'd be more relaxed."

I nodded. "Your job must give you a lot of freedom."

"Yes, I mostly work remotely. So, I do have freedom, but my socialization skills are getting rusty from so much time at home alone."

"On the bright side, you have flexibility. So, you came to Fox Island for the dating weekend. Did Clint give you advice on the men attending?"

"Yes."

I remembered Bess had said the same thing. "Did he tell you to be careful around Peter or Hank?"

She whipped around and faced me. "How did you know?"

"Just a hunch. And now those are the same men putting the moves on your mother."

"Yes. She refuses to listen to my warnings because she didn't like Clint."

"Was there some other reason for her not to like him?"

"Not that I can think of." She sniffed. "And now that he's gone, it's as if we never fought about him. It's almost like she was jealous, but that makes no sense."

It might make sense. "Jealous of your interest in Clint? Or envious of him paying attention to you?"

"I'm not sure. When it came to Clint, there was no reasoning with my mother."

"Is there a possibility that your mom ever dated him?"

Jennifer loosened her hair bun and massaged her scalp. "That would make her a liar, a hypocrite, and, well, I don't know what, but that would be terrible."

"I know it happens in movies, and probably real life. Don't judge your mom until you ask."

"Jennifer!"

We both turned toward the sound.

Erica's mouth moved, but I couldn't hear over the wind. "What's she saying?"

"The tour company is ready to drive us back to town." Jennifer trudged toward the others, dragging her life jacket in the sand and leaving a trail.

I hurried to catch up with her.

Jennifer said, "Mom, were you dating Clint? Or did you ever date him?"

Erica's posture slumped. "Why would you ask me such a question?"

"It would explain a lot about your attitude."

"I didn't want you to date a man that old. Now, hurry up before we miss our ride."

Jennifer looked at me. "Kate, will you drive me back to the resort?"

"Um, well, Allie drove us here, but I'm sure she won't mind."

Erica glared at me.

"Thank you." Jennifer handed her mom the life jacket. "I'll see you later."

When we joined the rest of the group, most had loaded onto the kayak company's van.

Allie spotted us. "Kate, are you ready to go?"

"Yes, but do you mind if we take Jennifer to the resort?"

"Sure." Allie smiled.

On the way, Jennifer sat in the backseat and muttered to herself.

I looked back. "Do you want to talk?"

She shook her head and sniffed. "It's too confusing. What is going on with my mother? She never wanted to discuss my dad, no matter how much I begged for information through the years. She didn't like my friendship with Clint. Are the two connected?"

Allie pointed to the glove compartment.

I opened it and pulled out a travel pack of tissues, and then passed them to Jennifer.

"I don't have the answers to your questions. You should talk to your mother, because she's the only one who can tell you the truth."

"She better tell me the truth this time." Jennifer groaned but didn't say anything else.

The remainder of the ride to Seaside Hideaway was a quiet one. When Allie stopped at the front, Jennifer thanked us and ran inside.

Allie said, "What was that all about?"

I shifted my body and looked at her. "It's possible Erica Fraser dated Clint at some point in her life. Erica never told Jennifer who her father is."

"Whoa, that's interesting." She removed her sunglasses and met my gaze. "But I might have something to top that."

Chapter Eighteen

I gawked at Allie. "Don't keep me in suspense."

A man driving a muscle car revved his engine behind us and honked.

I glanced back at the bright green vehicle. "Oh, look at that souped-up Charger. Sweet."

Another man tapped on Allie's window with his knuckles. "Ma'am, would you like me to park your car?"

Allie lowered her window. "Sorry, no. I didn't mean to hold up your line."

"It's no trouble. People shouldn't be in a hurry when they're living on island time." The man gave a two-finger salute and stepped back so Allie could drive away.

I tapped my foot to a Thomas Rhett country song on the radio.

Allie parked in the shade. "So, brace yourself for this story. Last night, Dwayne was playing his music on the terrace stage. He spotted Bess and Hank talking, and he didn't like the way Hank was leaning over her. Um, he might've said looming. Anyway, it rubbed him wrong."

I gasped. "Bess was here? Why would she have come to the resort if she knew she'd leave today? Sorry, please tell me more."

"Dwayne said Bess looked mad, so he cut his set short and walked over to them. He said that he tried to play it cool. Hank excused himself but told Bess that he'd be in touch."

"What time did this happen?"

"Dwayne said it was late. It would've been his last performance, but he promised to return for a bonus set. He's such a nice man."

"You're right about Dwayne. Let's think about the timeline. I went to

Bess's condo last night. We talked a bit. Then, something happened, and she went to the resort late last night. Why? Plus, she didn't show up for work. Again, why? Is it as innocent as going to care for her sister?" My stomach churned.

"I might know." Allie ran her hand over the steering wheel. "Dwayne walked Bess to her van, and she said Hank had lured her to the resort. He claimed he had her nice sunglasses."

I nodded. "She paid a fortune for them. Did he really have them?"

"Evidently, he did. Bess asked Dwayne if he thought Hank might be a pickpocket."

"Oh, my goodness. What did he say?"

"He had no idea, but he gave Bess his business card. Dwayne told her to call him if she ran into trouble with Hank. She thanked him, and he watched her drive away."

"It sounds like Dwayne was the last person to see Bess." The Sea Spray Kayaks van entered the parking lot, and the singles began to unload. "Allie, look at them. I see everyone except for Erica. Do you see her?"

"No. Maybe Dwayne knows where she is."

The van drove away, and the damp group of people slowly walked to the front door.

I jumped out of the car and hustled to the group. "Dwayne, wait up."

He turned and walked to me. "Hi, Kate. I talked to Allie."

"Yeah, she told me. I won't keep you long. Why didn't Erica get off with the rest of you?"

He pointed to the van. "Her car was at the store, and she's riding back with the crew. I heard you all gave Jennifer a ride."

"Yeah. The poor girl was upset with her mother, and she asked us for a ride."

"I don't have children of my own, but I've seen my siblings fight with their kids. Of course, most of them are teenagers."

"It'd break my heart if my son got that mad at me. Jennifer is struggling with Clint's death, and I think she can't deal with her mother right now." I decided not to blab everything I knew. "Thanks for watching out for Bess last night."

"Allie told me that she's out of town."

"We believe she left early this morning to help her sister. It's probably why she wanted her good sunglasses. Do you know much about Hank or Peter?"

"Peter's a player. Hank is bad news, but I haven't got a handle on him. I will, though." He crossed his arms, and his biceps flexed.

"I should let you go. Have a good rest of your day, Dwayne."

"If you talk to Bess, please tell her that I asked about her."

"Absolutely. See ya." I rejoined Allie in her Highlander. "Erica's car is at Sea Spray Kayaks."

"Okay." She pointed to her watch. "It's almost four. What do you want to do next?"

"I wish I knew. Who do you think killed Clint?"

Allie leaned her head back on the headrest. "To strangle Clint with a saxophone strap, the killer must have been strong. Maybe the person wore gloves, too."

"Why do you think the killer wore gloves? Most people don't wear gloves in Georgia in August."

"I thought saxophone straps were usually slick, making it hard to get a tight grip. That's what makes me think the killer would struggle to grip it with their bare hands."

"If gloves are involved, it was premeditated. Otherwise, it may have been done in the heat of the moment?"

Allie shrugged. "Dwayne would know about the straps. I hate to bother him again so soon, but I've got his number if you want to text him."

"Why don't you do it, Allie?" I texted Bess again while I waited.

"I may have embarrassed myself around him, fangirling and all."

I laughed. "He's probably flattered."

Allie handed Dwayne's business card to me. "I don't know. Please, you do it."

"No problem." I added Dwayne's contact information to my phone and sent him a text. Hi, this is Kate. Are saxophone straps slick? And what are they made of? Nylon?

His reply was immediate. Are you still here?

"Wow, that was a fast reply." I texted back. Yes. Parking lot with Allie.

Meet me at the outside restaurant in five.

Thanks. I flashed my phone to Allie, so she could read the conversation. "I guess we know our next step."

"Lead the way."

Allie and I walked through the resort's lobby and headed to the restaurant. The laughter and splashes from the swimming pools made it seem like a normal day. Beach music played over speakers and added to the festive atmosphere.

The outside restaurant was closed until five, but Dwayne met us from the inside and opened the door. "Come in, ladies."

"Thanks, Dwayne." I entered first, but Allie followed on my heels.

"For special events, I have a bigger band." He waved for us to follow. "This is our break room, and there are saxophones in those three cases. The guys won't mind if I show them to you. The answer to your question about the material is easy enough. It's a combination of nylon, neoprene, and leather. Some of the guys wear a harness if it's going to be a long set. The harness reduces strain on the neck and shoulders. Some musicians wear a padded strap."

I added the notes to my phone. "Thanks."

He opened the first case and found a black strap rolled up in a little compartment. He ran his fingers over it. "Hmm, only part of it feels slick to me."

I reached for the strap and ran my fingers over the material. "Oh, I bet this is the part that touches the player's skin because it's smoother, er, slicker."

Dwayne snapped his fingers. "I bet you're right." He replaced it and then opened another case. "Let's see if this is the same." He ran his fingers over the strap.

Allie said, "Well?"

"Slick in the same spot. So, the straps appear to only be slick where they're worn out from body contact. I don't believe the cops have Clint's strap."

I met his gaze. "I think you're right. Clint also only wore a simple strap. I don't believe there was padding, and it wasn't a harness. But for our speed dating event, he only played for a short time."

Allie reached out. "May I?"

Dwayne handed the strap to Allie, and she felt it. She said, "We all agree that there was no strap on Clint's body. Even as shook up as I was, I know that much to be true. If Gloria hadn't mentioned it, I wouldn't have given it a thought."

I nodded. "Yeah, I don't believe she found it."

"Gloria?" Dwayne's eyes grew wide. "Fascinating. Why would she care about such a minor thing when Clint was either dead or dying?"

My head began to spin, and I sat on a nearby chair. "That's a very good question, Dwayne. We'll try to find out."

Allie touched my shoulder. "Kate, you look pale. Are you okay?"

"Yeah, I'm fine." The dizziness was probably due to the heat.

Dwayne said, "You two wait here."

Allie sat beside me. "Do you want me to call Ethan?"

"No, I'm sure it's the heat. If you don't mind, could you take me home after this? I'll take a cool shower and rest."

Dwayne returned with fruity drinks. "Don't go falling out on me, Kate. I've met your husband, and I don't believe he'd appreciate it if I let you faint. Drink this."

"What is it?"

"A power smoothie. It's got almond butter and lots of fruit in it, and it should help if your blood sugar has dropped. I also brought one for your girl, Allie."

Dwayne straightened the room while we drank the delicious drinks. None of us said much, and I imagined we were all processing Clint's murder.

I slurped the remnants of the smoothie. "You know, I do feel better. Thanks, Dwayne."

He gave me a relaxed smile. "Good to hear it. I need to start prepping for tonight, but you two stay here where it's cool as long as you need."

My face warmed from embarrassment, and I stood. "I'm fine now."

Allie leapt to her feet and stood near me. "I'll drive Kate home."

"All right. Be careful." He held the door open for us, and we soon went our separate ways.

Once we were in Allie's vehicle, she said, "I already texted Ethan. He's going to meet us at your home."

"This is so humiliating. The heat got to me."

"Stress probably didn't help." She adjusted the air conditioner and pulled out of the parking lot.

"You might be right, but I'll be happy when my body adjusts to the hotter weather."

Allie turned onto my street, and Ethan stood in my driveway. He leaned against his Land Rover but pushed off to open my door after Allie parked in the drive.

"Mom, you gave Allie quite a scare."

She squealed and poked his arm. "Ethan!"

He laughed. "Sorry, but it's the truth. Mom, let's get you inside. I'll walk Lady."

Allie said, "If it's okay, I'll go back to Let's Get Organized and check for messages. What do you want to do about tomorrow?"

"We'll go to all the appointments together. It's time for you to learn more about our business."

"Yes, ma'am. See you in the morning." She waved and then sped away.

Ethan walked me to the door. "Something tells me your heat episode had nothing to do with work and everything to do with the murder investigation."

I shrugged. "There's no good response to your accusation. Although it's taking me a while to get used to this Georgia heat."

"How can I help?"

I unlocked the door, and Lady greeted us in the great room.

"Who's a good girl? I missed you today." I rubbed her sides. "Ethan, what do you think about meeting a man about jewelry?"

"Is this connected to the murder?" He leashed my goldendoodle.

"Yeah, what else?"

"As long as you're not trying to get me to propose—"

"Whoa. I'm not rushing you into anything." I thought Allie was wonderful and a good fit for Ethan, but I'd never push. "Plus, you told me not to interfere with your love life."

"Okay. Count me in on the jewelry thing." He led the dog outside, and I headed to my bathroom and a cool shower.

I couldn't wait to talk to Reid about the suspects and what I'd learned today. First, I needed to freshen up and check on Bess.

I fired off a short text. Did you make it to Ruth's safely?

After I showered and changed clothes, I glanced at my phone.

Nothing from Bess. Don't make me send Reid to find you. I knew Reid wouldn't mind checking on her if we decided it was necessary.

Bess's lack of response made me uneasy, but maybe she was too busy helping her sister to check messages. I wouldn't panic. Yet.

Chapter Nineteen

It was dark when I took Lady for her last walk of the day. She tugged toward the beach, but I didn't want to get far from home. I used my flashlight app, and we walked around the corner.

Lady's ears perked up, and she grew still.

I strained to listen. The rumble of a vehicle on my street sent a chill up my spine, and I tightened my grip on the leash.

Lady growled.

"Shh. It's going to be okay." I was good at recognizing cars with my eyes, but the nuances of sounds escaped me because of my hearing loss.

An engine shut off. That much I could discern.

I rarely saw any neighbors, and I couldn't imagine who would park on my street. Unless, it was somebody who'd driven over for the beach access. My anxiety lessened. That must be it.

Although it was high tide. It'd be hard to walk.

Could Clint's killer be here? I shivered.

I moved through the shadows with Lady and headed toward my home. If I could get inside and lock the doors, we'd be safe.

We stood behind a pine tree, and I looked toward the street. Nothing unusual. I glanced at my driveway. Relief swept through me at the sight of Reid's F-150.

Instead of the killer being here, it was my husband.

"Lady, let's go. Reid is home." I jogged across the yard, and Lady barked a happy welcome.

Reid stepped out of his truck and stretched. "Babe, I missed you."

I threw my arms around him. "I missed you, too. What are you doing here?"

"A little bird told me you weren't feeling great. So, I wrapped up business in Atlanta and hightailed it home." He kissed me like we'd been apart for months and not days.

When the kiss ended, I smiled at my husband. "I'm so happy to see you that I won't even get mad at the blabbermouth. Let's get inside, and I'll fix you something to eat."

"I picked up supper from The Varsity and ate in the truck."

"Oh, man. I haven't eaten there in years." I leaned my head on his chest, and he held me. We stayed like that until Lady tugged on the leash and barked. "I guess we should head inside."

Reid grabbed his duffel bag and his backpack briefcase, and we walked up the stairs and into the house. I locked and deadbolted the door.

"Seriously, are you okay, Kate?" Reid's concerned expression touched my heart.

"Yeah, I'm fine. Better now that you're home." My heart swelled with love for this wonderful man.

"I'm going to take a shower, and then I want to hear more about your investigation."

I glanced at my watch. Almost ten o'clock. I'd felt exhausted before Reid appeared, but now I was pumped. "Okay, and I'll fix us lemon balm tea."

"Wait, what?" He quirked an eyebrow. "Not chamomile?"

"Allie suggested I try lemon balm. You game?"

"I'll try as long as you don't get mad if I hate it."

I kissed his cheek. "I can't imagine getting mad at you."

"That's good to know, but there's also something to be said about making up." He left me standing there, with my mouth hanging open.

Lady nudged me, and I meandered into the kitchen. I started the tea kettle and prepared a plate of crackers, almond butter, and cherries.

Before long, Reid returned. His wet hair caused me to flash back to the first day we'd reconnected. His mother had hired me to organize his pantry, but Joy hadn't told him. He'd come home dirty from a job and had headed to the shower. Afterward, he'd taken my breath away. Honestly, it'd been the first moment before he'd cleaned up.

I said, "Do you want to sit on the couch?"

"Sounds like a good idea. You can update me on the murder while we snack." He carried the tray over, and I grabbed my journal.

"First, tell me what happened today. I still can't believe you're home."

"When I heard that Bess took off, I imagined you were upset. How are you holding up?"

"She's not answering any of my texts." I double-checked my phone. "Nope. Nothing. I closed the office today, and then Allie and I worked on finding clues to the murder. Bess was torn up when Paul questioned her, and I think if I can help solve the murder, we'll all feel better."

"But?" He reached for his mug of tea.

"It's possible she got herself in trouble."

"How?"

"What if Clint told her something, and she doesn't realize it's important? Or what if the killer thinks she knows more than she does? Is she the next target?" I paused. "Now, tell me what happened in Atlanta."

"They will make a donation to the home, but there has to be a vote on the amount. Also, there's a chance they'll take over running the place."

"How does that make you feel?"

"Terrific. I got it up and going, because I saw a need. Handling the day-to-day operations isn't my thing. I'd love for them to manage the place, because I'm out of my element." His relaxed posture reassured me. "Really, I'm just a man who likes to build stuff and protect the environment."

"Oh, Reid. You're so much more than that, but I'm happy for you." I reached for my mug.

"So, back to your investigation."

I looked through my notes and updated him. "Tomorrow, Ethan has agreed to contact Peter, the jewelry guy. He's going to pretend to want to buy a diamond ring."

"Okay, but what if instead of Ethan, you and I approach Peter? You'll see his reactions firsthand, and you might think of some new questions while we're with him."

I considered his suggestion. "I like your idea, but I've got to work tomorrow. Can we try to meet him at lunchtime or after supper?"

"If you have his contact information, I'll reach out to him tonight."

I looked at my watch. "It's getting late."

"True, but most people turn off their notifications when they go to bed."

"Okay. Here you go." I shared the info. "I saved it because of Bess."

"I understand. Neither of us trusts the guy." He tapped his phone.

"I'll let Ethan know he's off the hook for tomorrow." I texted my son.

Lady moved to her sleeping pillow and curled up.

"Done." Reid yawned.

"Let's go to bed. Tomorrow morning, we can develop a detailed plan."

"Sounds good to me."

I was happy to have my husband home, and I was glad we'd confront Peter together. I needed to organize my thoughts so I'd be ready to question him about the murder. But first, I needed a good night's sleep. Tomorrow would be soon enough to move forward in finding Clint's killer.

Chapter Twenty

Wednesday morning, Allie and I went to Brooke Young's law firm. Her assistant took us into the attorney's office and introduced us.

Brooke said, "Have a seat, ladies. I was expecting to see Bess Walker."

I nodded. "We had to adjust our schedule, but I can include Bess when we create plans for you. Do you know her personally?"

"She's a—friend." Brooke pulled a band from her top drawer and pulled back her thick, wavy hair.

Had Brooke almost admitted that Bess was a client?

Allie said, "Are you interested in organizing your entire office? Or a smaller area?" Allie was taking notes on a yellow legal pad.

Brooke pointed to a closet. "That's the first thing to address."

I stood and pointed at the door. "May I?"

"Yes, but brace yourself."

I walked over and opened the door. A gasp escaped me.

Brooke laughed. "You can't say I didn't warn you."

There were collapsing cardboard boxes, three-ring binders, folders, and loose papers. Oh dear. "What are your thoughts? Shelves? File cabinets? Do we have to sign any non-disclosure agreements before we go through the boxes?"

The attorney walked over and stood beside me. "I've lost control, but there are some confidential files in there. I'll go through them with my assistant before you return. I may even assign a law student to handle all the files under your guidance. Like when you see a collapsed box, you'll tell them to put the files in a new bin. You and Bess create a plan. Once you figure it out, you can tell my student how to implement it."

"Sounds good. Are these files related to current cases?"

"No. Why?" Brooke wore a white blouse with thin blue stripes, a blue skirt, and black pumps.

Allie joined us, and I moved out of the way.

I said, "This is prime space because it's in your office. It's convenient with quick and easy access. Is there a room in the building where you can store boxes of old files?"

"Follow me." Brooke swept past us.

Allie grinned. "She sure walks fast in those heels. I wish she'd teach me how to do that."

We followed Brooke out of her office and down a hall. At the last door on the left, the attorney stopped, opened it, and turned on the lights. "We used to have a private investigator in this office, but he outgrew us."

We entered the room. There was a desk and a chair. "Oh, this could be perfect. We can push the desk and chair to the side. We'll install strong shelves. You, or your student, can label the files with a code or case name. They can be arranged by date or alphabetically. If an attorney needs to review notes on an old case, she can move it to the desk and go through it. What do you think?"

Allie stopped writing. "Have you considered digitalizing files after you finish a case? That allows you to shred the papers and lessens your chance of a fire."

"Oh, that's a good idea. Let me think about it, but I do like your suggestion to empty my closet so it's more efficient. I'd like you to also help me create that space for optimal usefulness."

We discussed Brooke's needs and wrapped up our meeting.

Brooke said, "I do hope to see Bess next time. She's the one who convinced me to give your company a chance."

The three of us stood in the near-empty room. "Bess is out of town at the moment. Her sister was in an accident and needs Bess. I honestly don't know if it'll be for a few days or weeks. But we can ask for her input virtually."

Brooke's eyes widened. "She won't lose her job?"

"Oh, no. She and I are partners."

"Good. I heard through the grapevine that she might be involved with Clint Speck's murder, but anyone who ever met Bess won't believe those rumors."

How much should I share? Brooke would probably see through any lies or half-truths. "Unfortunately, Bess was one of the last people to see Clint. I'm glad you realize she's innocent."

Allie said, "The police questioned Bess but let her go."

"How did she get tangled up with Clint Speck?"

I grimaced. "Bess participated in the dating events. She didn't have a motive to harm Clint. In fact, he tried to warn her about one of the single men."

Brooke frowned. "Warn her? What do you mean, Kate?"

"I think he wanted her to be cautious of one of the men, but I don't know if he meant physically, emotionally, or financially."

Brooke crossed her arms. "I'd like to know the statistics on successful relationships versus broken hearts or scams with his company."

"Me, too." Plus, Bess had participated, so her sister would quit pushing her to find a man.

Brooke's watch beeped, and she looked at it. "Sorry. I've got an appointment. If you speak to Bess, please ask her to call me. She shouldn't talk to the police again without representation."

I shivered. My brother and his officers wouldn't be unfair to Bess, but Brooke was an attorney. She probably had to say that. "Okay. We'll be in touch."

Once we were back in Allie's car, she said, "The bookstore chick is next on our list. She said you offered to redesign the office at a discounted price."

"Madison Ledger. Did I offer her a discount? It's been a while since I've seen her, but we've got plenty of time before Reid and I meet with Peter."

Allie pulled out of the parking lot. "The jewelry man?"

"That's the one. I'd like to decide if he should remain on my suspect list."

"He's up to no good, but is he a killer? What about Hank?"

I opened my new polka dot journal. "Hank and Clint argued before speed dating. Only two words were clear."

"And they were?" Allie signaled to turn into the bookstore parking lot.

"Scam and proof."

"In my opinion, those are not good words."

"I agree." I spotted Joy's car. "Reid's mom must be working today."

Allie parked, and we went into the bookstore.

"Good morning! What a sweet surprise to see my daughter-in-love today." Joy put a small stack of books on a table, walked over, and hugged me. She wore a bright blue dress with orange swirls. On her feet were orange tennis shoes.

"Hi, Joy. We have an appointment with Madison." I stepped back. "Reid came home late last night. I didn't tell him about you and Sam, but please talk to him."

"We meant to call him last night but lost track of time." Her expression grew serious. "Thank you for keeping our secret, Kate."

"You're welcome."

Allie said, "I like your shoes, Ms. Joy."

Reid's mom lifted a foot. "I had to find something comfortable for the days I work here. I forgot how tiring it is to stand on your feet for hours at a time."

Madison appeared. "Kate, thanks for coming."

"I'm looking forward to seeing what you want to do. This is Allison Cameron. She's assisting me today."

Madison nodded. "We've met." Tension rolled off the young woman.

Madison and Ethan had spent some time together earlier in the summer, but they'd drifted apart. Was it possible Madison knew my son and Allie were hanging out? I couldn't call it dating yet, but there were sparks.

Allie said, "Hi, Madison."

An awkward silence settled.

Joy patted my shoulder. "I can take care of the store while you see what Madison wants to accomplish."

"Yes, ma'am." I looked from my mother-in-law to the store owner. "Lead the way."

Madison took us to the private area of the store. "Of course, you know my office, and I've begun converting this extra room into a stock room."

I walked around the space. "You chose good shelves. I'd suggest we organize this to match the store for maximum efficiency."

Madison crossed her arms. "I'm not sure what you mean."

I pointed to an empty shelf. "Let's say you don't have room for all the classics out front. The extras can go on this top shelf. What's the next section out front?"

"Science fiction."

"So, the next shelf can be designated for science fiction."

Allie stood to the side, taking notes.

Madison said, "Now, I understand what you mean about efficiency. What else?"

I didn't want to share all my thoughts. She could implement my ideas without hiring us. "Tell me more about what you want to do, and we'll come up with a plan. At that point, we'll discuss pricing."

"I'll show you my office."

I looked at Allie. "Will you make a note of how many shelves and tables before you join us?"

"Sure."

We left Allie alone.

Once Madison and I were in her office, I spotted a familiar brochure on a stack of papers. "Madison, did you attend some of the events for singles at the resort?"

She looked at me and then snatched the brochure. "I tried the scavenger hunt, but they paired me with a much older man. It was a complete waste of time and money."

"Bess was in the scavenger hunt, too."

"Yeah, she got the other old guy, but at least she's old." She shook her head. "I didn't mean for that to come out rude, but you know what I mean."

"I probably thought a person in their fifties was old when I was your age. Was Hank Ingram your partner?"

"Yes, and what a creep. He tried to get physical, and he wanted me to give him my money to invest for me. So he claimed. All my money's tied up in this place, and I wasn't even tempted." She shivered. "I don't want to talk about him."

"I understand. We should talk about something more enjoyable. What are your needs in here?"

We discussed her wants, and Allie joined us. We both took notes and left with a promise to return with organizing options.

On the short drive to Let's Get Organized, I added notes to my murder journal. It didn't feel like I was making progress, but I texted Paul and informed him about Hank Ingram.

My next suspect to question was Peter.

Chapter Twenty-One

Reid showed up at the store right after Allie and I returned. He was rubbing his chest and looked pale.

"Honey, are you okay?" I unlocked the front door of Let's Get Organized.

"Been better."

"Sit at my desk, and I'll get you a cool drink."

He flopped down and leaned back in my chair.

I poured him a glass of strawberry-infused water and took it to him. "Are you having a heart attack?"

"Nope." He drank the water.

Allie moved to his side and took his pulse. "Reid, tell the truth. What's going on? If you're in a crisis, we need to get you to the hospital. Have you been in the heat too long?"

"I'm used to the hot weather. Don't worry. This is about my parents."

Allie pushed back. "I still have a stethoscope in my car. Be right back."

Uh-oh. I knelt beside Reid. "They told me they want to get married. It looks like they got a hold of you."

He leaned forward. "You kept a secret?"

"No. In fact, I was very clear with them that they needed to tell you because I would not keep their secret. I only found out yesterday."

"But you didn't tell me."

I reached for his hand. "True, but it wasn't on purpose. We've been talking about other stuff, and it slipped my mind. When I saw your mom this morning, I mentioned you were home. I was going to let you know tonight.

How'd your mom get to you so fast?"

"My dad told me." He laced his fingers with mine. "Caught me completely off guard."

Allie appeared, carrying a stethoscope in one hand and a medical bag in the other. "Kate, I need you to move."

I stepped to the side.

After she listened to his heart, she pulled out a blood pressure monitor.

I reached for his cup and moved away to refill it. Tears pooled in my eyes. It was heartbreaking to see the effect of Sam's declaration on Reid.

"One-thirty-five over eighty. Given your appearance, I'm relieved. Plus, your heart sounds strong." Allie returned the medical supplies to her bag.

Relief swept through me. "Thanks, Allie."

"It's what I've been trained to do." She shrugged.

The front door swooshed open, and Peter entered. "Howdy, folks."

Allie said, "I'll be in the back room."

Reid stood. "Thanks for meeting us."

The three of us sat at my desk and chatted about the weather for a bit.

Peter said, "Why am I here?"

I crossed my legs. "Have you talked to Bess recently?"

"No. I figured she's dodging my calls. Maybe she prefers Hank, but you're her friend. Shouldn't you know?"

"Um, well, you see, she mentioned you sell jewelry. You know we recently got married."

Peter rubbed his bald head. "Yes, but she never explained why you were at speed dating."

Reid said, "We were there for moral support. So, Bess didn't tell you we wanted to discuss buying a ring?"

I smiled at Reid. Smooth.

Peter said, "No, but I can get anything you want. We're a family business with more than twenty stores. They all have different names because we want to keep the appearance of a small family business instead of a big, uncaring corporation. What kind of ring are you interested in? Diamond? Ruby? Sapphire?"

"Diamond." Reid's tone was firm.

I looked at my antique rose-cut diamond ring. It wasn't ostentatious, but it was beautiful. Plus, Reid had picked it out. Emotion welled up inside me. No murder investigation was worth hurting his feelings. "Wait, guys. I don't want a different ring."

Reid's expression relaxed. "Really?" His voice sounded hopeful.

"Yeah, I love the ring you gave me when you proposed." I smiled at my husband. "But, Peter was kind enough to come out here. How about something else, like earrings?"

Peter said, "Or a diamond tennis bracelet. I've got just the thing. Platinum with diamonds and an exquisite clasp. You want the best for Kate, don't you, Reid?"

I shook my head. "Maybe that'd be a good option if I had a desk job. But I don't. I often dig through cabinets and closets. I'm afraid I'd ruin a nice bracelet. Earrings are really what I'd prefer."

Reid reached for my hand. "You heard the lady. We'd like to see your selection of diamond earrings."

He tapped on his phone and then handed it to me. "Here are a few to choose from. If nothing suits you, I can bring some others over for you to examine."

I glanced from the phone to Peter. "Oh, I had imagined we'd go with you to the nearest store."

"No, that's not necessary. My company is aware of how valuable time is to our customers. I'll be happy to bring the earrings to you. Swipe left and show me some of your favorites."

There were round studs, dangling options with each diamond bigger than the one above, hoops, and much more. Lucky for me, the price was listed with most of the designs. "I prefer something simple, like these." I showed the men the pair of studs I liked.

"Right. I need a small deposit." He quoted a sum, and I almost gasped.

Reid opened his wallet. "Sorry, Peter. I don't have that much cash on me."

Peter's gaze dropped to the twenties in Reid's hand. "Credit card?"

"I don't have one with me. Those things can ruin people financially."

"I'll take whatever you have."

"Sure, as long as you can give me a receipt." Reid kept his posture relaxed.

Peter frowned, but his eyes were focused on the money. "Okay."

He pulled a receipt pad out of his pocket.

Why had he acted weird when Reid asked for a receipt if he had them handy?

Reid and Peter finished the transaction.

"I'll be in touch." Peter reached for his phone.

"Thanks so much for coming over. I'm curious if Clint ever bought jewelry from you for some of the prizes."

"Mercy, no. He couldn't afford to buy from me." He ran a hand over his buttons. "I mean, his budget didn't include giving away jewelry he purchased from me."

Reid said, "Are you saying it didn't fit the business budget, but what about Clint's personal budget?"

"Oh, was Diane his girlfriend?" I was prepared for a negative response.

Peter smirked. "Diane? In her dreams. She's more woman than he could've handled. Clint was into younger women."

"Really?" I had figured out that much. "So, did he buy diamonds?"

He puffed out his chest and took a deep breath. "Diamonds are for the rich or committed couples. Although some see diamonds as a good investment."

"What did Clint buy?" I scooted to the edge of my seat.

"We have some items that are more affordable for the average person. Clint mostly bought necklaces." Peter crossed his legs and chuckled. "Once he asked me to make a necklace to declare his love for a young lady. It was something along the lines of half a heart. I told him it wasn't unique, but he informed me that he wanted his fingerprint on the necklace he gave the young lady. The fingerprint would make it special."

I gasped. "You mean engraved?"

"That's right. Clint said exchanging heart necklaces with fingerprints would show commitment in a unique way."

"Did he tell you who he was going to exchange necklaces with?"

"Like a sailor has a woman in every port, Clint had a woman at every event. Some follow him around, and he meets new women all the time." Peter looked at his watch and stood. "If you'll excuse me, I need to meet another potential customer. I'll be in touch about the earrings."

I said, "Thank you."

After he left the building, I looked at Reid. "We need to be cautious about the information he shared. It could be true, but he could also be lying to protect himself."

Allie joined us. "I eavesdropped on y'all. It's possible that Gloria wasn't looking for a saxophone strap the day Clint died. What if she was looking for a necklace?"

I stood and paced. "If he had a necklace with her fingerprint, it would mean she was in a relationship with Clint. What do you all think?"

Reid rubbed his chin. "At the moment, my primary hope is that Peter is not on his way to sell a diamond ring to my dad. I'd hate for him to take advantage of Pop. Well, he shouldn't take advantage of anybody, but right now my focus is on Dad."

Allie said, "You two should go find out. I can run things here."

Reid stood. "This is something I'm capable of handling myself."

Allie shook her finger at Reid. "Yes, but it might be better for your heart if Kate goes with you. No matter what happens, stay calm."

I grabbed my purse. "We'll eat a healthy lunch after we contact your parents."

"Y'all are acting like you think I'll blow a gasket." Reid's gaze jumped from Allie to me, and then he sighed. "There's nothing wrong with me, but I would enjoy having lunch with my beautiful wife."

It'd be nice to eat at the resort's outdoor restaurant, but if Reid was dealing with stress, returning to the scene of the crime probably wasn't a good idea.

Chapter Twenty-Two

Sam met Reid and me at FUN Book Shop. Joy was busy wrapping gifts for a customer, but she told us to go into the empty area that used to be a coffee shop.

Sam stuffed his hands in the back pockets of his sagging jeans. "Son, I appreciate your support of me marrying your mother."

Reid said, "I'm curious about the rings."

"Your mother deserves a new ring. I'm working at the grocery store on the weekends, and Ethan helped me land a job cutting grass at one of the golf courses. It's going to take some time, but I plan to get her a nice ring."

"Pop, I don't know your financial situation, but if you need a loan, I can help."

Sam nodded. "Appreciate the offer, but this is something I've got to do on my own. I've actually got a little saved up from all the years I lived on the streets."

My mouth may have fallen open. "How?"

"Direct deposit. I may have been down and out, but I wasn't stupid. I have a checking account and use Joy's address. Reid, is this what you wanted to discuss? Are you worried I can't take care of your momma?" Sam's mouth morphed into a frown.

"No, sir. I wanted to warn you about a man who's on the island. He owns a small chain of jewelry stores, but I don't trust him."

I said, "We believe he might be some kind of scam artist." I didn't go so far as to reveal he was on my list of suspects for Clint's murder.

"Any chance this fellow's name is Peter Rodale?" Sam crossed his arms.

Air swooshed out of my lungs. "Yes."

Reid groaned. "Pop, please tell us you didn't give him any money."

"Not a penny, and I believe your hunch is right. He's up to no good."

I removed my glasses in hopes of reading his expression better. "How do you know?"

"When you get to be seventy-six and you've survived all I've been through, you just know these things." He tapped his head. "I've got a whole heap of street smarts."

Sam had abandoned his family when he returned from fighting overseas. He'd been angry, and it'd taken him decades to learn how to control his temper. I had no idea what he'd lived through all these years, but I trusted his instinct. "I'm glad you didn't believe him."

Reid said, "Pop, how did you run into Peter?"

"After I proposed to your momma, we went to have dinner at Seaside Hideaway. The waiter brought us champagne, and before you know it, Peter approached me. He said he could help me find a spectacular diamond ring at rock bottom prices." Sam rubbed his chin in the same manner that I'd seen Reid do many times. "Bunch of hooey, if you ask me."

Reid touched his dad's shoulder. "I'm glad you didn't fall for his trap."

"Me, too."

I watched the father-son duo. It'd been hard for Reid to forgive his dad, mostly because of his mom's pain all those years. Still, Reid had been hurt too. Joy had never quit loving Sam, and it'd been easier for her to have the hard conversations before welcoming him back. It'd taken Reid longer because he feared Sam would hurt Joy once again. It was easy to see all three sides of the story.

Joy came over to us. "What'd I miss?"

Sam said, "We're talking wedding stuff."

Joy raised an eyebrow. "Really? If that's the case, I would love for you to convince Sam that I don't need a fancy ceremony or a big ring to marry him. I want a simple ceremony on the beach with family and a preacher. For the record, Ethan is family."

I hugged my mother-in-law. "Thanks, Joy."

Sam said, "Reid, how about going with me to pick out a ring?"

"Sure, Pop. Call me tonight, and we'll compare our schedules. I know a reputable jewelry store in Savannah."

"Sounds good." He smiled and put his arm around Joy's shoulders.

We left the happy couple and jumped into Reid's truck. He said, "It's later than I expected. How about going to Sammy's Smoothies?"

"Smoothies to go? I like it." I fastened my seatbelt. "You seem in a better mood than earlier."

"I gave myself a firm talking to and prayed a lot. If Mom and Pop want a second chance at love and marriage, it's not my job to oppose them. They need my support. I'm a grown man and not a pouty kid."

I knew it'd taken more than one firm talk to himself. "I'm proud of you. Your mother loves both of you so much, and I know she doesn't want to choose one over the other."

"You're right, and she deserves to be happy. We got a second chance at true love. Why shouldn't they?"

"Amen to that." I squeezed his hand. "That was something about Peter approaching your dad."

"Yeah. That guy is a good actor."

"How do you figure?" I dug out my journal.

"Peter is very vague about his business. Different store names in different towns so customers will believe they are a small family business. Give me a break. There's more to his story."

"Do you think Bess is in danger?"

"It's doubtful he'd track her to Ruth's place. Have you heard from her?"

"Not yet. I keep telling myself that she's busy or that she lost her phone."

"Maybe she forgot a charging cord." Reid pulled into an empty parking spot on the street. "Why don't you call Ruth now, and I'll order our drinks." He grinned. "You can even keep the air on."

"Then you've got a deal. I'd like something with almond butter or some kind of protein."

"Protein. Got it." Reid darted across the street.

I called Ruth.

"Hello."

"Hi, this is Kate Sloan, er, Barrett."

"Un hunh. I know who you are."

"I'm sorry about your accident. Is Bess with you?"

"Yes and no. She made it here, but she ran to the pharmacy to pick up a prescription."

The tension left my shoulders. "Good."

"Why? What's going on? She seems off." Ruth's words were slurred, making me wonder how much pain medicine she might be on.

"You should ask Bess." I refused to get into anything between the sisters.

"Fine. I will. Why are you calling me?"

"Sorry, but Bess hasn't returned my messages. Did she forget her phone?"

"No, she dropped it at a gas station and broke the thang." Ruth yawned. "But Jonah plans to pick a new one up for her tonight. Do you need me to tell her anything?"

"Please tell her I called. Ruth, I hope you feel better soon."

"Thanks. I believe I'll take a nap, but I'll deliver your message. Bye."

"Bye."

Reid hadn't returned, so I made a list of goals. Go to Bess's place and see if I could find a clue about Peter. Maybe he'd given Bess a note or something. It could be a waste of time, but I had to do something. I might even follow him, but my old Wagoneer was conspicuous. I'd figure out something different.

At the sight of Reid carrying two drinks, I put away my notes. No need to add to his worry. Or was this considered a secret?

He got into the truck and handed me a smoothie. "Blueberry almond butter."

"Looks delicious. I know we're not keeping secrets, but do you want me to tell you every time I decide to do something in the murder investigation? Or just report to you at the end of the day?"

He slurped his drink through a straw. "This sounds like a better-to-ask-forgiveness-than-permission situation. You are free to do whatever you want, but I believe secrets ruin relationships."

"So, if I decide to follow Peter, you want to know beforehand."

He choked on his drink. "I'd prefer you not to follow him all by yourself. If you are about to dive into a dangerous situation, I'd like to be your buddy."

"Buddy system. Right. I'll keep that in mind."

I arrived at work and found Allie sitting at her desk, eating a burger. "We had a client reschedule her afternoon appointment. She's the client with triplets, but one baby spiked a fever. In case they are contagious, she doesn't want to expose us."

"That's nice." I swigged my drink. "Not nice that a child is sick, but that she doesn't want us to get sick. So, does this mean we have some free time?"

"Yeah. We don't have anything for the next two hours. Why?"

"Do you want to return to Bess's condo with me?"

"When I took this job, I thought it'd be boring and slow-paced." She wadded up the food wrapper. "There's never a dull moment, and I'm in. Want me to drive?"

"Yes, please." I grabbed my portable phone charger and tossed it in my bag.

"Did you expect the business to grow so fast?"

"Not really. With Bess gone, it seems busier. Thank goodness we hired you."

"Any word from Bess?"

"I spoke to her sister. She made it to Atlanta but broke her phone when she stopped to get gas. Allie, you are a great assistant."

"Thanks."

We locked up and took off in Allie's Highlander.

I rooted through my purse and pulled out some cash. "Gas money."

Allie glanced at it for a moment before turning her focus back to driving. "I hardly ever use cash, and you don't need to pay me."

"I want to. You're going beyond what you were hired to do."

She turned onto Ocean Boulevard. "Trust me, I'll tell you if I don't want to do something."

I laughed. "Good to know."

It didn't take long before we were at the condo complex, and a few seconds later, we entered Bess's home.

Allie clapped her hands. "Let's do this. Anything specific you want me to look for?"

"We should be respectful of Bess's property, but we've already searched for the obvious. I want to look under cushions, behind linens, in the freezer. Weird places."

"Why?"

"Bess was spooked about Clint's murder. He told her to be careful around Peter. Also, we believe Hank followed her in his car. Maybe we'll find something to help us figure out if she's in danger. She won't stay with her sister forever."

"Got it. I'll start looking for clues to Clint's death in the bedroom."

"Wait." I opened a drawer and absentmindedly moved things around. "I'd say look for anything that could be connected to Hank, Peter, or Clint. If they didn't commit the murder, they could still be dangerous."

"I'm confused. Like a receipt?"

I shut the drawer. "Yeah. Anything. Just grab it, and we can decide later if it's important. I'll begin in the sunroom and work my way in your direction until we meet."

The icemaker dumped ice, and I froze. "Did you hear that?"

"It was just the freezer dumping ice."

"The timing seems weird unless Bess—"

"Or somebody else?" Allie's eyes grew wide.

I gulped. "Yes. In the last few hours, somebody must've gotten a glass of ice."

"Hey, Kate, can we stick together?"

"Sounds like a good idea to me. Let's do a general sweep of the place, looking to make sure nobody else is in here."

Allie nodded. "Together?"

"You bet."

It didn't take long to confirm we were alone in the condo."

"Now what?" Allie crossed her arms.

"I'd like to check the kitchen first." I walked over to see if there was a dirty glass in the sink. No. I looked in the refrigerator. It was like Allie had described before. "Does the water pitcher look as full as it did the other night?"

Allie reached out.

"No, don't touch it."

She gave me a funny look.

"You know, in case somebody broke in and got a glass of water."

"Who would break in here just to get a drink?"

"Well, yeah." I opened the dishwasher and pulled out the top rack. My heart leapt. "Look. Only one glass is wet."

"Should we call the police?"

"Not until we search the place. You know what? Why don't you leave? I don't want to put you in danger or get you in trouble." Allie was too sweet to get dragged into my shenanigans.

"No, ma'am. We're in this together."

I appreciated her loyalty. Hopefully, I wasn't putting us in danger.

Chapter Twenty-Three

"A little more protection couldn't hurt. Let's push something in front of the door." I'd never been afraid in Bess's condo before.

Allie gave me a shaky smile. "Sounds good."

We pushed a heavy chair in front of the door. I said, "There's no way anyone will sneak up on us now. Why don't we start in here?"

"Yes, ma'am." Allie moved to the galley kitchen area and opened the cabinets.

The TV sat on a bookshelf, and I started my search there. I removed book after book. There were photo albums, paperbacks, and religious books. Nothing seemed unusual, so I returned everything to its place.

The condo was around five hundred square feet, so it shouldn't take long to search. I entered the sunroom but found nothing important. Back in the main room, I moved all the pillows off the couch and put them on the loveseat. Throw pillows were one of Bess's weaknesses. All had a beach theme and complemented the blues of the room. There was nothing hidden there, so I checked the loveseat.

"The kitchen is clear. I think I'm brave enough to check the bathroom by myself."

"Thanks, Allie." I lifted a cushion and spotted a journal. A quick look inside revealed it was a diary. I stuffed it inside my purse. If necessary, I'd read it and ask forgiveness later.

It took about an hour for us to look in every nook and cranny. On Bess's nightstand, we found a list of attendees for the singles' events, and I took pictures with my phone.

Allie looked over my shoulder. "Why don't we take the list with us?"

"I suppose it can't hurt. We'll make copies at work and save the original to return to Bess." I picked up the papers and moved to the dresser. In a decorative ceramic bowl, there was a toy ring, a business card from Hank, and breath mints.

In the closet was a laundry basket full of dirty clothes. A pair of muddy tennis shoes caught my attention. It was the same pair she'd worn to the scavenger hunt. They hadn't been muddy when we saw her, so where had Bess been to get her shoes so dirty?

Allie said, "I can't think of anywhere else to look."

"You're right." I stepped out of the closet. "Thanks for helping."

"Of course. She's my friend, too. Any other ideas?"

"No. Give me a minute to text Paul about the glass." I sent him a message and then joined Allie in the main room.

She said, "I can't believe somebody else was in here. It's a good thing you have a brother who's a cop."

My phone vibrated with a text from Paul. **I'm coming to you. Don't leave the condo.**

"Paul is on his way. Do you want to wait with me? If not, I can hitch a ride with him."

"What will you do afterward?"

"I'm not sure, but you said we have a two-hour break. We should reschedule and take off for the remainder of the afternoon."

"I can handle that. Then, if you really don't mind, I'd like to go home. I've got a migraine forming, and if I rest in a dark room, it might go away."

"Oh, Allie. I'm so sorry. You could've told me sooner. Are you okay to drive?"

"Yes, ma'am."

I gave her a quick hug. "Will you call me later, so I know you're okay? Or shoot me a text. Whatever's easier."

"Sure." We moved the heavy chair that had been blocking the door, and she took off.

While waiting for Paul, I sat on the loveseat and fingered through Bess's diary. So much for making myself wait.

The first page had been dated a month earlier. Bess was keeping a record of her dating life, and she stated that her sister had insisted she try harder to find a husband before she died an old maid.

"Good grief. Poor Bess." She had dated and maybe been in love once, but not everybody was destined to get married. If I hadn't reconnected with Reid, I would've remained single. I hadn't been looking to fall in love after my disastrous marriage, but I had fallen in love with Reid in my teens. When I saw him again, the feelings returned.

The doorbell rang.

I hurried to the door and raised my voice, "Paul?"

"Let me in."

I opened the door. "Hey, thanks for coming."

"No problem. So, you found a wet glass?"

I explained the situation to my brother and led him to the dishwasher. "I talked to Ruth earlier. Bess is with her, which means somebody else was here."

"It doesn't make sense." He put on gloves and slipped the glass into an evidence bag.

I opened the refrigerator. "In case the intruder used the water pitcher, do you want it for fingerprints?"

Paul said, "Why would someone break into Bess's condo right after she left town? She didn't broadcast her departure, so did this person plan on an encounter with Bess?"

"And how did they get in here?"

He walked to the door. He studied it and the doorframe. "No obvious signs of forced entry. I'll take the glass and water pitcher with me."

"Thanks for taking this seriously, Paul. Can you give me a ride to FUN Book Shop?"

"Where's your Wagoneer?" He bagged the pitcher.

"Allie drove us over, but I sent her home. I want to talk to Joy, and it's easy enough to walk from there to work."

"Let's go."

On the ride over, I considered my next move.

Hank seemed to be a good person to follow. I needed to figure out what he was up to. The main problem was my SUV. It didn't blend in with other traffic. Joy drove a nondescript car. If she consented to let me use it, I'd alert Reid and begin my search for Hank.

Chapter Twenty-Four

Around five o'clock, Reid and I sat in his mother's four-door, white Subaru sedan in Seaside Hideaway's parking lot. I'd driven around the island, looking for any sign of Hank before meeting my husband.

"Babe, it's too hot to keep sitting here. I know you want to follow Hank, but there's got to be a better way." Reid rubbed my knuckles with his thumb. "Plus, Mom's car isn't as roomy as my truck."

My husband was six-feet-two. No wonder he was cramped. Perspiration trickled down my hairline even though we sat in the shade. "You're right. Do you have Dwayne's contact information?"

"What are you cooking up?"

"Maybe we can meet him for a casual drink or light supper. We can look for Hank."

"We don't need Dwayne for that. Come on." He jumped out of the car and opened my door before I could even reach for the handle.

"Thanks." We held hands until we reached the outside bar. Fans spun counterclockwise, a breeze blew off the ocean, and I began to feel cooler.

The bartender walked over. "You two again. Still trying to solve the mystery?"

I said, "Hi, Mason. It can't hurt to try, but the police are the official investigators."

"Yeah, yeah, yeah." He winked. "What can I get you?"

Reid said, "Something energetic, so I can pretend to keep up with Katie."

Mason fist bumped his chest. "I've got you, man. Kate?"

"I like your raspberry spritzer."

"Coming right up." He turned his back on us and went to work.

I looked at Reid. "He's good at making fun tropical drinks."

"True. I imagine he gets good tips." Reid turned around, rested his arms on the bar, and looked around the outside areas of the resort.

I did the same. "I'll focus on the adult pool."

"My eyes are on the restaurant."

A dark-haired man dressed in khakis and a polo sat on a lounge chair. He was talking to a woman wearing a swimsuit and a wide-brimmed hat. The woman wasn't as thin as Diane, but she wasn't heavy. The man was Hank, but who was he speaking to?

I elbowed Reid. "I see Hank."

He said, "Go talk to him, and I'll get our drinks."

I hurried toward the adult pool section.

Hank stood and walked away.

I didn't want to chase him in an obvious way, but I did walk faster. The woman in the hat was Erica. "Hi, Erica."

She looked up from a magazine. "Kate. Why are you here? I thought you were a local resident."

"That's true. My husband and I stopped by for drinks, but I wanted to say hi. I noticed you were talking to Hank."

"Yeah. He has a strategy for me to invest my money and make big returns. I don't have much to invest, but I'm intrigued to hear more of his recommendations."

"Where did Hank go?"

"He's going to bring me more information and draw up a contract."

I gasped.

Erica removed her sunglasses. "What?"

"Nothing. I don't know. Just be careful." I hurried away before she could ask more questions.

Reid met me near the fountain, holding two plastic to-go cups. "Hank is on the move. We need to hurry if we're going to catch up with him."

"Yeah. I'll tell you what he's up to on the way." I took the drink he held out to me, and we hurried to the Subaru.

A red Camry turned west out of the parking lot.

"If we catch him, it works in our favor. He won't expect us in your mom's sedan."

"Right." He pushed a button on the fob, and the doors unlocked. We hopped in, and soon Reid was driving in the same direction we'd seen Hank go.

"There. He's pulling into the bank."

Reid turned into a convenience store parking lot. "We can see when he leaves. Are we certain that Hank doesn't live here?" He reached for his drink.

"I don't think so, but I'll look." I opened my journal and read over my notes. "I don't know where he lives. I'll text Paul."

"You already contacted him once today. How will he feel if you call about a suspect?"

"Good point." Cool air hit me from the vents. "I've been surprised that people who came to Fox Island for the matchmaking events didn't all stay at the resort."

"Hmm. You're right. It'd give them more time to mingle. It makes sense that the locals wouldn't stay on the property."

"I get that, but we know Peter rented a place because Bess gave him a ride."

The door to the bank opened. Hank walked to his car. After he pulled onto the road, Reid tailed.

I sipped my raspberry spritzer and kept watch on the red vehicle. "Whoa, he parked by the music store."

"There aren't any more empty spaces." He stopped at a crosswalk to allow a multi-generation group of people cross the road.

I spotted Dwayne on the sidewalk. "Do you mind if I speak to Dwayne? We'll meet you in the music store."

"Be smart, Katie."

"I will." I exited the car and walked to where Dwayne stood looking at a window display of homes for sale. "Are you thinking about moving to the island?"

Dwayne wore a black V-neck T-shirt over jeans. Three gold chain necklaces caught the light and sparkled. He looked at me and smiled. "Hi, Kate. Fox Island seems like a great place to put down roots. I've been inspired, and I'm writing songs like never before. So, yeah. I'm thinking about moving here. How are you today?"

"I'm good."

"Tell me about it." He chuckled. "I believe this is more than a chance encounter."

"It's not like I'm stalking you or anything. Reid and I were driving down Ocean Boulevard, and I hopped out when I saw you. He's looking for a parking spot. Are you performing tonight?"

"Got the night off." He crossed his arms. "What's really going on?"

"Would you go with me into the music store? I'll say you're helping me pick out a guitar." My face warmed. "Never mind. I can go in by myself."

Dwayne glanced at his watch. "Nope. We need to get a move on before they close. I'll ask more questions later."

"Thanks."

We traversed the short distance to the store, and once inside, we walked to the guitars.

Dwayne moved his eyes toward Hank, and then back to me. He must have figured out why I was here.

Hank was in a conversation with a beefy man with a dark ponytail. Hank said, "I noticed most of the chicks like music from the seventies and eighties. What do you have from back then?"

The clerk opened a drawer and removed a thin stack of sheet music. "It's not much, but over here, there are collections of songs from those decades. They include music, words, and chords." He led Hank to a rack of piano books.

"Cool." Hank's attention was on the music.

The clerk said, "Excuse me. I need to help these customers."

"Take your time." Hank gave him an absentminded wave.

The salesman lumbered over to us. "Can I help you?"

I said, "My friend and I want to look at guitars. I'm thinking about learning to play."

"Knock yourself out, but I close in fifteen minutes." He squinted his eyes. "Hey, you're Dwayne Gray. I'm bringing the wife to hear you this weekend. That's the main reason I'm in a hurry to close on time."

"Thanks, man. Be sure to say something to me during a break."

"That'll impress her. I appreciate it." A smile split the man's face. "Are we looking for a beginner's guitar?"

I nodded. "Yes."

He pointed to two options. "These are the ones I usually recommend, but ma'am, you're with a pro here. My advice is to buy whatever he suggests."

Hank joined the three of us. "Hi, Kate. Dwayne. Interesting seeing you here."

Dwayne said, "Why? It's a music shop, and I'm a musician."

"Maybe I should've said the timing is curious." Hank turned to the store employee. "I'll buy these." They shuffled to the counter.

Reid entered the store and joined us. The men talked, while I looked at the guitars. The prices weren't bad, but what business did I have picking up another hobby? Although kayaking hadn't been hard. Still, I had a new husband and a new business. Plus, I wanted to focus on solving Clint's murder. The investigation was the primary reason I had come here.

Reid stood on my left and touched my shoulder. "Do you want anything?"

"No. I'm good." I glanced at Dwayne. "Thanks for your help."

"It's my pleasure. It occurred to me that I need new strings. You two have a good evening."

We told him bye and reached the door at the same time as Hank. On the sidewalk, Hank said, "I thought you were going to buy a guitar."

I shrugged. "I'm not an impulsive shopper. It takes me time to make up my mind on big purchases."

Hank laughed. "You call a guitar a big purchase? We need to make you more money."

I removed my glasses and rubbed my nose. "That's right. You said something about day trading."

"Yeah. Music is my passion, but I'm not going to grow rich that way. I'd be happy to sit down and discuss finances with you while I'm in town."

"How long will you be here?" No way did I intend to give him one cent, but I wanted to learn more about Hank.

"I plan to leave this weekend."

Reid said, "We may not have time to meet before then. It's possible we can visit you at your office. Where do you live?"

"Jacksonville."

"That's not too far. Do you have a business card?"

"We can do an online meeting. I rarely keep normal business hours. If you want to get together this week, just let me know." Hank fished a card out of his wallet.

I reached for it. "We'll keep that in mind."

"How about your friend Bess? I haven't seen her in a few days."

I studied his expression. Was his question sincere? "Um, I don't know why you haven't run into her."

Reid puffed out his chest and crossed his arms. "Bess is like family to us."

"Right." Hank walked backward. "See you 'round."

"Bye." I waved.

Hank headed for his Camry.

Reid took my hand in his. "Mom's car is down the side street."

Thanks to my long legs, I kept up with Reid's fast pace. "We're still going to follow him?"

"Yep. Call it a hunch."

"I'm all for listening to gut instinct."

Soon, we were on Ocean Boulevard, following Hank once again. I put on my glasses and kept my eyes on Hank's car. "I can't wait to see where he goes."

Chapter Twenty-Five

Hank pulled into the pier parking lot.

Reid glanced at me. "What do you want to do?"

I sighed. "I was hoping to see him meet somebody, but if he spots us, his suspicions will skyrocket. We should just go home."

"Hold up." Reid parked near my old apartment. "What's wrong?"

I drank my raspberry spritzer before answering. "I'm tired and feel like my brain is about to short out. But I also want a clue so bad I feel like I can taste it."

He faced me, resting his left forearm on the steering wheel of his mom's car. "We can follow him on foot."

I met his blue-eyed gaze. "Thanks."

We trailed behind Hank and lost him in the crowds.

Reid said, "Do you see him?"

My heart raced. Where was he? "No. He must've darted into a shop or bar. Let's go back to the parking lot, and if he doesn't return soon, we'll go home."

"I'll stand watch if you want to look in the Camry's windows."

"Great."

Reid stood at the rear of the vehicle and watched the crowds.

I looked in the passenger window of the car. There were papers, the bag with the piano book, and a box of stationery. "Whoa, I've seen that before." I reached for my phone and snapped pictures.

"What do you think you're doing?" Hank snuck up on us from the ocean side of the lot.

I spun around. "Me? What about you?"

Hank advanced toward me. "I've had enough of your interference."

Reid stepped between us. "Step away from my wife."

Hank's eyes widened. "Why are you two following me?"

I said, "Why did you leave a threatening note at Bess's apartment?"

"What are you talking about?" Hank frowned, but his voice lacked force.

I pointed to his car. "I recognize your stationery."

"I often use it to thank my clients. You can find that anywhere."

A pickup truck cruised past us with noisy young adults crammed in the back.

"Why did you try to scare Bess? Did you murder Clint Speck?" My pulse pounded in my neck.

"No."

"Why did you leave the note for Bess?"

He leaned against his car. "It's related to the argument I had with Clint the night he was murdered. I'm not proud of myself, but I've been known to convince women to let me invest their money. The problem is, I've often lost their money. Clint knew the truth and didn't want me participating in the dating events."

"And the note?"

"I was afraid that if she dug into the murder, she might discover my, er, my—"

Reid cleared his throat. "Scam?"

"Not how I'd put it, but yeah. You might be amazed how often people trust me to invest their money."

I said, "Does anyone make a profit with you? Surely, you don't lose everybody's investments."

"Babe, it's a scam. There is no investing. He steals their money with a smile." Reid grimaced.

"Oh." How could Hank be so conniving? "Hank, you told me you make a living by day trading."

He shrugged. "What did you expect me to say? I'm a musician at heart. That much is true. The most important thing is that I am not a murderer."

It was early evening, but light enough to need sunglasses, and his eyes were covered. I couldn't decide if he was being truthful. "How did you convince Clint to let you participate?"

"I argued that he needed the numbers to be even. At last, we reached an agreement, and Clint allowed me to participate as long as I didn't try to con anybody."

I inhaled a deep breath. "You lied to Clint. You tried to talk Bess into giving her money to you."

He shrugged. "Liar. Yes. Killer? No."

Reid had begun tapping on his phone.

I said, "Is Hank Ingram your real name?"

"Yep." He turned from me to Reid.

Without looking up, Reid said, "Hank, who do you believe murdered Clint?"

"The man was a real Casanova. There could be a heck of a lot of women who wanted to throttle the man." Hank gave us a smug grin as if he were a better man than Clint.

"But?" Reid stuffed the phone in his pocket.

"If I were investigating, I'd zero in on Peter Rodale. That's not his legal name, though."

"Do you know his legal name?" Reid's relaxed posture put me at ease.

"He goes by more than one. Who knows what's legit?"

That explained why I couldn't find out much about him or his jewelry business. "Why?"

"Peter is way worse than me. He had to change his name and appearance—otherwise Clint would've recognized him—to get into events and to stay off the police radar."

A siren sounded.

Hank ripped off his sunglasses. "What did you do, Kate?"

"Nothing. I've been talking to you."

He turned his focus to Reid. "You low-down—" He charged my husband.

Reid stepped out of the way and twisted Hank's arm behind his back.

Hank's sunglasses fell to the sandy blacktop.

Two police cars appeared, and the fight left Hank.

His arrest was anti-climactic. One officer drove away with Hank in the back of his squad car, and Paul joined us.

Reid said, "Thanks for coming."

"Of course." Paul tugged on his belt. "Is he the killer?"

I answered, "Probably not, but he has stolen money from women. He left the note at Bess's apartment, and this is his car."

Paul peered through the car window. "Good to know. By the way, Bess's neighbor went into the condo. She was looking for a clam dip recipe and claims that she got caught up going through all of Bess's recipes and got thirsty."

"Angie Cornish?"

Paul checked his notes. "That's the one. Angie and Bess discovered that their keys open each other's doors one time when Angie got locked out of her place. We tried Angie's key, and sure enough, it worked. I'll take care of Hank's car, and I need you two to come to my office. I've got some questions for you."

Reid said, "We'll head over now."

We left my brother, and on the short drive to the station, I wrote down everything I could remember from our conversation with Hank. "Reid, did you believe Hank? Is it time to remove him from my suspect list?"

"I believe he's innocent of the murder, even if he's up to no good."

"I agree." Exhaustion hit me hard. I removed my glasses and put them in their case. "I know Bess is with Ruth, but I'd feel better if I could talk to her."

Reid said, "She'll call you when she can."

"When I talked to Ruth, she was loopy. They must have her on powerful pain medicine."

"Maybe the wreck was worse than we imagined. Give Bess some breathing room."

"You're right."

"And when she calls, it might be a good time to listen. Don't bring up the murder."

I nodded. "Yeah, it'll stress her out more. After Paul questions us, we need to take a break from this case. Go for a walk or watch a movie or something."

"It sounds good to me." He pulled into the police station parking lot behind Paul.

My brother got out of his Charger and pointed to us. "Guys, I'm afraid to ask whose car you're driving and why."

Reid chuckled. "There's nothing suspicious. It's my mom's car."

"I should've figured. Come on."

We followed Paul into the police station.

I truly needed a break from thinking about Clint's murder, and I'd make sure that happened as soon as Paul finished questioning us. Tomorrow would be soon enough to return to tracking down clues. With Hank off my list, I'd need to figure out who to consider next.

Chapter Twenty-Six

When I woke up Thursday morning, Bess was on my mind. I remained in bed reflecting on my best friend. Reid was whistling in the kitchen, and the aroma of coffee reached me.

I freshened up in the bathroom before joining Reid in the kitchen. "Good morning, honey."

He stopped whistling and turned down the music playing on our speaker. "Morning, babe." He gave me a kiss that stole my breath away,

I touched the counter to steady myself.

Reid poured a mug of coffee for me. "It's a new brew from a coffee shop in Savannah."

I blew on it before sipping. "Um, it's delicious. Do you have a busy day planned?"

"I woke up this morning with an offer to buy the veterans' home. They plan to run it as a non-profit, and that was my dream. I'm going to meet with my attorney this morning and meticulously go through the contract. I want to make sure there's not a loophole that I'm missing."

"That sounds like a good idea. Your attorney isn't by any chance Brooke Young?"

"No, but I've heard the name. Why?"

"I think Bess retained her, but I don't know why." Why did my friend need an attorney? "Anyway, Brooke hired us to organize two spaces at her office."

"Interesting." He opened the refrigerator and removed eggs, bacon, and peaches. "You hungry?"

"Famished. I can fix a bowl of fruit."

Reid looked at his watch. "I've got time to cook bacon and eggs. Another day, we can add grits or hash browns. What's on your agenda today?" He laid four strips of turkey bacon in a cast-iron skillet.

"I'd like to talk to Erica, Jennifer's mom."

"Hey, there's no need to explain. I'm keeping up with your suspects. What do you want to discuss with Erica?"

"She didn't want her daughter involved with Clint. In fact, she was vehemently opposed to them being together."

"Jealousy for a motive?"

I sat on a barstool and sipped my coffee. Jealousy? Or something more serious? "What would be worse than a mother and daughter dating the same man?"

"What?" Reid turned the bacon.

"Is it possible, that Erica had an affair with Clint and got pregnant? What if Jennifer is Clint's daughter? That would be the best reason for Erica to flip out when she discovered Jennifer and Clint had met and were in a relationship." I thought back to what Jennifer had told me after kayaking. "No, Jennifer said they were friends. She felt a connection to Clint, but it wasn't romantic."

He looked up from the sizzling bacon. "Is it possible to feel an immediate bond with someone before you know you're related?"

"I have no idea." I sipped my coffee again.

"What are you going to do with your theory?"

"I'm going to find Erica and ask some tough questions. Starting with her relationship with Clint."

"Please, meet her in a public place."

"The resort seems like a perfect place to catch her." I hopped off the stool and refilled my mug.

"Breakfast is ready. Biscuits would've been a nice addition, but this is healthier."

"Thanks, honey." I wasn't sure if I'd ever get over how good Reid treated me. He'd prepared our food while keeping my desire to eat healthier in mind.

We enjoyed our breakfast and avoided talk of murder.

An hour later, I parked the Wagoneer behind Let's Get Organized and opened the store. Joy had told me to keep her car for a few days in case I needed the air conditioning. With the scorching hot August weather, I'd probably take her up on it.

Allie and Ethan entered the store, carrying cups of coffee and laughing.

"Morning, Mom." My son gave me a one-armed hug. "I ran into Allie at the coffee shop and decided to stop by."

"I'm glad you did."

Allie moved to her desk and logged onto her computer. "Have you checked our email this morning?"

"Not yet."

"I'll do it." She tapped some keys. "Hey, this might be a message from Bess."

I hurried to her desk. "Really?"

"Yeah, but I'm not familiar with the email address. Anyhow, the person claims to be Bess. She has a new phone and is trying to set it up. She's going to get Ruth's kids to look at it, and then she'll be in touch."

"Oh, my. That sounds like Bess." I looked at Allie. "What does our schedule look like?"

"If I don't book more appointments, we have a few breaks to investigate Clint's murder."

Ethan said, "I was afraid of that. I'm going to leave so I'll have plausible deniability, in case you get arrested and Uncle Paul decides to question me. Just be careful."

Allie smiled at my son. "I'll walk you out."

He glanced back at me. "Seriously, reach out if you need me."

I blew him a kiss, then took Allie's seat and made notes on what needed to be done. When she returned, I said, "If you're ready to go solo, I'll send you to a young couple who moved into a new apartment. They need help with storage."

Her eyes widened. "Do you think I'm ready?"

"Yes, but call me if you run into trouble. It sounds like a fun project."

"Are you sure you want to risk this job by sending a rookie?"

"I trust you, but we can go together. I want you to be comfortable before going out by yourself." And it really wasn't smart to risk the reputation of my business by sending a rookie to take on a new job in order for me to investigate Clint's death.

Chapter Twenty-Seven

Thursday afternoon, Reid and I dropped off my Wagoneer at the local mechanic to get the AC fixed. Allie was at the office replying to online requests for information.

Cool air shooting out from the truck's vents felt glorious. "It's amazing how the heat can affect your mood and energy."

"You can't tell me it doesn't get hot in Kentucky."

"No, it gets hot, but not like this. Don't get me started on the gnats." I was still adjusting to the weather differences between Lexington and Fox Island. "How was your meeting with the attorney?"

"We signed the contract. They offered me a fair price for the house and land, and I'm ready to consider my next project. I'm psyched. Do you want to go for a drive around the island with me and look for my next challenge?"

"As long as your air works, count me in. What do you have in mind?"

"I may go for something simple this time. Like flipping a dilapidated home into a livable place. Low income and maybe handicapped accessible." He turned off Ocean Boulevard onto a side road with potholes.

"I'm proud of you." I rubbed my husband's shoulder. He was all about protecting the environment and leaving a small carbon footprint. He'd flipped my house specifically for me, and I couldn't dream of a better home.

"Thanks." He entered a rundown neighborhood and drove slowly enough for us to study each of the homes. "There's so much need here, and nothing appears to be for sale."

"The zoning laws seem different on the island. There are not many planned neighborhoods. When I sold real estate, one thing families preferred was safe communities with sidewalks and cul-de-sacs."

"We have some neighborhoods." Reid turned onto a different street. There were shops, convenience stores, and homes scattered in between.

I pointed out a sign. "Look, there. Didn't that used to be a dentist's office?"

Reid pulled into the parking lot and stopped the truck. "Yeah. First, it was a home. Then, it was a dental office for about twenty years. Let's walk around. It should be easy enough to convert back to a home, if the price is right."

"And there's a ramp to the front door." I walked around the property with Reid, and we looked in the windows.

At last, he said, "It has potential. What kind of person do you imagine would buy it?"

"An older adult? Maybe some people in their twenties. It'd be easy to walk to restaurants and shops. You can keep part of the parking lot, so they don't have to back onto the road. Maybe cover an area for a patio and put a fence around it for privacy. No, make that trees and azaleas."

"I can see it now. Sold. No wonder you were good as a real estate agent."

"Thanks. I enjoyed it, but organizing homes gives me a lot of joy, too."

"Now that you've helped me, what can I do for you? Have you questioned Erica yet?"

"No, I've been busy at work. Is there time to run to Seaside Hideaway?"

"Let's go."

I imagined the conversation I'd have with Erica when, and if, I found her. I needed to be polite but firm.

When we reached the resort, Reid parked under a shade tree. "Either Hank didn't get arrested or he made bail. He just entered the main building."

"Thanks for the warning." I glanced around. "Oh, there's Peter's Jag."

"I wonder what his real name is. What's on the vehicle registration, and are the papers in the glove compartment? And does that fancy car have a glove compartment?"

I laughed. "They call it a glove box."

Reid's phone buzzed. "Sorry, I need to take this. It might be a few minutes, because this will probably concern a mansion I'm building on the river for a musician's parents."

"I'll try to find Erica. I'll text you where I land." I hurried to the main entrance and bumped into Jennifer. "Hey, there. How are you doing?"

"I'm on the way to the spa. Hopefully, they can squeeze me in." Jennifer's long blond hair was pulled into a tight ponytail.

"Is something wrong?"

"I just had lunch with my mom, and my aunt is here now. They ganged up on me, and I can't take any more."

"Sorry to hear that. I came to the resort to talk to your mother."

"Be my guest, and good luck. They're at one of the tables near the bar." She broke away and entered the spa.

I meandered in the direction she indicated and slipped on my sunglasses. It was easy to spot Erica and her sister. The other woman had thick reddish hair, but she was as thin as Erica. They were sitting at a square table. I texted Reid before joining the women. "Hi, Erica. I just saw your daughter. May I join you?"

Her shoulders slumped, but she waved me to an empty seat. "Kate, this is my sister, Sydney."

I sat, and we got through the introductions. Besides thick curly hair, the women and Jennifer had similar noses and eyes.

I turned my full attention to Erica. "I can't get you and Jennifer off my mind. She's been so upset about Clint, but you seem almost happy that he's gone."

She took a deep breath. "Relieved is more appropriate."

"Oh, Erica." Sydney patted her sister's arm. "A man died. Don't be that way."

"He was a bad man. What kind of person pays so much attention to a much younger woman?"

Sydney pressed her lips together. "He was only sixty-eight."

Erica frowned. "Like I said, too old."

It didn't escape my notice that Sydney knew Clint's age. Had she consoled Erica all those years ago when he broke her heart? I looked at Erica. "Why do you believe he was bad? He held events to bring people together, and he seemed to be protective of the participants."

"Clint was a womanizer. People should have been worried about him and the trail of broken hearts he left in his wake. I didn't want that to happen to Jennifer."

"Shh. Don't work yourself up, sister. It's over and she's safe." Sydney patted Erica's arm.

I said, "Erica, were you jealous of your daughter's relationship with Clint?"

"Don't be ridiculous."

"Don't you feel sorry for her? The loss of a friend can be devastating."

"My daughter is young and vulnerable. Clint must've been up to no good." Erica crossed her arms.

"Do you want to hear my theory?"

A waitress came by and refilled their water glasses.

"I'm not interested in your hunches." Erica's nostrils flared.

"I think the reason you were so panicked about your daughter and Clint is that you dated him. Not only that, but you got pregnant. Was Clint the father of your baby?"

Erica cursed. "I never dated Clint Speck."

Interesting. She didn't deny that Clint was Jennifer's father. "Okay. Maybe you had a one-time thing. Did you blame him for taking advantage of your youth and inexperience?"

"I never had a relationship with Clint." Venom dripped from her voice.

"Why such strong feelings about him?" It had to be more than him paying attention to Jennifer. I glanced at Sydney. A chill crawled up my spine. "How did you know Clint's age? Did you meet him?"

Erica said, "Leave her alone. She would've been too young for Clint twenty-six years ago."

I focused on Sydney. "Did you know Clint? But that doesn't make sense. Jennifer is Erica's daughter. What's going on?"

"Nothing. We have nothing else to say to you." Erica stood. "Let's get out of here."

Sydney shook her head. "This needs to end. Please sit down."

"Don't say another word." Erica sat and leaned toward her sister. "Think about the repercussions."

Sydney waved to the nearest waiter. When he arrived, she said, "I'd like a whiskey. Neat."

I'd heard Erica drank whiskey, too. The sisters had more in common than their good looks.

Erica looked at her sister. "We've kept the secret all these years. Why ruin it now?"

My pulse pounded beside my eye, and I kept my mouth shut.

Sydney said, "At what cost? I made mistakes, and so did you. Jennifer deserves to know."

Jennifer took the last seat. "The spa is full."

I gulped. "Maybe I should go."

"What did I miss?"

Sydney clenched her fists. "There's something you should know."

I scooted my chair back.

Jennifer snagged my hand. "Please, stay."

I hesitated. Could she stand up to her mom and aunt? I married my first husband because of my mother. It'd been a mistake. Maybe my presence would encourage Jennifer. "Okay, but only if you're sure."

"Yes." She removed her sunglasses and stared at Erica. "Mom, what is the big secret?"

"Clint Speck was your father." Erica's jaw tightened.

Sydney said, "And I'm your birth mother."

My breathing stopped. I'd been correct about Clint, but Sydney?

Jennifer groaned. "What are you two babbling about?"

Sydney reached for Jennifer's hand, but the young woman yanked it away and sat on her hands. "I met Clint when I was young. He had a movie star quality about him, and I'd never met a person with so much charisma. He swept me off my feet. Back then, he was a pharmaceutical rep. We both lived in Atlanta, but he traveled a lot. When I discovered I was pregnant, I couldn't get him to answer my calls. It wasn't as easy to communicate back then as it is today. I was devastated." She crumpled her napkin.

Erica pounded the table with her fist. "You were young and innocent.

Clint took advantage of your naivete."

Jennifer's face lost all color. "Aunt Sydney is my biological mother? What other secrets are you keeping from me?"

The waiter placed a drink in front of Sydney, and she took a big gulp. "I was too young and immature to have a baby. Erica offered to raise her, er, you. It was the perfect plan, and it allowed me to be a part of your life."

Jennifer looked from Sydney to Erica. "That explains why you didn't want me to date Clint, but I wasn't attracted to him romantically. Mom, did you murder him?"

"Ack! Of course not."

People turned and looked at the four of us.

Reid approached, but I motioned for him to back away. H paused before heading to the bar.

Jennifer said, "It would've solved all your problems. Murder Clint, and he'd be out of my life. It makes sense now. You were even happy—"

"I was not." Erica spit out the words.

"Don't lie, Mom." Jennifer's eyes widened. "Or should I call you Aunt Erica now?"

"I raised you, baby. I'm your mother." Tears spilled down her cheeks. "There's more to parenthood than biology."

"What about you, Aunt Sydney? Did you kill Clint?" Jennifer stared at her birth mother.

"I wasn't even in town last week. I was attending a conference in Chattanooga. There are lots of witnesses." She signaled the waiter for another whiskey by lifting and tapping her empty glass.

Jennifer turned to me. "What do you think?"

"There's a lot to work through." My head was spinning. "Your aunt has an alibi. What about you, Erica? Were you with anyone Friday night?"

"No, but I didn't murder Clint." She frowned.

No alibi.

Paul and Officer Diaz walked to our table. Paul said, "Ladies, I have some questions for you. We can go to a conference room, or you can join me at the station."

Erica's mouth dropped open.

"I guess it's time to own up to my past." Sydney stood. "Kate, I can't say it was nice to meet you. Stay away from my family."

"Aunt Sydney, none of this is Kate's fault." Jennifer turned to Paul. "You're going to need a bigger notebook if you want to hear my story."

Paul glanced at me, and I nodded.

Soon, they left me sitting alone until the waiter appeared with Sydney's drink. "Charge it to her room. I don't think she'll be back anytime soon."

"Yes, ma'am."

The women probably imagined they'd gotten away with their secrets for years, but Clint's death brought all the lies and deceitfulness to light.

Reid walked over. "I guess that didn't go the way you had planned."

"Not hardly. Erica is guilty of a lot of things, but I'm beginning to doubt she murdered Clint. However, her sister Sydney could be a different story. I wouldn't want to be caught in a dark alley with her."

"That bad?"

"Wait until you hear. If she were Santa and had a naughty list, I'd be at the top of it."

Chapter Twenty-Eight

Reid and I sat at the resort's pool bar, eating pretzels and drinking healthy juices. Acai berry for Reid and pomegranate for me. I watched people, hoping to find someone to question.

A man walked past us, carrying a surfboard.

"Oh, hey, Kyle." I waved to Clint's son.

He squinted and then nodded as if he recognized us. "Hi, guys." He walked over to where we sat.

Reid stood and shook his hand. "Not sure if you remember us. I'm Reid Barrett, and this is my wife, Kate."

"Kyle Speck, but you know that. Sorry. It's been a few rough days. Surfing helps me forget about the bad and focus on the good, and the waves are killer today." He ran a hand over his face. "Bad choice of words."

I winced. "We're so sorry about your dad's death."

"You tried to save him, and I appreciate that." He pressed his lips together and stared toward the ocean.

"A friend was with me, but I'm sorry we couldn't do more."

An uncomfortable silence fell over us.

Reid pointed to an empty spot at the bar. "Can I buy you a drink? This place has more healthy options than hard liquor, but something tells me that's your thing."

"I could go for a green smoothie. Thanks." He laid his surfboard on the grass with the fin up.

Reid placed the order and scooted over so Kyle could sit between us.

When he rejoined us, I smiled at the young man. "Do you have much family?"

"My mother lives in Canada. She divorced my dad years ago."

"My first husband died, and I raised my son alone. I'm sure you missed having your dad around."

"I visited him twice a year. It was mandatory, but I did get to know him. I guess that's a good thing." He shrugged.

Reid said, "What brought you to Fox Island now?"

"I had business to discuss with Dad."

That seemed like an odd answer. "Did you two work together?"

"Nah. I started my own coffee shop in North Carolina, and I want to dip into micro-roasting."

I raised my hand to stop him. "I'm not familiar with that word."

"Sorry. Micro-roasting is a way to roast beans in small batches. You might say it's a marriage between science and art. It produces a taste like no other." He stood taller as he explained the process.

"One day I'll have to visit you in North Carolina and try your special coffee. Oh, but we've gotten off track. You were telling us about you and Clint."

"Right. We don't work together, but I came here to ask him about some of my money. I've had a savings account, CDs, and some stocks, but for some reason, there's hardly anything left in them. I'm not the best with investments and all that stuff, and I wanted to ask Dad his opinion about what could've happened. He told me I should go to college and get a business degree. That way I'd understand."

The kid really did need to go to business school, because it sounded like somebody had stolen money from his savings and CDs.

Mason, the friendly bartender, brought the smoothie and fresh pretzels. "Dude. How's it going?"

"The waves are gnarly." Kyle fist bumped Mason. "I rag-dolled once. You should go out on your break."

He laughed. "No, thanks. I'm not as cool as you, and I don't enjoy pain."

"Don't forget my offer to join me in North Carolina."

"It's too good an opportunity not to consider." He took Reid's credit card and stepped away.

Kyle gulped his drink. "Man, this is exactly why he needs to come work for me. My barista can't make anything this good."

We chatted more about Kyle's coffee shop and his dreams of expansion.

Kyle studied his drink. "Money is always an issue when you want to grow."

I said, "A friend and I recently started an organizing business, and I understand the money pressure. Thinking about return on investment can freeze me in my tracks."

"Dude, that's a real head-scratcher, for sure." Kyle finished his drink. "I need to bounce."

"Wait a second. Who do you believe murdered your dad?" I studied his expression.

"No idea. Probably some woman with a broken heart. Nothing else makes sense to me." He stared at the ocean again.

"Any one woman in particular?"

"My dad and I weren't that close, but if I was going to investigate, I'd begin with his assistant."

"Diane Field?"

"That's the one. She tried to manage me once—"

"Manage you?" I wanted to be clear on his meaning.

"Yeah, like keep me from my dad. She and I have been sideways for years." Kyle's hair had dried into a salty, stiff style, and he touched it. "That doesn't mean she's guilty. Why are you asking so many questions?"

Reid said, "You might say it's a hobby of Kate's."

"Cool. See you 'round." He sauntered over to his surfboard and picked it up before disappearing onto a path that led to the guest rooms.

I looked at Reid. "He wasn't completely upfront with us."

"What's he hiding?"

"Who knows? I'd hoped to scratch him off my suspect list. I'm not making much forward progress today."

"But you've eliminated Erica."

"I've at least put her on the back burner."

Mason reappeared with Reid's credit card and receipt. "Sorry that took so long. A woman started crying, and I always struggle when somebody begins to cry."

"No problem. It's a beautiful day." Reid signed and took the credit card. "How much do you know about Kyle?"

I kept my good ear toward the conversation but glanced down the bar.

Erica must have been the crying woman. Her face was red and splotchy. Paul's questioning hadn't lasted long.

Mason said, "The first time Kyle made me an offer to come work for him, the salary was too good to ignore. I'm a loyal employee, and I'm content working at the resort. At least, for now. I'm saving money and hope to open my own bar one day and feature country singers."

Reid nodded, "But Mason's offer interested you."

"Yes, in the beginning."

I picked up a pretzel. "What changed?"

"He started backpedaling. He claimed his money had disappeared, and he was convinced his dad would help him find it." He raised a finger. "Give me a minute."

I looked at Reid. "Curiouser and curiouser."

He nodded.

I watched Erica while we waited for Mason. Her sister appeared and touched Erica's shoulder. The two exchanged words, and then they left.

Mason returned to us. "I don't have much time. Bottom line is that Kyle thought a lot of his money was missing. He asked his dad for help. Clint basically blamed Kyle for not having a better head for business, and he refused to invest in the micro-roasting business. Kyle came down here and started drinking beer. No, I take that back. He was already half-sloshed when he came to me. As the night wore on, he began to question if his father had stolen his savings."

I had wondered the same thing. As a kid, he would have had an adult on his account. "When was this?"

"Thursday night."

"The night before Clint died." I reached for my journal, thought better of it. So, I typed the words into my phone. "Do you believe Kyle could've killed his dad?"

"Given the right conditions, anybody can kill another person. I gotta go."

"Thanks, Mason." I turned to Reid.

He said, "Maybe you need to look into possible reasons for Kyle to harm his dad."

"It sounds like money is at the top of the list. I wonder if Diane can shed light on the situation?"

"Don't you have an appointment soon?"

I glanced at my watch. "Yes. I'm going to the senior center to discuss downsizing."

"It sounds like we need to return to our real jobs."

"You're right. I've been excited about meeting this group for weeks."

Reid drove me to the store, and I picked up what I needed for my speech. I pushed all thoughts of murder from my mind for the moment. Sydney and Kyle had moved to the top of my suspect list. Tonight, I'd try to find out more about them.

Chapter Twenty-Nine

I walked Lady on the beach, and for once, it wasn't crowded. "I'll let you off your leash if you behave."

My goldendoodle wagged her tail, prompting me to trust her.

I held her collar for a moment and looked her in the eyes. "Stay by me."

Lady had been a stray when I adopted her. In no time, we bonded, and there'd been no looking back. I trusted her not to run off.

I'd contacted Jennifer about meeting here if she wanted to talk. So, I walked with my dog toward the resort. It was still daylight even though it was almost seven o'clock. The sea spray added a beautiful touch to the already amazing beach view. We skirted sand art. Someone had created a sea turtle and a mermaid. I snapped a picture with my phone because the tide would wash them away.

A woman in the distance was wading through the waves as they crashed onto the shore. It was Jennifer, and she was alone.

"Come, Lady." I changed our direction, and we joined the younger woman. "Hi, Jennifer."

She turned to me. "Hi, Kate. Thanks for reaching out."

"How are you holding up?"

She shook her head. "I feel like my life is one big lie. Can you believe the secrets my mom and aunt kept from me? The pregnancy, the birth, my father, and the woman who raised me—"

I patted her shoulder. "It's a lot to absorb."

A wave splashed us, and Lady barked at the ocean.

I pulled a tennis ball out of my shorts pocket and threw it into the water.

My dog ran into the waves and chased it down.

"Your brother talked to me longer than he did Erica and Sydney."

"I saw them in the pool area."

"I don't know how to address them anymore." Jennifer swiped at a runaway tear. "Why are you so nice to me?"

"I understand family drama. Erica and Sydney are probably questioning their decisions right about now."

"Aunt Sydney, er, my birth mother, is married and has two sons. They always seemed to have the perfect life, while Mom raised me as a single mother. But I was never jealous. We had a good life. Now, I have so many questions. Why did Erica sacrifice having a family, and why did my birth mom get everything?"

"I don't know. You are amazing, and Erica may not have considered it a sacrifice."

Lady returned and dropped the ball at my feet. I rubbed her head.

"Do you mind if I throw it?"

"Go ahead." I handed her the soggy ball.

Jennifer heaved it farther than I ever had.

My dog ran into the waves with a happy bark.

"This is her favorite game. I'll have to give her a long bath when we get home to get the sea salt and mess off her body. It's totally worth it because running into the ocean gives her so much joy."

Jennifer gave me a trembling smile. "I wish there were an easy way to clean up my messy life. I was drawn to Clint the first time I met him, but I couldn't explain it."

I was sure Jennifer was relieved it had never been romantic. "You two formed a beautiful friendship, and that's rare."

"You're right. We had a solid friendship. Pure and simple."

Three pelicans flew over the waves in a straight line. "Is it possible Kyle knows you two are related?"

"Nah, that guy hasn't given me a second look. Clint introduced us, but Kyle was distressed about a business problem. Kyle asked Clint what happened to his money. It was very awkward, and I left."

"Is it possible that Clint stole money from Kyle?" I threw the ball again for Lady.

"This will sound crazy, but I followed Clint around to different events. You know that I work remotely, and I couldn't help myself. He wasn't perfect, but I can't believe he stole money from his son." She shook her head. "It just hit me. I have three half-brothers. One by Clint, and two from Sydney. And who knows? There may be more half-siblings out there."

Poor, Jennifer. "I guess it's possible, but you may never know."

"Kyle is the only child that Clint acknowledged."

"He could be the only one Clint knew about." I watched Lady play in the water. "I don't want to be insensitive, but have you thought any more about who might have murdered Clint?"

She shook her head. "I suppose Sydney, Erica, or Kyle could be guilty, except Sydney has an alibi. She was at a conference in Chattanooga."

"Yeah. She told me the same thing. But you believe Erica could be guilty?"

Jennifer stared at the waves. "Maybe."

Lady returned, dropped the ball, and then lay at my feet, panting.

Jennifer said, "I'm going to head back to the resort. I paid for the week, so I guess it makes sense to stay."

"One more question, please." When she nodded, I asked, "Is Erica strong?"

"She doesn't lift weights or anything like that, but she rides her bike a lot. Why?"

I shrugged. "It seems like you'd need a good bit of strength to strangle somebody."

"Yes, but don't forget that Clint was sick to his stomach. I keep imagining he was too weak to fight back, and it breaks my heart." Jennifer sniffed.

I gave her a quick hug. "It's pitiful to imagine. Did you ever date any of the participants in the events? Could it have been one of them?"

"Most of the men were too old for me, but I have gone on a few dates. They were people Clint approved of."

"Any chance you went out with Peter or Hank?"

Jennifer grimaced. "No, ma'am. Dad told me not to date those guys. He said they were grifters. I had to look that word up, but I stayed away from them. It seemed like a normal thing for a dad to do, and I felt special."

"You're right." Why had Clint allowed the men to participate? "Do you feel safe walking back to the resort alone?"

"I'm not afraid in the daylight. See you later, Kate."

"Bye." As the younger woman walked to the resort, I texted Paul. **Do you know what made Clint sick to his stomach?**

His reply was quick. **No comment.**

Well, I guess if you couldn't shoot a brusque reply to your sister, who could you send one to?

"Come, Lady. Bath time." Her tail swished in the sand. "Let's go."

She stretched before standing. At last, she moseyed over to my side and walked with me on the firm sand.

No comment? Did that mean Clint had a health condition? Ulcer? Or was he poisoned? What kind of poison would only affect his stomach? He'd been able to speak, argue, and play the saxophone in the hour before his death. So, it was probably a health condition.

We reached the house, and I led my dog to the outdoor shower and sudsed her up. Thoughts of murder swirled through my mind as bubbles whirled down the drain. Did it matter what had made Clint sick? He'd been murdered. That's where I needed to focus.

Chapter Thirty

When Reid got home Thursday evening, we ate salads and then went for a drive.

"Thanks for doing this." I rubbed his arm. "I'm not going to solve the murder sitting around the house."

"No, problem. It's hard to believe it's been a week since we met Peter." He turned off Ocean Boulevard onto the street where Bess lived.

"What are you doing?"

"If somebody is watching Bess's condo, maybe we'll see them. We still don't know if she's in danger or not."

"Ohhh, good idea." I pushed my glasses up my nose. "I guess these things aren't horrible. They do help me see better."

"Good." He drove slowly.

I looked right and left. "Nothing looks suspicious."

"And there are no lights on in her place." He turned at the next intersection. "Tell me more about your conversation with Jennifer."

I got him up to speed as he drove around town. "No sign of any suspects. Where to next?"

"How about the new beach bar?"

Reid rubbed his chin. "Are you serious?"

"Don't you want to know if Hank is working the crowd?"

"Okay, but I'm bushed. Can we make it an early night?"

"Absolutely." I freshened my lipstick and ran a brush through my hair.

Foxy Beach Bar had a simple name and a simple, but obvious, theme. There were rafts, palm trees, and bright colors. The place looked over-the-top beachy, but the parking lot was almost full. It was easy to see how it appealed to visitors.

Reid parked the truck. "You sure about this?"

"Yes." I squeezed his hand. "How about a quick look? Then, we can do something fun."

"It seems like a good night to sit outside and look at the stars."

"I'm up for that." Our home was far enough away from businesses and close to the ocean, and it never ceased to amaze me how many stars shone in the sky.

We walked into the loud bar. There were picnic benches outside, a rock band playing inside, and people flowing back and forth. I blinked to adjust my eyes to the dark room and covered my good ear with one hand. I probably looked silly, but at least I wore appropriate clothes. White shorts, a blue T-shirt with white polka dots, and white sandals completed my outfit.

Reid tapped my shoulder. "Hey, I think I see Dwayne."

"We should speak to him. You lead the way."

I followed my broad-shouldered husband through the crowd to a standing cocktail table. The men greeted each other. When Dwayne spotted me, we shook hands, and then he pointed to the exit.

We walked outside and meandered through the rows of white picnic tables until we found a quiet spot. The setting sun created shadows in our area.

Dwayne said, "Shoo wee. That was so loud. I came to check out the competition, but we have very different vibes. I don't believe we're competing for the same audience."

I smiled. "Thank goodness for that. Your music is much more to my taste."

The musician nodded. "Thank ya. I appreciate it. Where's your friend Bess?"

"She's with her sister. Did you see anyone you know inside?"

A deep chuckle rumbled out of Dwayne's chest. "Related to Clint's murder?"

My face warmed. "Well, yeah."

Reid said, "Because when a killer is on the loose, my wife has a one-track mind."

"Understood." Dwayne nodded. "Hank's in there hitting on women who are sitting alone."

"You don't say." Reid rubbed his chin. "Have you seen anybody else from Clint's events? For instance, Peter?"

"Nah. Jennifer's mom and another woman are in there."

"You know Jennifer? Of course, you do. She was on the kayak trip." I was amazed at his observation skills.

He finished his drink and placed the glass on a nearby picnic table. "There's a lot of drama between Jennifer and her mother. I'm trying to figure out the other woman's role in the relationship."

I said, "She is Sydney Randal, and she's Erica's sister."

"Family emotions can be the worst."

Reid stopped rubbing his chin. "My family has some challenging issues of our own. I don't judge other people on their dynamics with loved ones."

"Right, right, right. Never good to judge." He crossed his arms. "It doesn't mean I can't imagine and put their situation into a song."

"Dwayne, have you ever been married?" I wondered how his career as a singer affected his relationships.

"Came close once, but life on the road isn't easy, and it's not easy on relationships."

"But you seem interested in Bess. If she went on a date with you, how do you see it working out?"

He shrugged. "I turned fifty this year, and it's led me to reflect on my life. It's one of the reasons I'm staying for an extended period at the resort. The combination of a beautiful setting and being in one place for a bit has inspired me to write more songs. I've discovered it's time for me to settle down."

He'd convinced me. "Any chance you—"

Reid shook his head. "Katie, stop."

I laughed and reached for my husband's hand. "You are so amazing, and I just want everybody to fall in love and have what we do. Love."

He gave me a quick kiss.

Dwayne said, "You two make me want to fall in love myself."

Hank walked to a table and sat down with a forty-something woman. She had short gray hair in a stylish cut. She placed her arms on the table and leaned toward Hank, as if she wanted to hear everything he said.

I tuned out the guys and studied the two at the other table. The woman wrote something on a cocktail napkin and handed it to Hank. He folded the napkin in half, put it in his shirt pocket, and patted his chest.

A young woman bumped into me and spilled her drink down my back. Cold stickiness pulled my shirt against my skin, and liquid flowed down my back.

I squealed.

"I'm so sorry." She giggled.

"It's okay. Don't worry about it."

She waved and caught up with her friends.

Reid and Dwayne stared at me with surprised expressions. Dwayne spoke first, "You took that well."

"Getting mad won't change the outcome." My cold shirt clung to me, and I shivered.

Reid said, "That's our cue to head home. Dwayne, nice talking to you."

"I won't shake your hand, because a trickle of liquid ran down my arm. My hand is sticky." My gaze darted to Hank's table. The woman was sitting by herself. I walked her way.

She looked up from her phone and glanced at me. "That was terrible, but you handled it with grace. I'm impressed."

"Thanks. Earlier, I noticed you were with Hank Ingram."

Her eyes widened. "Um, are you sure? I thought he said his name was Hank Durham. It's loud inside, but it's hard to believe I misunderstood. Durham. Ingram. I guess it's possible, but are you certain?"

"I'm fairly confident. I've met him a few times."

Her eyes narrowed. "Oh, are you dating him?"

I laughed. "No, I'm happily married. Be careful if he offers to invest your money."

"He did offer. In fact, I was just looking at his list of references. He's a financial advisor to some of the richest people in Georgia." She shut her eyes. "Momma mia. I know better. I should leave before he returns. I don't like confrontations."

I glanced inside the building. "He's still in line at the bar. My husband and I can walk you to your car."

She narrowed her eyes again. "How do I know you're trustworthy?"

Reid and Dwayne joined us.

I said, "You don't. Maybe call the police to escort you to your car, if you're worried."

"That seems extreme." She stood and focused on our friend. "I know you. Aren't you the singer at Seaside Hideaway?"

"Yes, ma'am. Dwayne Gray." He stuffed his hands in his pockets.

"Okay, I trust you. Will you walk me to my car?"

"Of course. You can also trust my friends here. This is Kate and Reid Barrett."

I patted Dwayne's arm. "We need to scoot before Hank spots us."

The four of us hurried to the parking lot, and once the woman was buckled into her SUV, she took off faster than normal circumstances required. At least she was safe.

We parted ways with Dwayne and drove home.

I thought about Hank. Did the police still have his Camry? If he didn't murder Clint, that didn't mean he wasn't guilty of committing financial crimes or fraud.

I sent a text to my brother. **Hope you're doing okay. We're leaving Foxy Beach Bar, but Hank Ingram is there. He tried to convince a woman to let him invest her money. She got away, but he may look for his next target.**

"Who are you texting?" Reid stopped at a red light.

"Paul. Don't you think he needs to know about Hank?"

Reid's fingers tightened on the steering wheel. "Yep."

I hit send.

"Sorry that we didn't get to dance." He eased off the brakes when the light turned green.

"I'm not sure we could've danced to that music even if it hadn't been too loud."

"I'd rather dance on the beach to the music of the waves."

My heart swelled with love for my husband. "You're so romantic. Let's do that another night."

"You've got a date."

I continued to think about Clint and his murder.

Paul replied to my text. **Thanks.**

I laughed. "My brother can be a man of few words when it comes to murder investigations."

"What's next since Hank's not at the top of your murder list?"

"Kyle or maybe Sydney. I'll decide tomorrow." I sighed. "I'm going to clean up and then enjoy a cozy night at home with my husband and dog."

"That's the best thing I've heard all day."

Chapter Thirty-One

Reid and I kayaked in the ocean early Friday morning because the water was flat. We rented a two-person kayak from the resort and enjoyed the adventure.

Back on land, I squeezed salty water out of my ponytail. The waves had sprayed us more than once, and we were wet. "I'll carry the paddles."

"That leaves the easy part for me." Reid chuckled and hauled the orange kayak toward the resort. "You did good out there. I believe you can handle a boat by yourself, but—"

"Don't go out by myself. The buddy system. I got it." My husband was all about safety, especially where I was concerned. After a couple of close encounters with death earlier this year, I didn't mind.

"That's my Katie." He wrapped his arm around my shoulders.

"You've always been good about reminding me to do things with a partner, especially if I could get hurt."

"No need to take unnecessary chances." He slowed his pace. "You think we'll run into Kyle?"

"Hopefully. He's in good shape. I figure he runs, and early morning is the best time with the August heat." One paddle slid out of my grip, and I bobbled it for a moment.

"Need help?"

"No, I got it." I regained control. "If we don't see Kyle, it's been a lovely morning."

A bark of laughter escaped from Reid. "I'm glad you don't consider it a waste of time to hang out with me."

"Never." I spotted two runners. One seemed familiar, but I hadn't wanted to risk losing my glasses in the ocean. "Can you tell who those guys are?"

Reid squinted. "Oh, it's Ethan and Kyle."

"I don't know how those two got together, but yay. It won't seem as odd if we approach them."

"True." He put the kayak down, and I placed the paddles on it. I waved to Ethan and walked toward him.

The two guys jogged our way.

"Hey, Mom. Reid. Were you guys kayaking?" He breathed heavily, but he didn't labor to catch his breath.

Reid smiled. "Yeah, your mom did great out there."

Ethan gave me a quick hug. "Way to go, Mom. I'm proud of you."

"Thanks, honey. Seeing you is a nice surprise." Wow, a compliment, and a hug. I stepped back before I got mushy. "Hi, Kyle."

"Hi, Kate. Reid." He stood with his feet spread out and propped his fists on his hips.

Reid said, "Can we buy you guys a quick breakfast? I know that at least three of us need to get ready for work. What about you, Kyle?"

"I've got a lead on an investor. He said that he and my dad were good friends."

Uh oh. "His name isn't Hank Ingram, is it?"

"How'd you know?"

"Just a feeling. Don't be too hasty to give him control of your money. He fought with your dad last Friday night before Speed Dating about investment scams."

"Are you serious? He acted like they were the best of friends."

"Maybe you should ask Diane. She can probably give you more details."

Kyle frowned. "Do you think Hank murdered my dad?"

"Not really." I kept my tone soft. "In fact, you have a better motive to want your father dead than Hank did."

Ethan gasped. "Mother."

Reid said, "Easy now."

Kyle fisted his hands. "Please explain."

My brain scrambled for the right words. "First, just because you have a motive, it doesn't mean you're the killer."

"Thanks for that, but tell me more about my motive."

"Primarily money. Did your dad lose your investments or borrow from you without your knowledge? Or maybe you wanted a loan to grow your business. If he has a will, it seems like you'll get the money." I didn't know if it was my nerves or if the day was already getting hot, but I removed my life jacket. "Not that I'm accusing you."

"Anything else?" Kyle crossed his arms.

"Do you have any siblings that your dad might include in his will?"

"No, but wouldn't I be more likely to murder them than my dad?" He looked at the ocean. "On second thought, my dad seemed to have a lot of relationships. Maybe I should ask Diane about that, too."

I shrugged. "Maybe so."

Kyle said, "For the record, I didn't murder my father. No matter how angry he made me at times, I could never harm him."

"A witness reported that you and Clint were arguing last week."

"About the money. Anything else?"

"The other day at the bar, I felt like you were hiding something. Can you share?"

He took a deep breath and released it. "A girl around my age approached me the other day. She suggested that we might be related. She made me mad. I figured she wanted to squeeze money out of me through blackmail or a scam. Now you've got me wondering if she really might be a stepsister."

His admission surprised me. I wanted to ask if it was Jennifer, but it was possible there was another young woman in the same situation.

Reid said, "It's been a few days since your dad died, and you've met more of the players. Who do you think murdered Clint?"

He shook his head and studied the ground. "I have no idea who the killer is, but I need to finish my run."

Ethan looked at us. "See y'all later."

Kyle and Ethan ran toward the lighthouse, and Reid and I returned the kayak, paddles, and life jackets."

CHAPTER THIRTY-ONE

On our walk home, I said, "Do you believe Kyle?"

"Yeah. I've been angry with my dad for deserting us for most of my life. No matter how hurt and angry I was, there's no way I would've resorted to murder. He's my dad, and that's what Kyle said. That's why I believe he's innocent."

I nodded. "When we thought he was being secretive the other day, he was dealing with the issue of Jennifer, or another potential sister."

"Clint's philandering ways are more than any child should have to handle, even if the child is a grown man. And especially after his death. Kyle can't discuss it with his dad, so it's like an albatross around Kyle's neck."

"I agree." We reached the path to my house and took it. "Why don't you shower first, and I'll take Lady out?"

"Thanks. I have an appointment in forty-five minutes. You know the abandoned house near the creek with the beautiful views?"

"Yes."

"The mayor's wife is a real estate agent, and she asked me to meet her there with a couple to discuss the possibilities of renovating it."

"Then you better hurry up. I know there's nothing you like better than to save old homes."

He turned and took me in his arms. "Time with you beats restoring old houses every day."

I kissed him. "You say the nicest things."

Chapter Thirty-Two

The exhilarating morning had energized me. I arrived at Let's Get Organized, unlocked the front door, and fixed a pot of coffee.

"Good morning." Allie entered the store and sat at her desk. "I'll check today's schedule."

"Good. Would you shoot an email to Bess? Let her know we're thinking about her."

"Sure." Allie began tapping keys on her computer. Her thick ponytail swayed with the movements. "The way Bess has talked about her sister, they don't seem to get along."

I pulled caramel creamer out of the refrigerator. "Ruth has always been bossy. I hope she behaves, especially after Bess put her life on hold to care for her. Don't get me wrong, Ruth loves her sister, but she also likes to tell her when and how high to jump. I hope she doesn't crush Bess's spirit. Most of the time, Bess is a strong, independent woman."

Allie nodded. "Except when it comes to her sister?"

"Exactly. If Ruth's involved, it's never good. In fact, Ruth is the reason Bess entered the singles events."

Allie said, "After the major car accident I got called to, I could barely get out of bed. If my parents hadn't come to town and forced me to see a therapist, I might still be curled in a ball. I'm so thankful they were supportive. I hope you don't think I'm weak because I didn't go back to my job as an EMT."

"No way. You're one of the strongest people I know."

Allie didn't reply immediately.

I gave her a moment to process our conversation. I poured coffee into a mug and added the creamer. "Would you like a cup of coffee?"

"Not right now."

I moved to my desk and booted up the computer. We discussed the appointments on our schedule.

"I need to go over the plans I made for the bookstore with Madison. If she gives me a deposit and signs the contract, I'll return and place an order for the supplies."

"Would you like me to try to add registries on the website?"

"Yes. Will you start with weddings? I can ask Joy to test drive it for us."

"That will be fun. When is the wedding?"

"They're being cagey about a date."

Allie laughed. "They may decide to elope like you and Reid."

"I have a hunch they want Reid to be part of their wedding." I drank my coffee and gathered my supplies, including my laptop, to take to FUN Book Shop.

Allie said, "Do you plan to continue your investigation?"

"Yes. I saw Kyle this morning, and we talked. I think he's innocent."

"So, you've ruled out Jennifer and Kyle?"

"And Hank. He's a scammer, but I don't think he murdered Clint. Tonight, I'll decide who to focus on next. It's been a week, and I'm making slow progress."

"What does Chief Wright think?"

"He's not sharing much with me, but I always contact him if I think there's something he needs to know."

My phone alarm sounded.

"It's time for me to go to the bookstore. Would you like to have lunch together?"

"Sounds good."

I gathered my belongings and drove to the bookstore in Joy's car.

The parking lot was full, so I parked on a side street. When I reached the front door, there was a flyer taped to it. FUN was hosting an event. It involved picking a blind date with a book, and somehow it'd connect you to a blind date with a person. Thank goodness I didn't have to jump through those hoops. I entered the store and made my way past a woman with two small children. They were looking at a display of books and corresponding toys.

Joy said, "Kate, darling, how are you?" Joy wore a hot pink top with three-quarter sleeves over white jeans.

"Hi, Joy." I gave her a quick hug. "This is quite the crowd."

Joy whispered in my good ear. "Madison is banking on this event to increase sales."

"Good luck. I believe she is expecting me."

"Yes, why don't you go back to her office? I'll let her know you're here."

"Thanks." I worked my way to the back rooms and landed in the office.

"Hi, Kate. Sorry to keep you waiting. We need to make this quick. I hoped hosting an event to attract singles would be a good idea, but I never imagined the wonderful response."

"I can do quick." I opened my computer and we proceeded to review the plans.

Madison agreed to most things, signed the amended contract, and wrote me a check. It was one of the smoothest presentations I'd participated in.

"Thanks, Madison. I'll let you know when the supplies arrive, and we can come over when it's convenient and implement the organization design."

"Good." She stood and motioned for me to follow.

In my hurry, I fumbled stuffing the samples into my bag. "You don't have to wait for me. I'll be right out."

She left me alone, and I got myself organized.

Movement on the security screen drew my attention.

It appeared there were four security cameras. Two outside, and two inside. The parking lot remained full, and I shifted my attention to inside the store. FUN carried fine, unique, and new books. Erica and Sydney stood at the shelf featuring local history books. I'd missed an opportunity the night before at the loud bar. I should be able to catch them this morning.

Plenty of people mingled near the books wrapped up for blind dates. I edged past them and approached the sisters. "Hi, you all."

Erica and Sydney turned and looked at me. Sydney held a book on the history of railroads in Georgia. She also had an old copy of Mary Kay Andrews' *Savannah Blues*. A sticker on the cover claimed it was a signed, first edition.

Erica said, "Hi, Kate."

"How are you doing?" I adjusted my head to hear them better.

"I saw you talking to Kyle Speck this morning. Did you explain our situation to him? How did he take the news about Clint and Jennifer?" Erica's expression showed no emotion.

"That's not my news to share. I want to help catch the killer, but I'm not a busybody." I shivered at her narrowed eyes. "I don't butt into everything."

Sydney's fingers tightened on the book. "What did you discuss?"

I wanted to tell her it was none of her business, but it seemed hypocritical, considering how many people I'd questioned. "Kyle was running with my son, and they were impressed I'd been out kayaking this morning." I saw no need to mention the conversation between a young woman, probably Jennifer, and Kyle. "I didn't see you all on the beach. Where were you?"

Erica said, "We were near the resort but close enough to see you."

I suppressed a shiver. Had they spied on me? "Um, do you know Peter Rodale very well?"

"I know him."

"Have you discussed Clint with him? Do you think he could be the murderer?"

Sydney raised her chin. "I would not have gone to dinner with Peter if I believed he was involved with Clint's murder."

The emotion in her voice gave me chills. "Were you in love with Clint?"

Erica took the book from her sister. "You two need to have this conversation outside. I'll pay for the books."

"No, it's too expensive." She handed a credit card to Erica and then motioned for me to follow her.

Sydney and I headed out the door and sat on a bench in a shady spot near the building. Sydney inhaled sharply. "I did love Clint, and I believed he loved me. Clint didn't mean to hurt me, and one day I realized he'd never made me any promises. I dreamed of a bright future with him, and in the end, I realized how foolish I'd been. Still, I don't regret what happened because Jennifer is such a precious gift."

Her declaration was hard to believe. "Why did you give her to Erica?"

"I wouldn't have been a good mother to her back then. I had planned to give her up for adoption. I loved Clint too much to consider abortion. A part of me always believed Clint would learn about the baby, find me, and declare his love. As you know, that didn't happen." She looked at the ground. "Erica stepped in and saved the day."

"Were you ever jealous of Erica?"

"Of Erica? No." Sydney pulled a tissue from her purse and dabbed her eyes. "I was grateful. Her sacrifice allowed me to watch Jennifer grow up, even though it was from a distance."

I remained quiet. Was Sydney serious? She claimed she didn't blame Clint, and she wasn't jealous of her sister raising her daughter. She'd lived a lie for over twenty years. "Have you put any more thought into who murdered Clint?"

"Diane was in love with him. Maybe she finally cracked under the pressure of constantly watching Clint carry on with other women."

Erica joined us. "Sydney, are you ready to leave?"

"Sure." She stood and flipped back her hair. "This is the last conversation we're going to have about my family."

I didn't reply. On the way, in Joy's car, it hit me. Sydney admitted she'd gone on a date with Peter. Jennifer told me that Sydney was married. What was going on?

I texted Jennifer to clarify.

Chapter Thirty-Three

After lunch with Allie and Ethan at the pier, I returned to the store. Allie showed me what she'd created for wedding registries. When I approved, she contacted Joy, who agreed to test the program.

My phone vibrated with a text from Jennifer. I just learned that Sydney and her husband are separated.

Interesting. Why hadn't Sydney told me earlier? I updated my notes on Clint's murder based on the conversation with Sydney and what I'd just learned. I called Diane.

"This is Diane. How may I help you?" Her tone was crisp and businesslike.

"Hi, this is Kate Sloan Barrett. I'd like to meet with you and discuss a few things. Do you have any free time today?"

"I'll be at the resort pool this afternoon if you want to meet me there."

"Great. I'll see you soon." I ended the call and checked the schedule. "Allie, I need you to order the supplies on this list for Madison's store." I handed the paper to her. "I'm going to Seaside Hideaway to meet with Diane."

"Okay. Bess emailed me and said we don't need to continue checking on her. She's fine."

"I'm glad she reached out. Do you need me to do anything before I leave?" It occurred to me that Dwayne had asked for an update on Bess. I'd look for him at the resort and tell him she was okay. I might even ask if he'd stumbled across any clues.

"Nothing I can think of. Call me if you run into trouble." Her eyes sparkled.

"I never expect to encounter problems, but thanks for offering." I got into Joy's sedan and headed to the resort as soon as the condensation cleared from my glasses.

I turned the AC button to high and waited for cool air to pump out of the vents. Perspiration ran down my back. Soon, the car began to cool, and I drove off. My Wagoneer was nice and big, but I couldn't live on Fox Island without air conditioning. If I looked for a new vehicle, it needed to be big enough to haul around my organizing supplies. Yeah, that sounded better than admitting I was scared of driving a little car after a previous accident.

Once I reached Seaside Hideaway and entered the lobby, I got a complimentary glass of water. Gloria stood at the registration desk, and I headed over to speak. "Hi."

She glanced up from the computer screen and smiled. "Kate, how are you?"

"Good. And yourself?"

She pushed a loose strand of hair behind her ear. "I'm okay. Actually, I need to schedule a meeting with you, but I can't seem to get a day off."

"I can meet you one evening when you get off work. What do you have in mind?"

"My rent is going to increase in September, and I will need to find a roommate. I've been used to living alone for a few years. If I'm going to survive, I need help to move my clothes from two closets to one. Would you be interested in a job like that?"

"I'd love to help you." I drank my water.

"Thanks. I'll be in touch."

"Do you have a second?"

Gloria spoke to the other lady working and then came around the counter. "I can't talk long. What's on your mind?"

"Clint's murder. You went through his pockets when we tried to save him. What were you looking for?"

She gripped my elbow and led me away from the counter.

I said, "Was it his saxophone strap?"

"Why would I want that?" Her reaction seemed authentic.

"Then why did you look through his pockets?" I jerked my elbow out of her grip.

Tears welled up in her eyes, and she touched a gold chain around her neck. "We had exchanged necklaces as a symbol of our feelings for each other. They had our fingerprints engraved on them, and I didn't want anyone to find the one I gave him."

"How did you know he wasn't wearing it?"

"I watched while you and Allie tried to help. I didn't see it."

"Did you find it in his pocket?" I leaned in to hear her answer.

"Yes. I managed to palm it when you weren't watching me."

I took a deep breath. "Earlier that night, you saw Clint kissing another woman. Who was it?"

"Nobody important." She sniffed. "Let me rephrase that. No woman was important to Clint. He and I had recently exchanged necklaces, and then I saw him kissing her. I should've been smarter. I don't know the other woman's name, but she was here for the dating weekend."

"Is that why you wanted your necklace back?"

Gloria nodded. "Yes. It was humiliating."

"Humiliating enough to murder Clint?"

"No, I could never hurt the man. Like the necklace indicated, I gave him a little piece of my heart. I wanted the necklace back so the police wouldn't suspect me."

"I guess it makes sense, but you need to tell the police. If you don't, it'll look worse for you."

Her eyes narrowed. "If I don't, I suppose you'll tell them."

"I won't withhold evidence from the police." I walked out the door leading to the pools. The sweltering heat fogged my glasses again. Once I could see, I strolled to the adult pool and spotted Diane. I walked to her, but the chairs on each side of her were taken. "Hi, Diane."

She looked up from the celebrity magazine she was reading. "Kate, you're not dressed for the pool."

"I think it's only for guests. Do you have time to sit at a shady table? I'll treat you to a refreshing drink."

"That's an offer I can't pass up, even though I'm sure you're here to discuss Clint's murder."

My face warmed. "You've got me figured out."

I stepped to the side, giving Diane room to get out. She slipped into her swimsuit cover-up and flat sandals.

I reached for the resort towel and deposited it in a nearby towel-return bin before following Diane.

She was tall and thin. Her short hair was feminine, and she carried herself with assurance. Heads turned as she walked by. Diane pointed to the tables. "They're all taken. Do you mind sitting at the bar?"

I tapped my left ear. "As long as you don't mind sitting on this side so I can hear, I'm happy to sit at the bar."

We found two seats and got settled.

Mason walked to us. "Ladies, what can I get you this afternoon?"

Diane ordered a strawberry daiquiri.

Mason looked at me. "Kate, what about you?"

"Something light, refreshing, and non-alcoholic. I'm driving. Oh, if you see Dwayne, would you tell him I'm looking for him?"

"Yes, ma'am. Be right back with your drinks."

I swapped my glasses for sunglasses.

Diane said, "You should get contacts or have laser surgery."

"My husband suggested contacts, too. I might have to try them because my glasses are bugging me."

She laughed. "I get it. What do you want to discuss?"

"Where were you during the break when Clint was murdered?"

"I was in the restroom with about ten other women from speed dating. We can all provide alibis for each other." She tilted her head. "Did the police confirm it happened during the break?"

"I think so. What's going to happen to Clint's business now that he's gone?"

She reached for a peanut and then dropped it back into the bowl. "With my luck, it's going to be auctioned off to pay off Clint's debts."

"Did he owe money to a lot of people?"

"Not exactly, but we were just beginning to recover from a financial hit we took last year."

Mason appeared with our drinks. "Kate, this is a frozen non-alcoholic pina colada. I believe you'll enjoy it."

The pink straw and mint sprig added a colorful touch to the icy drink. I took the first sip, and the deliciousness gave me happy vibes. "Mason, you're a genius."

"Thanks! I'll be back to check on you two in a bit." He moved down the bar and waited on two men wearing polo shirts and golf shorts. Both looked hot and sunburned.

"Diane, did Clint take money from his son?"

"Steal? No. Did he borrow and not mention it to Kyle? Yes. He had good intentions of paying him back." She took a drink of her strawberry daiquiri. "I'm sure he would've if he hadn't died."

So, Kyle had been right. "Did he do the same thing to anybody else?"

"I doubt it." She stared at her daiquiri. "It's hard to imagine he had control of another person's money. His parents were gone, and no siblings."

"Did Clint have more children?"

"You asked me that the other day. Kyle's an only child."

I picked up the pink cocktail umbrella and twirled it in my fingers. The last time I'd asked, I hadn't known Jennifer's story. "I understand he was involved with many different women. Did anyone ever come to Clint and say they were his offspring?"

"Over the years, a few people approached him claiming to be his child and asking for money. Clint never worried. He usually offered to do blood work at their expense. Then the kid would disappear." She adjusted her sunglasses. "Why do you continue to ask?"

"I'm trying to figure out Clint's life. Is there anyone else you think might have a motive to murder him?" I sipped the icy drink.

"I keep circling back to Peter and Hank because Clint didn't want them to participate. He knew they'd pulled scams in the past. The fact that Peter uses different names nags me. How else would I have allowed him to participate?" She clenched her hands.

"Diane, I have a good friend who worked for a man for years. She had a crush on him and couldn't bring herself to look for a different job. Is that the same sort of thing that happened with you and Clint?"

She almost smiled. "The thing is, when Clint gave you his full attention, he was so charismatic and pulled you in. No other man came close to having the same effect on me. Believe me, I tried to walk away. I was so miserable. So, one day it occurred to me that I could either be content with the snippets of time Clint gave me or I could be lonely. Clint asked me to take my job back, and I agreed. By coming back to work, I spent more time with Clint than any of the other women who came and went. It was enough for me."

I didn't know how to respond to her sad story. I slurped the rest of my delicious drink.

Diane said, "Good luck to your friend. Falling for the wrong man can be heartbreaking."

"Did any of the other women ever threaten to harm Clint?"

"We never stayed in one city very long. There was a scene or two, but I never witnessed a woman threaten Clint."

"How about a disgruntled boyfriend or unhappy husband?"

"No. Clint was only interested in women with no attachments. That's where he drew the line."

"Good to know. Thanks and good luck in your future endeavors."

"I appreciate that, Kate." Diane picked up her glass and carried it to the pool.

I removed my credit card from my purse and waved to Mason.

It didn't take long for him to join me and swipe my card. "I see Dwayne over yonder." He pointed to the stage where the musician sometimes performed.

"Thanks, Mason." I signed the receipt and included a nice tip. "See you later."

I hurried toward Dwayne, but before I could reach him, Erica and Sydney had him surrounded.

Chapter Thirty-Four

Sydney and Erica stood on each side of Dwayne. His head turned from one lady to the other. He scooched back. His action made me think of a kid on the playground trying to get away from the school bully.

I joined them. "Hi, Dwayne. Did you get my message?"

"Yes." He glanced at his watch. "Look at the time, will ya? Ladies, please excuse me. Time got away from me."

We exchanged polite words, and the sisters walked to the beach entrance.

Dwayne's shoulders relaxed, and he smiled. "Can't thank you enough. How can I return the favor?"

"No need. I wanted to let you know that Bess is doing okay with her sister."

"Shh." Dwayne shifted.

Peter appeared and shook Dwayne's hand. "Have you given any thought to the gold necklace I showed you? Or how about the chunky bracelet?"

Dwayne rubbed his neck. "Nah, man. I've got a lot on my mind these days and never gave the jewelry another thought."

Peter's eyebrows shot up. "Think about it. I'll be around through the weekend." He strolled away without glancing at me.

Once he was out of earshot, I looked at the musician. "Are you going to buy jewelry from him?"

"Not a chance. I don't trust him. People are heading home, and it seems like Peter is growing anxious to sell his jewelry. I don't know if it's stolen or fake, but it's not a legit operation." He pointed to the lobby door. "Let's go inside where it's cooler."

"Great idea." We walked into the resort lobby and found a quiet corner.

"You and your husband should come out dancing tonight. I'm featuring love songs from the seventies in one of my sets."

"That sounds mighty tempting. If Reid doesn't come home exhausted from the heat, we'll be here."

I left Dwayne and walked to the car. I needed time to think, so I headed home.

Hank and Peter were both taking advantage of single people, possibly lonely people, to make money. Hank stole it by pretending to make investments. Peter could be selling ill-gotten jewelry.

After taking care of Lady, I fixed a glass of water and climbed the stairs to my office and murder board. My goldendoodle followed at a leisurely pace, circled the room, and then plopped down on her dog pillow.

"Girl, maybe if I write things on the board, something will jump out at me."

I added Sydney's name to my suspect list. Paul called them persons of interest, and I'd bet some lawsuit somewhere led to the distinction.

According to Diane, Clint never went after women in other relationships. That should rule out significant others. Before I considered other people, I wanted to decide about Sydney and Peter.

"Whatcha doing?" Reid appeared wearing athletic shorts and a clean T-shirt.

I squealed. "Oh, you startled me. Did you take a shower? I didn't hear the water running."

Lady hopped up and greeted my husband.

After Reid rubbed her head, he turned to me and took me in his arms. "I used the outdoor shower to avoid bringing dust and sand inside. I missed you, Katie."

"I'm so glad you're home, and I'm happy you don't have to take many work trips."

"Me, too." He kissed me. "Catch me up on your investigation."

"It's been an interesting day. I'm moving Diane, Kyle, and Jennifer off my suspect list."

"What about the lady at the spa?"

"I think Lauren Lee was being a friend to Clint, and there doesn't seem to be a motive."

"Okay, but Gloria is still a suspect?"

"She had a romantic relationship with Clint, and she acted jealous about Diane and Jennifer. I'm not ready to rule her out. She sounded the alarm that something was wrong with Clint. Plus, who knows their way around the resort better than Gloria?"

"What about Diane? I bet she knows the resort layout pretty well." He settled into his recliner and kicked up his feet.

Lady jumped into his lap, and Reid laughed. "We may need a second recliner for her."

I couldn't stop myself from smiling. "She didn't pay it any attention until you sat down. She wants to be near you."

He stroked the dog's side. "Back to Diane. Why did you remove her?"

"She claims she was in the restroom with a lot of other women during the break. For now, let's take her off the list. I wish we could find out when Erica and Sydney arrived at the resort."

"Is there any chance Gloria would tell you?"

"Doubtful. I bet Paul would need a search warrant to learn the check-in times." I stepped back and studied the board. Why was I trying to solve another murder? I sighed. "Let's drop the case. Do you want to discuss your feelings about your parents getting married?"

"I'd rather do anything else than talk about my parents." He chuckled. "I've accepted it, that's enough."

Okay. No need to push. "Dwayne invited us to come to the resort and listen to him. He's going to play love songs from the seventies. We can dance."

"Is dance code for look for clues? What happened to dropping the case?

I laughed. "Dwayne mentioned he watches people and learns stuff. We can do the same thing. Eat a nice dinner, listen to good music, and observe people."

"You do enjoy watching people." He grinned and shook his finger at me.

"Oh, I almost forgot to tell you. Erica and Sydney ganged up on Dwayne. He looked very uncomfortable, and I kinda rescued him. Sydney and her husband are separated, and it doesn't look like she's interested in saving the marriage. She even went on a date with Peter. Diane confessed that Peter changed his name for this event and slipped past her scrutiny."

He snapped his fingers. "I took a deep dive into the Rodale Jewelry Store. Peter's picture isn't on their website or social media. Now it makes sense."

"Another weird thing happened today. While I was talking to Dwayne, Peter came over and spoke to him. He completely ignored me, and I was standing right there. Peter was trying to talk him into buying some jewelry. How is he making enough money to drive a Jag? Is he selling or buying jewelry?" I wrote the question on my board.

"Not sure." He motioned for Lady to get out of his lap and then pushed the footrest down. "We'd better get ready if we're going to get a good table. In fact, I'm going to call Dwayne and see if he can have the staff save a place for us."

We discussed our mission for the evening as we changed clothes. It wasn't long before we were seated at a table near the stage. It had a great view of the band and the restaurant.

I said, "Tonight's goal is to watch for Peter, Erica, or Sydney."

Reid tapped the table. "And have a good time."

"Babe, if I'm with you, I'm having a good time."

He laced his fingers through mine. "Nice recovery. Don't look now, but Peter is at the bar talking to women."

I adjusted my glasses and looked toward the bar.

Peter worked the crowd, speaking to a few men but mostly women.

Erica and Sydney entered the bar portion of the restaurant and sat at a raised table.

When Peter noticed the two of them, he spoke to the bartender and pointed to the sisters.

I said, "Are you seeing this?"

"Yep. It looks like he's buying drinks for Erica and Sydney."

"Dwayne said that he thought Peter was getting desperate for sales before everyone left. It could be the reason he's changing the script by paying for their drinks."

Reid reached for my hand. "This could be interesting. Instead of dinner and a concert, we've got dinner, a show, and a concert."

I adjusted my glasses to read the menu. By the time we ordered, Peter was sitting at the high-top table with the women. Dinner and a show. But what kind of show?

Chapter Thirty-Five

The sound of children's voices at the pool and the ocean breeze added to the festive mood at the resort's outdoor restaurant.

Peter, Erica, and Sydney had been moved to a table near us. Erica made eye contact, and I waved.

She replied with a tight smile.

The waitress appeared with our food, breaking the moment.

I leaned toward Reid. "They've seen us, so it'll be more of a challenge to watch them."

He shrugged. "It sounds like I need to focus on eating my sirloin."

I smiled. "I'm excited to try my fig-and-prosciutto flatbread.

'You don't look excited." Reid put a dollop of butter on his potato. "You're doing great with your investigation. In some true crime shows, it takes the police years to catch the bad guy. You're only six days in."

"True, but the suspects in Clint's case will leave town soon. If they had been able to get refunds from Seaside Hideaway, they probably would've taken off already." I took a bite of my flatbread. The sweetness of the fig combined with the salty prosciutto made a delicious combination.

"I get it. You want to solve the mystery before the remaining suspects leave."

"Yes."

Dwayne took the stage, and people clapped.

"Folks, it's good to see you. Our theme tonight is love. I'll play a few of my songs as well as hits from the seventies and eighties." Dwayne picked up his guitar and adjusted the strap. "Sit back and enjoy this beautiful Georgia evening."

I focused on my food and the music until Reid tapped my hand and pointed to my right.

Jennifer said, "Hi, guys. May I join you?"

"Yes, please do. I'm deaf in my right ear and didn't hear you. Are you hungry?"

"Yes, but mostly I couldn't stand to hide out in my room any longer."

Reid waved down our waiter and asked for another menu.

Jennifer shook her head. "There's no need for that. I'd like a cheeseburger, fruit, and sweet iced tea."

After the waiter walked away, Jennifer pointed to the table. "Please, finish your food while it's hot. Cheeseburgers are my comfort food, but your steak looks good."

"It's everything a steak should be. Juicy, tender, and flavorful." He cut a bite. "Your mom, er, family, is sitting over there."

"Yeah, I had hoped to avoid them. I mean, what do I even call them? They've lied since before I was born. I'm twenty-six. Maybe I can understand keeping the arrangement secret in the beginning, but I've been an adult for years." She took a deep breath. "I am so very sorry. You're trying to enjoy a nice dinner, and I'm acting like a whiney baby."

I patted her arm. "I'm impressed you can put one foot in front of the other. You were brave to come down, and you stayed even though you saw Erica and Sydney."

Reid nodded. "Yep, I know grown men who aren't as tough as you."

Her eyes traveled from me to Reid. "I wish you'd been my dad. Do you want to adopt me?" She smiled, but her lower lip trembled.

"I never had children of my own. We got married this summer, and now Ethan's my son. I'd be honored to be your father, but that won't solve your problem."

"What will fix this crazy situation?" She slumped back in her chair. "I can't move on with my life and act like nothing happened."

Reid set the fork and knife on his plate. "If you mean the lies your family told you, forgiveness is the best way to move forward. Believe me, I know it's hard to forgive. But carrying a grudge weighs you down. Now, if you're talking about Clint, the killer will eventually be caught. Again, you can be bitter, or you can forgive."

"Hmm. Are you a preacher?" Jennifer's shoulders hunched.

"Not even close. These are lessons I've learned over the years." He shrugged. "In fact, I'm still learning to forgive. It's a process for me."

"A process? Maybe I can figure it out."

I squeezed Reid's hand. I was so stinking proud of him. "Jennifer, I don't want to put a wedge between you and your family, but you're invited to spend time with us whenever you like."

"Thanks."

The waitress arrived with Jennifer's order.

I glanced toward Erica and Sydney. Both frowned. The look Sydney shot me sent shivers up my spine.

The music set ended, and Reid stood. "I think this is a good time to ask Peter about the earrings. After all, I gave him a deposit."

A knot formed in my belly. "Oh, man. It was cash. We'll probably never see that money again."

Jennifer added mustard to one side of the bun and then cut the burger in half.

Reid said, "Good thing my brother-in-law is the police chief. Truth and justice are on my side."

I snorted. "Good luck with that."

"Challenge accepted." Reid ambled toward the others.

Jennifer bit into her burger.

I said, "It was very nice what you said to Reid. You have an open invitation to join us for visits or holidays."

"I might come visit you one day. Y'all have been very kind."

"We'd love for you to think of us as family." I gave her time to chew and reflect on my words. "You're staying at the resort, and I was wondering if you've observed anything helpful concerning Clint's death."

She covered her mouth with one hand. "Can't quit investigating?"

"I'm an amateur and aware of my limitations. But I am curious."

"Most of the attendees are on the same floor. Diane is in the room next to mine, and she's been ordering room service lately. When Clint was alive, she ate meals with him as much as possible. Sometimes I joined them. The other day, when I returned from a run, a resort employee was pushing a wheeled cart out of Diane's room. There were dirty dishes, empty alcohol bottles from the mini fridge, and a clear plastic bag of trash. In the trash was a white plastic bottle of weed killer. Isn't that odd?"

"It's definitely interesting. Do you think a maintenance person put it in there?"

"No. This is a classy place. We don't have flowers or plants in our rooms or on the balconies." She took another bite of the burger.

Just when I'd taken Diane off my suspect list, Jennifer gave me a reason to put her back on. But Diane had an alibi, and what would be her motive? "Jennifer, this could be a big clue. Have you told anyone else?"

"No." She finished chewing. "I've also avoided people after I learned about the family lies. Am I overreacting? It seems like the earth has spun right off its axis, and I can't make a good decision. Do you think I should tell the police?"

"Yes. Would you like to talk to my brother? He's a good guy."

"But he's also the police chief." She sighed. "I've never been involved in anything that required a conversation with law enforcement. Will you go with me?"

"Yes. Enjoy your supper, and then I'll give him a buzz."

She snatched my hand. "Are you leaving me here?"

"No, sweetie. We're sticking together." Her panic broke my heart. How cruel for her mother and aunt to have lied to her all these years.

I punched Paul's number into my phone.

"Hey, sis. What's up?"

"Are you on duty?"

"Kinda. Until this murder is solved, I won't take much time off."

"I've learned something interesting, and I want my new friend to share it with you. Can you come to the resort in non-cop clothes?"

"Will it make the witness more relaxed? I'm still kicking myself for upsetting Bess."

"Yes, and don't worry about Bess right now. When she gets back from taking care of Ruth, you two can make up. She'll understand you were only performing your professional duties. She'll forgive you." I paused. Forgiveness seemed to be a popular topic this week.

"Good. I'll change clothes. ETA twenty minutes. Thirty tops." The call ended.

"What did he say?" Jennifer popped a grape into her mouth.

"He'll be here in a few minutes in regular clothes. Hopefully, most of the guests won't recognize him out of uniform."

"Thanks, Kate."

The waitress refilled our glasses, and Reid returned. "What a moron."

"No earrings?"

"No, ma'am." He sat in his chair. "I reminded him that I have a receipt, and he finally agreed to meet us tomorrow with earrings. It's a good thing I approached him with witnesses around, because I think he wanted to deny everything. It's not even that much money. It just grinds my gears that Peter thinks he can get away with ripping off innocent people."

I said, "Jennifer may have stumbled onto a clue, and Paul is coming over to hear her story. We're going to stay with her for moral support."

Jennifer gave us a weak smile. "Thanks, guys. Reid, did my mom mention me? Um, Erica."

"No, but Peter did most of the talking. Erica raised you, loved you, and did all the things a mother does. Don't be so quick to write her off."

She sniffed, and a tear flowed down her face.

I said, "I need to freshen up while we wait for Paul."

Jennifer stood. "I'll come with you."

I looked at Reid. "Find out if Gloria talked to him."

"Will do."

We went to the restroom closest to the space used for the speed dating event. There were six stalls, an area with sinks, and a sitting area with chairs. It seemed like Diane's alibi was possible.

I washed my hands and freshened my lipstick.

CHAPTER THIRTY-FIVE

Jennifer moved from a stall to a sink without saying a word.

The main door swooshed open, and Erica appeared.

Jennifer squealed. "Mom, I can't deal with you right now."

"Honey, give me a chance to explain."

"Not tonight." She raced past us.

I wanted to follow her.

Too bad Erica blocked my path to freedom.

Chapter Thirty-Six

My pulse throbbed in my temple as I faced Erica in the cold restroom. "Please move."

"What are you doing with my daughter?" Her angry words bounced off the bathroom walls.

"She joined us for dinner." I licked my dry lips. "It wasn't planned. It just kinda happened."

"She should've sat at my table." Anger rolled off the pretty woman. "You're trying to drive a wedge between us."

"No, I'm not." My legs shook, but I managed to keep my voice calm.

"You gave her a ride after the kayak adventure."

Of all the nerve. "She asked me for a ride. You must know this problem began with you and your sister keeping a secret from Jennifer. Maybe if you give her a little breathing room, she'll be ready to talk. You must have imagined this day would come, but it's hit her out of the clear blue sky."

Erica slumped against the wall. "Most of my life, I helped clean up Sydney's messes. You have no idea. But, raising Jennifer was nothing but joy."

"Did you ever consider having more children?"

"I was in a car accident in high school. There was internal damage, and I survived, but the doctors told me I could never get pregnant. When Sydney told me she was pregnant, I saw it as an opportunity to help my sister and have a child of my own."

"Why do you think your sister came to the resort?"

"She's made a mess of her marriage and started looking back at her relationship with Clint through rose-colored glasses. I had no idea who the father of her child was when I told her how worried I was about Jennifer and Clint."

"Jennifer told me it was not a romantic relationship."

While positioning herself between me and the door, Erica grabbed a paper towel, wet it, and dabbed her neck with it. "She told me the same thing, but I didn't believe her."

"Clint never tried anything. I wonder if he guessed she was his child? They may have felt a father-daughter bond."

"If she suspected he was her father, she would've thought I had been in a relationship with him." Erica shook her head.

I scooted to the side, hoping to brush past her. "You didn't answer my question about Sydney. Did she come to get back together with Clint? Or were you worried she wanted to tell Clint he was Jennifer's biological dad?"

"Sydney didn't arrive at the resort until Wednesday night."

"Clint had already died by then." Air whooshed out of my lungs. It seemed like that should take her off my suspect list, but doubts lingered. "Reid is probably getting worried. Let me out of here."

"Fine." Erica threw the paper towel into the trash can.

I hurried out before she changed her mind and tried to stop me again.

"Kate." Dwayne stood in the hallway. "Your husband asked me to look for you. He didn't want to leave Jennifer alone with your brother, but he was concerned."

"Thanks. I was a little worried myself when Erica appeared." We walked down the hall toward the outdoor restaurant.

He whistled.

"Erica was questioning me about Jennifer. She blames me for their conflict."

"Hunh. She should blame herself and her sister."

I stopped walking. "You know?"

He nodded. "I keep telling you it's easy for me to notice things. I also keep my ears open when I'm not singing. Sydney had a baby. Clint's the dad. Erica raised the baby as her own child. How am I doing?"

I said, "You're probably a better detective than I am. Maybe you should add amateur sleuth to your list of accomplishments."

We continued walking. "I haven't solved a murder, and you're welcome to keep the title of amateur sleuth." He opened the door for me. "See you later."

"Thanks again." I walked to my table, and Dwayne moved to the stage.

Sydney had taken my seat and leaned toward Reid, talking rapidly.

I took the empty chair.

"He wanted to buy my wedding rings and said he'd get top dollar for them."

Reid's eyes met mine. "She's explaining why she went on a date with Peter."

"It wasn't a date." Sydney's nostrils flared, and she turned my way. "It was a business meeting. I could use extra money for a divorce attorney. I believed Peter wanted to help until your husband came over asking about his deposit and the earrings."

Jennifer crossed her arms tightly around herself.

"What happened?"

"I told Peter the deal was off." She stood and stalked to the bar.

"Looks like I'm interrupting something." Paul's comment drew my attention away from Sydney.

"Thanks for coming."

Paul hugged me. "Hey, sis."

"Seaside Hideaway could use a full-time security staff." I motioned for my brother to take the empty seat.

Paul said, "Why am I here?"

"I witnessed something," Jennifer repeated the story about the cart coming out of Diane's room and the fertilizer bottle in the clear trash bag.

I said, "What do you think, Paul? Was Clint poisoned?"

"I can't say, but this is good information. Thanks, Jennifer. Is there anything else?"

Reid pointed at Peter and Sydney. "Let me tell you about Peter. Stop me if you already know."

Dwayne began to play music. I tuned out the conversation between Reid and Paul and allowed myself to enjoy the song.

After the first two songs, Jennifer tapped my arm. "I'm going back to my room. It feels like you know who is staring at me."

"I'll walk with you."

"I appreciate it."

I told Reid where I was going.

"I can come too."

"No, stay with Paul. I won't stop and question anybody."

Paul shook his head. "You better not."

The trip to Jennifer's room proved uneventful. While I waited for the elevator to take me down to the lobby, Diane exited her room.

Gulp.

"Hi, Kate. Are you staying at the resort?"

"Um, no. The owner is a friend of mine, and I'm—"

Ding.

The elevator doors opened.

A family with four children scooted back so we could get on, and our conversation ended. Thank goodness.

When we reached the lobby, I exited and hurried to the restaurant.

Dwayne played a slow song, and Reid stood when I reached the table. "May I have this dance?"

"Absolutely. This is going to be the best part of my day."

We joined two other couples on the small dance floor.

"Where's Paul?"

"He left to track down a clue. He said that Gloria had contacted him about the necklace. Katie, let's forget about the murder and enjoy the music." Reid hummed along with the song. I relaxed as we moved together to the beat of the music. Stars shone in the sky.

Thoughts of Clint's death drifted away, and I was completely focused on Reid.

A blood-curdling scream broke the mood.

The music ended.

Chairs screeched as people jumped up to see who had yelled.

Shouting followed, but it was muted to me.

"Oh, no." Reid stood on a chair and scanned the area. "Erica and Sydney are fighting by the adult pool."

"Arguing?"

People ran past us.

Reid said, "No. It's a girl fight with hitting and hair pulling."

I texted Paul. Erica and Sydney are in a physical fight by the pool.

Reid said, "Two waiters are trying to break up the women."

"What should we do?"

Reid got off the chair. "Peter is running away from the fight even though everyone else is running toward it. Let's follow him."

I couldn't stop myself from smiling. "Let's go."

Chapter Thirty-Seven

"You're doing a great job of following Peter without being obvious." I kept my eyes glued on the Jag.

Reid said, "Hope you're right. It helps that I know the island so well."

"Yeah. You surprised me when you turned onto another street."

"Knowing the ocean is to our east, it didn't seem like a risk. There are only so many directions he can go."

"Clever man." I was always impressed by how smart Reid was. He was book-smart and had a good dose of common sense. "Oh, he's slowing down."

"There are lots of bars between here and the pier. Maybe that's his destination." Reid slowed enough to allow a car from a side street to pull in front of us.

"Peter has probably worked over the resort crowd with a fine-tooth comb. He needs fresh victims." The light turned yellow, and Peter turned left toward the pier, restaurants, and noisy bars.

Reid tapped the steering wheel. "If you plan to keep solving mysteries, we need a nondescript vehicle."

"More and more, I realize buying the Wagoneer was a knee-jerk reaction to my accident. I need a safe, boring vehicle."

"I couldn't agree more." A green arrow appeared on the stoplight, and Reid turned. "Your reaction makes sense to me. I still don't like to ride in little cars after my wreck, and I was in my teens. However, I think you've got a lot of options available besides the tank you're driving now."

"I'm ready to consider other vehicles." I pointed to the other side of the street. "Peter must've done a U-turn. He's parking over there."

"Keep looking forward in case he sees us."

As much as I wanted to see what he was up to, I focused on the car in front of us. "There's so much foot traffic."

"Yep, and they're darting across the street every which way." He stopped for two guys who stumbled into the street in front of us.

A car behind us honked.

Reid remained calm. "I'm parking at the first available space."

The guys made it to the other side, and Reid drove slowly down the street. I said, "They're all taken."

"Not a problem." He turned onto a side street and parked in front of a small apartment complex. "Do you mind walking?"

"Not at all." What a blessing to have a husband who wanted to help me solve a mystery.

We met on the cracked sidewalk and walked to the busy street.

Reid said, "Our goal is to find Peter and observe."

"Right. Nothing good can come from a confrontation." We reached the crowded street. "I'm surprised so many people are still on the island. In Lexington, the university students are back on campus by now, and the town is flooded on home football game weekends."

"The island will be crowded until after Labor Day. Then it will begin to slow down, but November is when you'll notice a big difference." He stopped walking. "Don't look. Peter's on the front porch of the apartment building where you used to live."

"Let's go into the ice cream shop. I think we can watch without him spotting us."

"Sounds like a plan." Reid opened the door and allowed me to go first.

I said, "I'd like a small dip of rocky road. I'll grab a table and try to watch." Reid nodded. "Go for it."

There were three big plants near the window, and I picked a table near the artificial Ficus tree. I sat in a chair and scooted it so I could observe Peter without being seen.

Peter pulled out a pack of gum, removed a piece, unwrapped it, and popped the stick of gum into his mouth. Each motion was slow and deliberate.

What was he up to? A scam or murder?

Another man walked up the front stairs of the building and stopped in front of Peter. The new man wore a green hoodie with the sleeves cut off and striped surfer shorts. The hood was pulled up, preventing me from seeing his face. The second guy handed a small box to Peter.

"What's going on?" Reid patted my shoulder.

I jumped. "You scared me. Watch. There may be a deal going down."

Reid pulled a chair beside me and behind the Ficus. His breathing tickled my neck. "Who's the second guy?"

"I can't tell."

Peter studied the box's contents and then closed it. He removed an envelope from the pocket of his shorts and handed it to the stranger.

The second guy thumbed through the contents. Most likely it was cash, but I couldn't see.

Peter said something while stuffing the box into his pocket. They walked down the steps. Peter walked west toward town, and the stranger jogged toward the beach.

Reid said, "We're sticking together."

I understood Reid wasn't being bossy. One time, we had split up for an investigation, and the situation turned dangerous. Almost deadly. "How'd you know I wanted to follow them?"

"Katie, I know how you think. It's why I ordered you a milkshake instead of a cup of ice cream. It'll be easier to follow, but we need to move."

I reached for my drink, and we darted out of the ice cream shop and toward the beach. "Shall we go to the pier unless we see the second guy?"

"Yeah, we don't want it to appear we're looking for that dude."

We walked between people on the crowded sidewalk, and I took a sip of the milkshake. "Yum. A rocky road milkshake. Who knew it was possible?"

"You don't know if you don't ask."

"Kinda like my investigations. I learn by asking and organizing the information."

We crossed the street when the light gave the Walk signal.

I glanced toward the parking lot and spotted the green hoodie dangling on the lip of a public garbage can. "Oh, no. We lost him."

"How do you know?"

I pointed to the hoodie. "Paul needs to know."

"We must be wearing him out tonight, but you're right."

I texted my brother. **Found a clue.**

My phone rang, and Paul's face flashed on the screen.

I swiped right. "Hey. Reid said I'm probably getting on your last nerve."

Reid leaned toward the phone. "Not my exact words."

"I just lectured Erica and Sydney. Where are you, and what's going on?"

"It involves Peter." I explained what I'd witnessed.

"I'll meet you at the trash can. Try not to let anyone tamper with the potential evidence." He ended the call.

"There's no way we can prevent people from throwing away trash."

"I've got an idea." I handed him my milkshake and rushed into the nearest gift shop. I went to the checkout counter. "Can I buy a bag from you?"

The young girl pulled out a big white shopping bag. "You mean like this?"

"Yes. That's exactly what I need."

"I wouldn't know what to charge you. Just take it and shop here another time."

"Terrific. Thanks." I exited the store and looked both ways. My pulse pounded in my neck. Was I being watched? My knees locked. Should I go out? Or stay put?

There were so many people laughing, smoking, crying, and talking loudly. My gaze bounded from one person to the next, but I couldn't spot anyone suspicious.

A person bumped me.

I swayed.

If Peter, the other guy, or somebody else was watching, I'd be a sitting duck unless I blended into the crowd.

A family walked by, followed by a group of young women wearing sashes and crowns for a bridal party. They'd been drinking, and it was easy to push into their rowdy group.

At last, I reached the can. "Did you see Peter or the other guy?

"No, but I was about to look for you. What's your plan?"

I turned the store bag inside out, picked up the hoodie, and secured it without contaminating the evidence with my fingerprints. "There."

A group of young, giggling girls stepped between us and tossed empty food bags into the can. They walked away without ever saying a word to us.

My pulse began returning to normal. "Looks like we saved the evidence in the nick of time."

Reid handed me my drink. "Yeah, those girls swooped in here before I could react."

"I'm probably overreacting, but it felt like somebody was watching me."

"It's good we're together."

I took a drink of the rocky road milkshake. Chocolate always helped. "There's a slim chance we can spot the guy who took money from Peter. Look for teal, white, and maybe orange surfer shorts."

"Got it."

We finished our milkshakes and chucked the cups into another trash can. "There's your brother."

Paul pulled into the parking lot and double-parked. He walked over and looked at the can. "I don't see a shirt."

I handed the bag to him and explained the situation, including the sensation that I had been watched. "I wonder if he took the money out of the envelope. If so, it might be in there."

Paul put on gloves and returned the bag to me. He said, "You two hold your phone flashlights so I can look for the envelope. I doubt it's related to Clint's murder, but I'm not willing to take that chance."

We shone our lights, allowing Paul to look.

A car came to a stop behind Paul's Charger and honked.

Reid said, "I'll handle it."

I kept my light focused on the garbage.

Paul retrieved a grimy envelope. "We'll test this and the hoodie for fingerprints and possible DNA. Anything else?"

"Aren't you going to look for the guy?"

"You gave me a description, and I'll alert my officers."

"What about the fight between Erica and Sydney?"

"I think it's a sister thing. Hey, I'm holding up traffic. Gotta run." He left me, patted Reid on the shoulder, and spoke to the driver who'd honked. At last, Paul hopped into his car and drove away.

Reid joined me and reached for my hand. "Are you ready to call it a day?"

"Yeah. Tomorrow is Saturday, and we can get an early start on the investigation."

"Please, not too early."

I laughed. "You'll probably be up long before my feet hit the floor, so I'm not worried about dragging you out of bed."

We walked to Reid's truck and drove home listening to country music. Reid parked but left the motor running. "I think somebody's sitting in a rocker, and it's not Goldilocks."

My breathing grew shallow as I looked at the porch. "You're right. I think it's a woman."

"You have women on your list of suspects."

"True. I'll call Paul and keep him on the line until we identify the person." I dialed my brother.

"What?" He sounded tired and cranky.

"Someone is on our front porch. I'm going to keep you on the line until we see if it's safe."

"I'll stay on the phone, but I'm coming your way." His hoarse voice made me wonder if he'd gotten any sleep this week.

Reid said, "We can wait until Paul gets here."

I sighed. "I'm not worried if it's a woman. Let's see who it is."

"There are prisons full of women who committed horrible crimes. Don't let your guard down."

He made a decent point, plus I had women on my suspect list. "I'm on full alert."

Chapter Thirty-Eight

R eid and I got out of the truck. A streetlight illuminated the way to the stairs. "We should've left the porch light on."

"Lesson learned." He went up the stairs ahead of me. "Who's there?"

A woman stood and walked to the railing. "It's me. Bess."

Relief swooshed through my veins. "Bess, oh my goodness. What are you doing here, sitting in the dark all alone? I thought you were still in Atlanta."

Reid reached her first and gave her a brotherly hug.

I focused on the phone. "Paul, it's okay. Nothing to worry about."

"Yeah, yeah. I heard you say Bess's name. I'm heading home. Call me if you need me, but please try not to need me for the rest of the night."

"Get some rest. I love you, Paul."

"Love you too." The call ended.

I moved to Bess and gave her a long hug. "I'm so happy to see you. Let's go inside."

We entered the house, and Lady barked.

Reid attached the leash to the dog's collar. "I'll take her out, but don't say anything important until I return."

I said, "Don't dawdle."

"Yes, ma'am." Reid and Lady went out the front door.

"Bess, have a seat. Are you okay?"

"I'm good. Your hubby said not to talk about anything important until he's here."

She sat on the white linen chair and propped her feet on the ottoman.

"You're right." I handed her a throw even though it was still hot outside. I fixed three glasses of water and set them on the coffee table. "Did you eat on the drive? Are you hungry?"

"I'm good."

Reid and Lady returned, and we sat on the couch.

I said, "Okay. Tell us what's going on."

"Hank was following me around the island, and it freaked me out. Plus, I was worried that Paul thought I was involved in Clint's death. I'd never taken time to process Tom's final rejection. I started dating to get my sister off my back, but meeting so many strangers at one time doesn't suit me. I think I'm more into becoming friends first."

None of this explained why she was here and not at Ruth's place. "Dwayne said he saw you at the resort the other night after we'd been together. Talking to Hank."

"Yes, but he lured me there, saying he had my good sunglasses. That was Monday night. I think he stole them, but it doesn't make sense. At least I got them back. Anyway, I shouldn't have gone to meet him at night. Dwayne was kind enough to walk me to my van. Ruth had asked me to help her through the recovery process, and I would've done it anyway, but it also seemed like a way to escape my immediate problems. You know what I mean?"

Reid said, "Knowing your sister, you landed yourself in a different kind of mess."

"Oh, brother. You don't know the half of it." She shook her head. "Even so, I wasn't in danger. I've tried to keep up with the news. It doesn't sound like Paul has caught the killer yet."

"Not yet. Do you feel like telling us more about Hank?"

She reached for a glass of water and took a long drink. "That's good. I got hot waiting for you to come home. I know I could've texted, but I wasn't sure how much to share. I don't want to put you in danger."

"Oh, Bess. You're my best friend. I'll always be here for you. What happened to make you so scared?" I leaned forward.

"When I met Hank on Monday night, he had a funny look in his eyes. I won't go as far as to call them crazy eyes, maybe a little desperate. He asked me to have a drink with him, but I made up an excuse about needing to leave. He insisted that I would want to hear about his investment opportunity. I debated if it was safe to leave or if it was better to be around people. I followed the sound of music and walked to the outside restaurant where Dwayne Gray was performing. Hank followed me. He accused me of lying when I told him I had to leave. That's when I shifted from being scared to mad. I asked him to leave me alone, but he continued to follow me. The music ended, and Dwayne joined us. Hank left, and Dwayne walked me to my van. I was surprised to discover how safe I felt around him. When I got home, I called Ruth. I didn't turn on any lights, and sure enough, a red car parked across the street. I didn't tell Ruth about the murder or Hank. Instead, we discussed my going to Atlanta. I fell asleep on the couch while watching Hank's car. Next thing I knew, the sky was growing lighter. There was no sign of the car, so I fixed a travel mug of coffee and hightailed it out of here." She swiped at a tear.

Guilt hit me. "I should've helped you."

Bess shook her finger. "You can't solve all of my problems. I'm a grown woman, and Hank was my problem to handle."

I sighed. She made a good point. I was her friend. Not her mother. "Hank's guilty of some crimes, but I don't think he murdered Clint. Still, we should be cautious around him."

"Oh." Her voice squeaked.

Reid said, "Why come home now?"

"Oh, y'all know how relentless my sister can be. She harped on me about everything from breaking my phone to the temperature of her coffee. Her argument should've been with her fancy coffee maker and not me." She took a deep breath and released it. "Jonah finished his project and told me to come on home. I can't tell you how relieved I was."

I nodded, understanding how Bess shriveled up in the presence of her sister.

"I wanted to stop by here first and share what I witnessed at the resort on Monday."

My heart sped up. "You mean there's more?"

"Yes, ma'am. When I first arrived at the resort, I heard voices arguing. I couldn't resist a little sleuthing of my own. While trying to listen, the voices grew louder. Not like madder, but like the people were getting closer to me. I was standing by the complimentary water station. So, I got busy filling a cup. It was Hank and Peter, arguing about Clint. Hank accused Peter of committing the murder. Then Peter accused Hank of larceny and fraud. I knew the minute they saw me because the argument ended."

"It's interesting they suspect each other. What did you say to them?"

"Girl, you would've been proud of me. I acted like I had just arrived and was about to look for Hank to get my sunglasses. He and I walked away from Peter, and that's when Hank launched into his investment opportunity speech." She took another drink of water. "I think that gets you up to speed."

"You've had quite an emotional week."

"That's the truth."

"Watch out for Hank. He left you a warning note." I explained the note. "He thought if you dug into Clint's death, you'd discover he was a fraud."

"And here I was more scared of Peter." Bess stood. "I might need a couple of days to recover, but my goal is to return to work by the middle of next week. Is it okay to leave my van here and contact a ride share? In case Hank's out and about, he won't see me driving home. I don't have the energy to deal with him."

"Bess, are you concerned he might hurt you?"

"He's pushy and wants my money. I don't know how desperate he is, but there's nothing to give him. My money is invested in our business."

"It makes sense he'd back off if his primary concern was you probing into Clint's murder and discovering he was a conman. Do you want to stay with us?"

"No. I need some alone time." Her smile was lopsided. "Once I'm home, I'll be okay."

Lady meandered over to Bess and gazed up at her.

Bess rubbed her head. "I bet you always make people feel better."

Reid said, "I'll give you a ride and go inside with you to make sure your condo is safe."

I moved into the kitchen and pulled out a reusable grocery bag. "Let me get you some food."

"Oh, thank you."

I filled a bag with bagels, cream cheese, apples, creamer, and peaches. "Um, I noticed your tennis shoes were muddy. That doesn't seem like you. Not that I'm judging or anything."

"I went for a walk around the marsh and ended up in the mud. It had nothing to do with the mystery." She pointed to the bag of food and laughed. "That should hold me. I appreciate it."

Reid said, "You should lie low as long as you think it is necessary. When you're ready, we'll bring the van to you. In fact, I'll probably move it to one of my sites where it's not obvious."

I said, "We can bring you more groceries."

"Wait a minute. You saw my muddy shoes? Have you been snooping in my house?"

I hugged Bess. "When your phone was broken and I couldn't find you, it seemed like an emergency. Allie and I went over and made sure you weren't injured and unable to call." I didn't tell her some of my wilder worries.

"Thanks for checking. I'll see you later." Her shoulders drooped, and her voice lacked enthusiasm.

"Hey, Bess. I'm sorry about the times I've acted over-protective. I'll do better."

"It's no big thing. Your heart's in the right place."

"Wait. I need you to forgive me."

"I forgive you."

"I know you're smart and capable." The fact that she hadn't dated much and that she wasn't used to me dragging her into murder investigations didn't make it okay for me to act like her mother.

"You're nothing like Ruth. Please, quit worrying about it." She squeezed my hand.

"Okay. I'll do better, but if I slip, you need to tell me."

"Deal."

I stayed at the house with Lady, hoping that if anyone spotted Reid, they'd think I was with him. With a little luck, nobody would suspect he was driving Bess. Once they left, I went upstairs to my office and added her comments to my murder notes.

Had Hank or Peter said anything that would truly put my friend in danger? Was that why Hank followed Bess to her condo on Monday night after she'd met him at the resort? In her position, I would've called Paul. But Paul wasn't her brother, and he'd questioned her about the murder. Easy to see why she didn't turn to him.

For now, I'd focus on catching the killer and hope Hank and Peter would have to answer for their crimes.

Chapter Thirty-Nine

On Saturday morning, Reid and I took Lady for a walk on the beach. It was a sweltering August day, and it was only nine. "How hot is it going to be this afternoon? Are you sure I'm going to survive the Georgia heat?"

"You'll adapt. This will probably be the worst summer."

Lady came to a complete stop.

I reached for a bottle and poured water into a bowl for her. "Drink that up."

She lapped the bowl dry, so I gave her more.

Reid said, "We should take her home."

I heard a noise, but wasn't sure what direction it was coming from. I turned in a circle, trying to locate the sound. At last, I spotted Ethan and Kyle. "Hi, guys."

"Hey, Mom. We finished our morning run and we're trying to cool down."

I laughed. "Good luck with that."

Kyle's shirt was soaked. "Kate, you might like to know the attorney has gathered everyone, and she plans to read the will today."

"Are you expecting any surprises?"

He shook his head. "No, but you never know, especially with Dad."

Ethan said, "Hey, man, we should meet for dinner afterward."

"Cool. There's no funeral because he donated his body to the university for research." He grimaced. "It'll be nice to have somebody to decompress with."

Reid said, "Why don't you guys come to our house, and I'll cook steaks?"

Kyle smiled. "Thanks. I've never turned down a steak."

"We should get Lady inside, but Ethan can tell you how to get to our place." We left them and headed home. I said, "It's interesting that Ethan and Kyle have become friends."

"Think about it. Ethan's twenty-seven. He's not a party guy, he's not married, and he's not local. It's probably been a challenge to make friends here with people his age."

We walked through the thicker sand to the path leading off the beach. "I see your point. When I moved here, I had friends from my past and family. And then there was you. I haven't been lonely for even a minute. With Ethan living on the island, there's nothing more I could ask for. I see how it could be challenging to start a new life here."

Reid said, "I imagine in Texas, he had gym memberships, bars—"

"I could be wrong, but I don't think Ethan drinks much. He's so focused on only putting healthy stuff in his body. He did attend a huge church and made friends there."

"I've noticed some of his healthy food choices. Speaking of which, we should discuss the impromptu cookout and a menu."

For the rest of the walk, we talked about what to serve and created a grocery list.

Reid said, "I'll give Lady a shower out here."

"Thanks, honey." I handed the leash to him. "You know what? This seems like a normal day, doesn't it? We're not discussing murder, suspects, or clues."

"What do you know?" He rubbed his chin. "No, we can't go all day without trying to solve the mystery. It's been a week. I know you well enough to realize we'll try to track down some clue."

"Yeah, and it's weighing on me. One week ago, Clint was murdered. I'll clean up and try to decide my next step." I moved to the stairs but turned back. "It will be interesting to hear from Kyle about the reading of the will."

"That's not why I invited him."

"I know. You're a good man." I gave him a quick kiss before heading inside.

By noon, we'd conquered the grocery shopping. Reid had insisted on going with me so he could pick out the steaks. His grilling skills were an art form. The meat was now in the refrigerator, marinating. I'd begun food prep, and I had baked beans in the crockpot.

Reid sat at the kitchen counter, sipping coffee and watching a sports channel.

"What would you like for lunch?"

"I thought about calling Peter and seeing if he'd meet us for lunch."

"That's a great idea. I'll get ready."

"Hey, he may not agree." Reid reached for his phone.

"I bet he will because he wants our money." I paused and looked at my husband. "How will we know if the diamonds are real?"

Reid rubbed his chin. "I'll tell him they need to be appraised by an independent source for our insurance. However, I won't mention that until we're together."

"Brilliant." I went to our bedroom, changed into nicer clothes, and applied fresh lipstick. A cute blue and white polka dot hat hung on a hook in the closet, and I grabbed it. It'd protect my skin and maybe help me deal with the heat better. Plus, it was super cute and went with my outfit.

Reid joined me and brushed his teeth. "We're going to meet him for a quick lunch at Island Perk. What kind of food do they serve for lunch?"

"Mostly sandwiches unless there's quiche left from the breakfast crowd. I'm sure you'll find something you can eat."

"At least I know we're going to have a hearty supper. Let's go."

Reid's truck was parked in the shade with the windows down. It wouldn't take us long to drive to Island Perk, and I didn't want Peter to catch me off guard. "Do you find it peculiar that Peter wants to meet across the street from Sand Piper Apartments? He couldn't have known we were watching him from the ice cream shop. Right?"

"If he'd thought he was being watched, he wouldn't have finished the deal."

"It's so weird, though. Why meet in the shadows if you're going to be in the middle of the action?"

Reid turned onto Ocean Boulevard. "Hmm. Maybe because it's easy to blend into the crowd."

"Good point. It worked for them. We lost the other guy."

"Oh, there's a space big enough for my truck. Do you mind walking?"

"Sure. It's not that far."

After he parked, we walked to the coffee shop.

I said, "Do you see Peter?"

"Not yet, but we're on the early side. Why don't we grab a table and study the menu?" He opened the door.

I entered, found a table for four, and walked over to it. We sat down and picked up menus from the clip on the napkin dispenser. "I need to make a healthy choice. We've been eating out too much lately."

"I'm doing better than when I was single, but you're right. We should eat at home more."

I glanced out the window and spotted Peter crossing the street. He wore a straw hat, probably to protect his bald head. "Here he comes."

Peter jaywalked like it was no big deal, and in the grand scheme of things, it probably wasn't, especially if he was guilty of murder. He entered the coffee shop and joined us. "Hi, folks." He fanned himself with the hat and undid one of the buttons on his shirt. He wore various gold necklaces of different lengths. "A buddy called me on my way here, and I forgot we'd scheduled to get together. If you don't mind, let's cut to the chase." He placed a wooden box on the table and lifted the lid. It was a bigger box than the one from the previous night. The inside was lined with gray velvet, and diamond earrings were displayed nicely. "Have a look."

There were teardrop earrings, studs, huggies, and hoops. There were small diamonds and bigger ones.

Reid said, "That's quite a selection. Is your store in Savannah?"

"Which one catches your eye?" Peter nudged the box closer to me, ignoring Reid's question.

I reached for a pair of studs. "How much are they?"

"You pick your favorite pair, and then we'll discuss the price."

A lady approached us from behind the counter. "If y'all aren't going to order, I need the table for paying customers."

Reid nodded. "I understand."

Peter stood. "I'll place our order while you decide on the earrings."

The woman said, "You'll have to get in line. We don't wait on tables. Sorry." She walked behind the counter to help another employee.

Peter said, "Can I get coffee for you both?"

"Iced for me." I put down the pair of studs and studied another pair of earrings.

"Make that two iced coffees." Reid propped one ankle over his other leg and draped his arm on the back of my chair.

Peter made his way to the back of the line.

I said, "They're very sparkly."

"Yep. They're beautiful. Which one will you pick?"

"Life on Fox Island is pretty casual, and I don't need a pair of diamond earrings." I picked up another pair and held them in the light. "Peter's watching. I suppose you noticed he didn't answer your question."

"Sure did." He picked up a pair attached to a card and held them to the light. "I understand that you don't want a pair of diamond earrings, but I think we need to see this through. Also, he has my deposit money."

"That's unfortunate." I shifted my focus from Reid back to the studs. "This is my favorite pair. Not too big or ostentatious."

"Okay."

"Oh, Reid." My eye twitched. "I feel like this investigation is forcing you to buy me earrings. I'm usually careful about money."

"Shh. Don't worry. We'll ask the price. Depending on how expensive they are, I'll do the spiel about the insurance, and we'll see how Peter reacts."

The jewelry man had worked his way to the front of the line. He handed the girl his credit card and soon came to our table with three small black coffees. Two were iced and one was hot. "Guys, that woman said there's a station to add cream and sugar in the back corner. Did you decide?"

I passed my selection to him.

"Really? I thought you'd pick something flashier." He closed the box with the rest of the jewelry and set it in the empty chair.

"It doesn't fit my island lifestyle. Peter, I have a store in town, and I'm curious how you can sell jewelry, well, I guess, you know, off the street. How do you manage your inventory? Um, do you need a professional organizer, or what kind of system do you have?"

"What are you getting at?" Peter frowned.

"Yesterday, you didn't seem to have earrings in your inventory. Today you do. How'd you get them so fast?"

Reid reached for his phone and appeared to open an app. His fingers swiped across the screen.

Peter's nostrils flared. "To meet the needs of my customers, I have systems in place. It was no problem to contact a colleague."

"So, they brought you this nice selection? I'm just asking because sometimes I show up at a client's home with products that I think they'll like. If they don't, I have to go all the way back to the store and select different things. This is after we've had conversations and reviewed their style. It wastes time, but in the end, they're happy with the outcome."

Peter met my gaze. "You probably have bulky storage stuff. Jewelry is small and easy to transport. As you can see, I was able to offer you a wide selection."

"Yes, and I appreciate it. Please thank your co-worker for me. So, Peter, how much are they?"

Peter quoted a price that made me gasp.

Reid said, "My insurance agent says I need to get them appraised by one of her people. Do you mind if I set that up?"

"No, way. I'll provide the paperwork for your insurance."

Reid sat straighter. "That could be a problem. The pictures you showed me at the resort are not the same as the earrings here. How will I know if you're giving me the proper appraisal? Where are the earrings you showed me at the resort?"

"You must not be remembering correctly." Peter smiled, but it appeared forced.

"No. You showed me pictures of different earrings." Reid turned his phone so we could see it. "I don't see this pair." He swiped the screen, and a different photo appeared. "Or this one."

Peter yanked the phone from Reid's hand. "Let's see." He moved his finger to the bottom of the screen near the delete button.

I leaned forward to grab Reid's phone. In the process, I knocked over Peter's coffee.

The mug tipped over, coffee spilled, flowed across the table, and landed on Peter's leg.

"Yeow." Peter dropped the phone. "You—"

Reid said, "Be careful what you say there."

"I'm sorry. I didn't mean to do that." I snagged the phone and wiped the coffee off.

Peter grabbed napkins and blotted the coffee off his shorts and legs.

"Again, I'm so sorry."

Peter glared at us. "I don't need your business this bad."

It was a relief to be out of the deal, but I was sorry for the coffee spill. "Peter, remind me where you were at the time of Clint's murder."

"I was with your friend, Beth."

"Bess. Not Beth." I tried to tamp down my irritation. He didn't even know her name.

"Whatever." Peter stuffed the pair of earrings into the pocket of his short-sleeved, button-up, green fishing shirt. He picked up the jewelry box. "This deal is off. Don't bother me again."

I opened my mouth to apologize, but Reid touched my hand and shook his head.

Reid said, "Peter, it's too bad we couldn't buy from you, but good luck in the future. When can I expect my deposit back?"

Peter left without uttering another word.

I slumped back in my chair and sighed. "That was ugly. I was trying to stop him from deleting your photos. Who knew I'd spill his coffee?"

"It worked in our favor, and it might be a good thing we ordered iced coffees. Try yours."

I took a sip. "It's good, just like always."

"Yeah. So, did we learn anything related to Clint's murder?"

I replayed the conversation in my mind. "No, but I'm glad Bess didn't fall for Peter. He's mean."

"I agree. We'll never see the deposit money, but we could've lost a lot more. What's our next move?"

"I wish I knew."

Reid's phone vibrated, and I slid it to him. "It's a bit sticky from the coffee."

"No worries." He swiped the screen. "Hi, Mom."

He nodded. "Um, hmm. Yes, ma'am. If it gets physical, call the police. We're on the way."

"What's wrong?"

"Things are coming to a boil." Reid leapt to his feet and reached for my hand. "Mom is at the bookstore, and Sydney and Erica are in another argument. Come on. Maybe we can get there before they leave."

"It might be quicker to run than maneuver through traffic." I grabbed my purse but left the coffee.

Chapter Forty

I was out of breath by the time Reid and I entered FUN Bookshop. We'd power walked and even jogged the last couple of blocks.

Joy pointed to the sisters. "Erica is calmer than Sydney. I don't know what's happening, but we're losing customers." Her tone was flat, and normally her voice had a lilting quality.

Where was Madison? There wasn't time to ask, but I'd circle back. I patted my mother-in-law's arm. "Thanks, Joy."

"Of course, hon. I thought you'd want to know in case it's connected to the murder." She hugged Reid. "I'm glad you two are together. I better work on damage control."

I cut my eyes to Reid. "It doesn't seem so bad at the moment, but it must have been terrible. I've never seen your mom come undone."

"It's rare. We should approach them before anything else happens." He touched my shoulder.

Two women had their phones directed at the sisters. Had they recorded the conflict?

"I'll go first." I joined them in the section of healthy living books. "Hi, Erica. Sydney."

In unison, they whipped around and faced me with murderous looks.

"What do you want?" Erica hissed.

"You two are scaring the customers, especially the children. Maybe you should leave the store and continue your fight somewhere else."

Sydney said, "She started it."

Erica shook her finger at Sydney. "I'm tired of cleaning up your messes."

"Shh. Come on, ladies."

Sydney turned on me. "What gives you the right to insert yourself into our family?"

Madison appeared. "You need to leave. All three of you. I'm calling the police right now."

I turned to leave. The truth would sort itself out.

Sydney grabbed my hair.

I stumbled backward.

"Leave my family alone." She screeched.

Erica leapt toward her sister. "Let go of Kate."

Sydney pulled harder on my hair.

I fell toward Erica, and my glasses slipped down my nose.

Children screamed.

I clawed for Sydney's arms, hoping she'd release me and end the pain ripping through my head.

Reid appeared and clamped his hand on Sydney's arm. "Release my wife."

Her fingers eased their grip.

Blessed relief. The pain ceased, but I fell forward. My glasses hit the floor.

Reid's arm shot out and stopped my fall. "Oh, baby. That was close."

I fell against his strength and wrapped my left arm around his waist. "I thought I was going to faceplant for sure. My glasses fell off."

"You're safe." His arms circled my shoulders, and he kissed the top of my head.

Madison reached for my new glasses and handed them to me. "Here."

"Thanks." My heart raced. I held them in my hand and rested my head on Reid's shoulder.

Officer Collins and Officer Diaz entered the store, and a hush fell over the place. They led the sisters outside.

The customers who had remained in the store clapped.

Madison wrung her hands. "I'm so sorry, folks. This isn't how I usually do business. Um, how about for the next hour, we'll give you five dollars off your purchase?"

The people clapped again.

Joy said, "Madison, I'll go tell the officers what I witnessed. After I finish, you can go out."

"Thanks." She moved behind the checkout counter.

"Hey, Joy. Be sure to mention that some of the customers got the fight on their phone cameras."

"Sure thing."

I looked at Reid. "I never had sisters, and now I'm glad. Paul and Bobby never would've treated me like that."

"I know. It's probably a good thing Paul didn't show up. There may have been some—"

"Yeah. He'd probably read them the riot act." I rubbed my head. The pain was not as sharp, but it was there. "Do you mind if we go outside? I'd like to give my statement and head home."

"Good idea." We exited the store.

I put on my glasses along with the clip-ons to shield my eyes from the sun.

Paul had arrived and was in a conversation with Joy.

For the next hour, we waited, told our version of what happened, then waited some more. Finally, Paul joined us. "How's your head?"

"It's fine. Do you need us to stay?"

"No, but do you want to press charges?"

"It never occurred to me. I don't think Sydney intended to harm me. It was a heat-of-the-moment reaction."

My brother frowned. "We won't be able to hold her as long if you don't."

"I kinda feel sorry for her. She has a broken heart."

"Good grief. We have your statement, so you're good to go." He gave me a quick hug. "I've got some news, but we're not going public with it."

"What?" I held my breath.

He stepped closer. "Clint was poisoned with glyphosate. It's an ingredient in weed killers. Not enough to kill him, but enough to make him sick."

I nodded. "Thanks for sharing. See you later."

"Be careful."

Reid said, "Katie and I will stick together today, but we were together when this happened. So, I'm going to be hyper-alert."

"Sounds good." Paul shook Reid's hand before he joined his officers.

"Home?" Reid's expression was hopeful.

"First, we need to talk to Bess. Do you think she's really Peter's alibi?"

"I'm not sure, but I don't believe anything Peter says unless I have proof. Why don't you call Bess? We should warn her we're coming over."

"You're right."

We walked to the truck at a much slower pace than when we'd hurried to the bookstore. I dialed my best friend. "No answer. I'll text."

Reid opened the door to let out the hot air.

I texted Bess. **Peter Rodale says you're his alibi for the time of Clint's murder. Were you?**

Three dots appeared.

No.

I moved closer to the truck but stood in the shade, hoping to catch a breeze on the blazing hot August day. "Bess said she's not his alibi."

"Okay. Another lie from Peter, but this is directly related to Clint's murder. Not a fraud scheme."

My phone rang, and Bess's face flashed on the screen.

"Hey, Bess. Reid's with me." I tapped the speaker button.

"Listen, you know that I gave Peter a ride home after the event. But I thought Clint was murdered during the break. If that's the case, I was not with Peter."

"Good to know. Thanks for calling."

"You're welcome. I'm going back to my nap. See ya later."

"Bye."

Reid reached into the truck and turned on the air. "What next?"

"I'd like to talk to Diane one more time. I've got a hunch on the poisoning."

"Katie, Paul trusted you with the information."

I sighed. "Yeah. You're right. So, let's see how soon Paul can get together." I texted him, requesting that he meet us at Seaside Hideaway to discuss the murder.

Reid nodded. "That's good."

This murder case was more than a simple crime of passion to be solved.

There was also a poisoning and two conmen running around. Clint and Peter were fraudsters. If we solved the poisoning, and I had a strong hunch about that, we'd be free to focus on the murder.

"It's cool enough to get in." Reid waved and got my attention.

I slid into the passenger seat and buckled my seatbelt. "I still believe we should go to the resort. Hopefully, we'll hear from Paul soon."

"Seaside Hideaway, here we come. Are you going to tell me your big idea?"

"I believe Diane poisoned Cliff."

Chapter Forty-One

"Come again?" Reid stopped at a red light and looked at me. "Why in the world would Diane poison Clint? Don't we think she was in love with him?"

"Yes, but don't forget that Bess heard somebody say that the more Clint drank, the more he flirted. What if Diane only gave him enough of the weed killer to make him sick? If you have stomach problems, you probably cut back on alcohol. Less alcohol—"

Reid nodded. "Means less flirting."

The car behind us honked.

Reid stepped on the gas and drove through the intersection.

"Plus, there's the possibility he'd need Diane's help. Both physically and with the events. Maybe she thought it'd bring them closer together."

Reid rubbed his chin. "It makes sense in a twisted way."

"Right?" I patted his thigh.

"Okay. Let's say you're right. Diane is responsible for the poison. Who strangled Clint?"

"After today, I'd say Sydney is strong enough to strangle Clint. Plus, he was in a vulnerable state because of the poison."

"Glyphosate."

"Right. Sydney's attack today was a spur-of-the-moment reaction. And it got me thinking. We never decided if Clint's murder was planned or spontaneous."

"Meaning it could've been Sydney. What was her motive?"

Reid signaled his intention to turn onto Seaside Hideaway's property.

"Unrequited love? She and her husband are separated. Did she want to try to get back with Clint?"

"Maybe, but she never had a real relationship with Clint. To my knowledge, he didn't realize that Jennifer was his daughter."

"I hear you, but what was going through Sydney's mind? Did she believe Clint had deep, buried feelings for her after all these years?" He backed into the parking place.

"I don't know. Is her motive better than Peter's motive?" I stared at Peter's Jag parked in the shade. "Don't answer that. It doesn't matter who has the better motive. What counts is who committed the murder."

"True."

"Wait a second. Erica told me Sydney didn't arrive until Wednesday evening. If Erica's correct, Sydney can't be guilty."

My phone vibrated. "It's Bess calling."

"I'll keep the motor running while you talk."

I swiped the screen. "Hey, Bess. What's going on?"

"I can't sleep. Where are you?"

"We're at the resort. Can you join us?"

"Yes. In fact, I should be there in ten minutes."

"See you soon." I turned to Reid. "Bess is going to join us."

"She doesn't have her van."

"I bet she gets an Uber."

"Seems like a waste of money when we could've picked her up."

"True, but it probably makes her feel better to be independent."

"Okay. Well, we never really ate lunch, and I'm starved."

I laughed. "We should eat. It's already been a busy day, and we're having the cookout tonight. You know what? We should invite Bess and Dwayne."

"Playing matchmaker?" He turned off the truck.

"They're both interested, so it shouldn't take much effort on my part." A text dinged on my phone. "Paul's on his way. I need to warn Bess so she doesn't think we planned to ambush her."

I dialed her number, but it rolled to voicemail. "Hey, we're going to find a table at the outside restaurant. Paul just let us know that he's on his way here. I hope you still come. Bye."

Reid and I strolled into the lobby, past the water station, and out the door to the back patio.

He said, "I see available tables."

"Good. I'm surprised it's not more crowded." I walked to the hostess stand. "Hi, we'd like a table for four. Two more people will join us."

"Follow me." She shuffled through a stack of menus and stopped with four.

I trailed behind her, studying the few people sitting at tables.

"Here you go. Your waitress will be with you soon. And we have a special treat. Dwayne Gray is going to play a short set and feature a new song he's written since he arrived at the resort."

"Cool." Reid picked up a menu. "I'm going to try the club sandwich. What about you?"

"It didn't take you long to decide. The BLT with avocado sounds good." I looked toward the entrance. "Oh, Paul and Bess are both here."

They joined us, and before long, we had placed our orders.

Paul said, "What's on your mind?"

I leaned forward. "I can't quit thinking about the—"

Paul motioned for me to continue.

"Can I mention poison in front of Bess?"

He ran a hand over his face. "You can now."

Bess patted his arm. "Don't worry yourself about me. I want nothing to do with Clint's murder investigation. I also don't gossip."

I said, "Paul, what if the poison is not connected to the murder? Suppose somebody, say Diane, poisoned Clint only enough to make him sick. Then he might turn to her instead of focusing on other women. It'd bring the two of them closer, and maybe he'd fall in love with Diane."

He propped his arms on the table. "I like your theory. You went straight to suspecting Diane. Anything else?"

"It'd be nice if we could nail down a motive for the murder."

Paul gave me a half-smile. "I've got all kinds of motives. Evidence is what I need."

"I'm working on it." I had been the one to bring the poison from Diane's room to his attention. "If my hunch about Diane is correct, you can move her off your persons-of-interest list."

He grimaced. "Maybe. Maybe not."

The waitress brought our food, and the conversation shifted to other topics.

Bess finished her spinach salad. "That was very good."

Reid said, "Guys, we're cooking out tonight, and we'd like you to join us."

A woman bumped into my chair.

I looked up at Sydney.

She sneered at me before following the hostess to a nearby table.

Bess gripped my arm. "Who was that?"

"Sydney."

Paul said, "To be specific, Sydney Fraser Randal. She's Erica Fraser's sister and Jennifer's aunt."

I raised a hand to stop him. "Erica raised Jennifer, but Sydney is her birth mother. Jennifer only learned this a few days ago. Sydney arrived Wednesday night."

"That's not true. I saw her in a conversation with Clint on Friday, and it wasn't pleasant."

Paul pulled his notepad out of his shirt pocket and clicked his pen. "Friday? The day he was murdered?"

She nodded.

"Do you remember what time it was?"

"It was in the afternoon. I also saw her that night."

Paul scratched his jaw. "With Clint?"

"No. She was alone, and she wasn't dressed for a dating event. For some reason, I assumed she'd been trying to convince Clint to allow her to enter the event despite missing the entry deadline. Clint was always nice, and I imagined he'd allow her to join. I guess that's why it surprised me to see her wearing shorts and a tank top."

Paul pressed his fingertips above his eyebrows. "Another alibi bites the dust. Is there any chance you saw her with Clint that night? Not the afternoon, but the night."

"No, but I was focused on other things. Did Kate tell you that I wasn't with Peter at the time of the murder? I gave him a ride after speed dating. We were not together during the break."

"Thanks, Bess. I hear you loud and clear." He stood. "I need to get back to work, starting with Diane."

Reid said, "Don't forget the cookout at our place."

"I'll do my best to make it." He walked away.

Dwayne stepped onto the little stage, carrying his guitar. "Hi, folks. I wasn't sure if I'd be singing to myself or not. Good to see you." He strummed the strings and launched into a song.

I felt the tension ease from my shoulders, and I enjoyed listening to the melody.

Reid tapped my hand and pointed at the bar.

I turned and spotted Peter.

He faced us with a frown.

Chills broke out on my arms. If he saw us, he saw Bess. Most likely, he realized we'd asked her about his alibi.

Would he slink out of town? Or would he come after us?

Chapter Forty-Two

When Dwayne finished his short set, he joined us at our table. We all complimented him on the new song, and we chatted about his music.

The waitress brought a ginger ale and placed it beside Dwayne. "Your usual."

"Thanks." He returned his focus to us. "The staff here is terrific. What's going on with you guys and Peter?"

I said, "We caught him in a lie, and when he saw Bess, he figured it out."

"No wonder he disappeared. The man usually works the crowd in the bar."

I looked around the bar and restaurant. "You're right."

Reid stretched his legs. "We're having a cookout at our place this evening. We'd love for you to join us."

Sydney stood behind me on my right. I felt her before I heard her, and I angled my head to distinguish her words. "Am I invited too? It seems like you're inviting everyone else."

Reid stood and faced off with the woman. "You are not welcome in our home after the stunt you pulled earlier today."

My scalp tingled.

It took a lot to make Reid this mad.

Sydney said, "I'll see you around."

Dwayne said, "Mind letting me in on the secret?"

Reid sat in his chair. "She and Erica got into an argument today, and before it was over, Sydney was pulling Kate's hair and not letting go. Watch yourself around that woman. If she thinks you're our friend, she might go after you."

"I appreciate the heads up. As far as your cookout, I'd love to drop in. Can you give me the deets?"

Bess tapped the table. "Kate, you just got a text."

I swiped the screen and read the message from Paul. He had no luck with Diane and asked me to try.

When the conversation fizzled, I said, "Paul asked me to look for Diane."

Reid nodded. "Give me time to pay, and I'll go with you."

"Paul struck out. It might be better if I approach her alone. Woman to woman."

Reid rubbed his chin. "Okay, but holler if you need me. Better yet, will you stay in a public area where I can see you?"

"That shouldn't be a problem." I left them and walked around the pool area, looking for Diane. When there was no sign of her, I decided to try her room. It was beside Jennifer's. Not public, though. I texted Reid, sharing my intention, and then got on the elevator. When I reached her room, I knocked.

"Come in."

I opened the door. "Diane? It's Kate."

"I was expecting room service. What do you want?" She wore a white robe provided by the resort. Her short hair was damp, and she wore no makeup.

"We need to discuss your relationship with Clint."

"He was my boss. We could never be more than co-workers."

"I don't buy it." I walked to the glass door that led out to a balcony. The view of the ocean was breathtaking, but I was here for a confrontation. "You were in love with Clint. I think something caused you to snap a while back."

"Stop right there. I did not murder Clint. Did you forget I have witnesses?"

"I remember." I took a deep breath. "But I'm not accusing you of murdering him. Something else was going on."

"I don't have time for your theatrics, Kate." She roughly blotted her hair with a hand towel. "I was a good and loyal employee. Maybe I was too loyal."

There was a knock at the door. "Room service."

"I'll open it myself. It turns out you can't be too careful or the wrong person will walk in." Diane crossed the space and opened the door.

A familiar figure pushed a cart into the room. Officer Collins wore the hotel staff uniform. "Hello. Where would you like this?"

"Over by the balcony."

I remained quiet and looked around the room for weed killer, a syringe, or a dose cup. I needed a clue.

Drake said, "Would you like me to empty any trash on my way out? Or is there anything else you need at this time?"

Diane huffed. "I don't suppose you can make her disappear, can you?"

The undercover officer said, "I can call the police."

"No, that's fine." She ushered him to the door and handed him a tip. "Thank you."

"Yes, and thank you." He left us alone.

But I wasn't alone. No doubt Drake was waiting in the hallway with Reid, and they'd probably alerted Paul. I said, "It must have hurt to watch Clint flirt with women everywhere you went. He had short-term relationships, and then you'd go to the next city. What was your breaking point?"

"Your imagination is running rampant." She stalked into the bathroom. When she returned, she wore a white fishnet cover-up over a black swimsuit.

"You began to poison Clint. Why? To make him feeble? He couldn't drink alcohol in his weakened state and with his gastric issues. It's possible that he blamed it on nerves. Maybe it didn't happen every day. Did you only poison him on event days?"

"Why on earth would I do such a thing?" She stood by the food cart and picked up a white frothy drink with a chunk of pineapple on the rim. She took a sip. "Umm, the bartenders around this place are excellent."

"You were the one constant in Clint's life. You're the one he turned to when he was sick."

"It's a nice theory, but you can't prove anything."

"I became friends with Jennifer—"

"That child was like a groupie. She's been following us for the last few months, but Clint swears they're not in a romantic relationship. I think he felt sorry for her." She popped the pineapple chunk into her mouth.

"He asked her to follow you all so they could get to know each other better. Were you jealous of her?" I paused. "Wait a minute. That's it. You were used to Clint's other women. You had learned how to deal with his romantic affairs. But Jennifer was different. Did you figure out she was Clint's daughter?"

Diane choked. Deep coughs were followed by the sounds of her trying to take a breath. She dropped the drink on the carpet and coughed more.

I hurried over and patted her back firmly. "Diane, I'm going to Heimlich you."

I stood behind her and wrapped my arms around her waist. I cupped one hand over the other fist and pulled them inward and upward.

She spat out the chewed piece of pineapple but continued to cough.

I kept patting her back because the fruit wasn't blocking her air passage any longer.

At last, she moved away and sat on the edge of the bed. "I'm fine."

I reached for a box of tissues and passed them to Diane. Her nose had started running through the ordeal.

"Thanks." Her voice rasped.

I pulled a chair over from the desk and sat in front of her. "It must have been so hard to see Clint spend time with another woman. They probably shared meals and did things he usually did with you."

"It caught me completely by surprise, and you're right. She began to take my place. Clint had less and less time for me. After all the years I'd devoted to him. It wasn't fair." Her voice trailed off.

"I know. How did you come up with the idea to poison him?"

She reached for a new tissue and dabbed her eyes. "I was listening to a true crime podcast while traveling. I thought if I did it once, Jennifer would disappear. She was young and vibrant. It didn't make sense she'd want to hang around an older man, especially if he wasn't healthy."

"You gave him more than one dose of poison, though."

"Yes. Jennifer didn't leave, but Clint did turn to me. He didn't want her to see him in such bad shape. So, my plan worked."

CHAPTER FORTY-TWO

"She's his daughter. They took a test."

She inhaled. "I wondered about that possibility."

"Diane, did you murder Clint?

She wailed, "No. I loved him."

"The authorities need to know what you did so they can make the poisoning case different from their murder investigation. Are you ready to confess?"

"Yes. It's been exhausting trying to keep my secret, and I miss Clint so much." She fell back on the bed and wept.

I gave her a moment. Had Clint realized the depth of Diane's feelings for him? Did he not care? Or was he so self-absorbed that he never knew?

"Kate, do you think if I hadn't poisoned him that he might still be alive?" She hiccupped. "Would he have been strong enough to fight off his attacker?"

"Possibly." I paced at the end of the bed. Diane's actions had endangered Clint, but who was I to say they contributed to his murder?

"Why couldn't he have loved me?" She sobbed.

"I'm so sorry, Diane." My chest ached. She wasn't alone in falling for the wrong man. Clint had taken advantage of her feelings, even if he wasn't fully aware. Tom had done the same to Bess. Peter and Hank preyed on lonely women by showering them with attention right before they took their money. "The police want to talk to you."

Diane clutched a pillow to her chest.

I walked to the door and looked in the hallway. Reid, Paul, and Drake stood near the door. "I believe she'll talk now. Can Reid and I go home?"

"Sure, but write down your statement of what happened while it's fresh on your mind." Paul patted my shoulder.

Reid and I left the resort in a somber mood.

"Diane's broken." I scrounged around in his backseat and found a notebook. "Can I use this to write my report for Paul?"

"Of course. Use whatever you need. I'll drive around the marsh so you won't feel rushed." He turned the air on high, and soon the truck's cab cooled.

I wrote down everything I could remember. When I finished, I turned to

Reid. "After talking to Diane, I believe Clint probably could've fought off his attacker without poison in his system. Even if no charges are filed for her part in his death, she'll have to deal with the guilt."

"That's the truth. You should be proud of yourself for figuring out what Diane was doing, and you got a confession."

I shrugged. "You're giving me too much credit. It seemed like she wanted to talk."

"I'm still proud of you. So, what's your next step? Who do you think committed the murder?"

"Peter seems like the logical choice. His business isn't legit, Clint didn't trust him, and he goes by different names."

Reid said, "But?"

"My gut says it could be Sydney. Her emotions are over the top. I think it's possible she left her husband, hoping to reunite with Clint. When he wasn't interested, she realized how much she'd given up to be with him. She lost it and strangled him. It fits my heat-of-the-moment theory."

"She attacked you when she was angry. If Peter murdered Clint, it was probably a cold and calculated action." He hummed to a song on the radio.

"It's got to be Peter. He's a smooth operator. Can't you see him slipping into the quiet room, strangling Clint, and then rejoining the group? He asked Bess for a ride and acted like she was his alibi."

"I agree. Sydney's a loose cannon. It's hard to imagine her doing it quietly and escaping."

"Yes. So definitely, Peter." I relaxed in the seat. "I know we're hosting a cookout, but do you mind if I set up a meeting with Jennifer?"

"Not at all. We've done most of the prep work for supper. You've got plenty of time." He drove us home.

I texted Jennifer. This is Kate. Can you meet me?

Yes. When and where?

My place? We can go for a walk on the beach.

See you soon.

We hadn't known each other for long, but we'd been through some rough things. I wanted to see how she was doing.

Chapter Forty-Three

"I'm so glad you reached out. You'll never believe what happened." Jennifer's voice held a note of excitement.

We walked on the beach and headed toward the lighthouse. It was less crowded and seemed better for a private conversation. "What?"

"I was invited to the reading of Clint's will."

A breeze caused my hat to shift, and I tugged it down. "You sound surprised."

"I kinda was. You're the first person I'm telling my secret. I'm not ready to share the news with my mother and aunt." She picked up a shell and held it in her hand. "Clint and I felt such a connection. He had been a love 'em and leave 'em kind of man, and he began to wonder if I was his biological child. When he broached the subject with me, I wanted to do a backflip. We had lab work done, and the results proved that he was my dad. This was way before my family spilled the beans the other day. So, I wasn't shocked by the fact that Clint was my dad, but my mom and aunt changing places threw me for a loop. It never occurred to me to ask if he'd been with Erica or Sydney."

"It probably never crossed Clint's mind either. How long did you two know?"

"About three months."

"Jennifer, did you have any concerns about Clint's health?"

She stopped walking and looked at the ocean. "Not at first because he seemed to be in good shape. He acted much younger than sixty-eight. One day, he got sick. At first, I thought he might have an ulcer. He wasn't a heavy man, but he had a little belly. Then, he began to lose weight. I begged him to see a doctor, but he refused. Blamed it on stress."

That much lined up with Diane's story. "It's a shame that he got sick around the time you two met." Although if they hadn't found each other, Diane would not have resorted to poisoning Clint.

"I know, but at least we got to meet. I'm so glad I followed him around these past few months. He wasn't a perfect man, but in his own way, he loved me." Jennifer faced me. "That brings me to my big news. At the reading of his will, I discovered he left me some money and his Volvo SUV. He never thought my little car was safe. That seemed like such a normal fatherly reaction, and I loved him for caring." Her voice wobbled with emotion.

"Did Clint think he was dying?"

Jennifer's smile disappeared. "Yes, but I don't believe he expected to be murdered."

We resumed our walk. I said, "What about Kyle?"

"He seemed defeated. It was like he knew there were potential siblings, and now he had to admit it. He accused Dad of stealing money from him, but the attorney was only in charge of the will. Kyle did get the bulk of the estate, but that's not saying a lot. There was a financial problem with the business, and it affected Dad's personal money."

"Diane mentioned they'd taken a hit, but she seemed confident they were coming out of the red." I paused for a wave to flow over my feet. It was an adjustment wearing my glasses and dodging waves. It made me a little dizzy, but I was more scared of falling. "Kyle told me about plans to grow his business. The reason he was in town was to discuss money with Clint. Do you think you and Kyle will stay in touch?"

"I hope so. In fact, I asked if we could discuss my investing in his coffee shop. I don't need the money, and he does. The car is the most important thing to me. I see it as a symbol of my dad's love."

"That's nice of you to want to help Kyle. I hope you two can form a solid relationship. I have two brothers, and I love them dearly." We reached the path to the lighthouse. "We should probably head back. I'm having a small cookout tonight."

"That's nice." She turned and remained on the side of my good ear.

"Kyle is coming. If not for that, I'd invite you. I just don't want to blindside him in case he's processing the will."

"I completely understand."

A family of six rode toward us on their beach bikes.

"What are your plans, Jennifer?

"I'm going to sell my car and drive the Volvo back to Atlanta. It's time to reconnect with my friends. You know what?"

"What?"

"The people I thought were my friends haven't kept in touch. Is that part of life in a big city, or are they not real friends?"

"Only you can answer that. If you leave Atlanta, where will you go?"

"Fox Island, or maybe North Carolina. But I shouldn't make a hasty decision. Between Clint, Sydney, and Erica, my world has been rocked. They lied to me, and I know I need to forgive them, but it may take time to trust my family."

"Stop!" The father of the bike-riding family yelled at a young boy with a wonky helmet.

Two of the children were racing their bikes on the firm section of the beach, and the boy seemed to have lost control. He zigged toward us and then zagged away.

"Uh oh." I froze, uncertain which direction to go.

Jennifer jumped out of the way and fell.

The kid crashed into her. "Ow!"

The father was the first to reach them. "Son, are you okay?"

"Yes." His voice shook. "But I don't think the lady is."

I knelt by Jennifer. "Are you hurt?"

She groaned. "I twisted my ankle."

The rest of the family circled around us. The young boy and his parents apologized profusely. Jennifer assured them that she'd be okay, and they finally left us alone.

"I saw them the other day at the resort. They seem nice, but I'm sorry you got injured." Chills raced up my back. Was somebody watching us? I scanned the beach.

"Kate?" Jennifer gave me a questioning look.

"Sorry. That's where we get off." I pointed to a beach access. "Can you make it?"

"It's doable."

I helped her stand while keeping watch for trouble. "Put your arm around my shoulders, and we'll take it nice and slow."

"Are you sure you can support my weight?"

"Absolutely. This is something one friend does for another."

"Thanks, Kate." She put her arm around my shoulders.

We took our time hobbling to the house. The sound of the waves crashing soothed my nerves, and we made the journey in silence. We reached the street and picked up a bit of speed, but I kept my arm around her waist.

Ethan pulled his Land Rover into the driveway and parked. He hopped out and jogged to me. "Hey, you all. Um, Kyle is with me. I'm not sure—"

I raised my hand. "Shh. Don't worry. Jennifer is leaving."

Ethan looked from me to Jennifer and down to her ankle. "Are you hurt?"

"Just a little mishap on the beach, but it's throbbing."

Ethan moved to her other side. "It'll be easier with both of us helping. Then we need to elevate your leg and ice the ankle."

Kyle appeared. "Kate, I'll give you a break. What happened?" He traded positions with me.

Jennifer told the guys the story of getting run over by a kid on a bike. "I'm going to head back to the resort. I never intended to crash your cookout."

Kyle said, "Don't leave on my account. I'm cool if you want to stay, Jennifer. That is, if it's okay with Kate and Reid."

I nodded. "We'd love to have you, and there's plenty of food."

Ethan's posture relaxed. "Good, because Allie is coming too."

"Sounds like a party." It was time to quit thinking about murder suspects for a few hours. Later, I would find a way to dig deeper into Sydney's alibi and explore the timeline of her arrival.

Chapter Forty-Four

Our first party as a married couple had been a success. Bess left early with Dwayne to listen to him perform at Seaside Hideaway. Ethan, Allie, and Kyle had gone for a beach walk with plans to listen to bands perform at a country music festival at the lighthouse. Reid was giving Jennifer a ride to the resort because her car wouldn't start. Allie had wrapped Jennifer's ankle like she'd learned in her medical training. She also warned her to elevate and ice it.

Lady had enjoyed all the activity, and she was snoozing inside.

Reid had speakers outside and inside the house, and Harry Connick Jr. crooned. I sang along as I cleared the outdoor patio table. I filled a tray with serving dishes and leftover food.

Kyle and Jennifer had gotten along. Maybe she felt the same kind of bond with Kyle as she had with Clint. Too bad he wasn't alive to witness their connection.

If Clint hadn't been murdered, and if there'd been time for Sydney to tell him about their baby, would they have reconnected? Kyle's mother had been married to Clint, and their relationship hadn't lasted. If Clint had as many relationships as people claimed, would he have remembered Sydney?

He must've questioned Jennifer about her mother. How had she felt when he didn't remember Erica? There was no way he could've known her because he'd been with Sydney.

I swiped the silverware clean with a rag and placed each piece on the side of the tray. The pieces weren't clean, but they'd be easier to wash by removing unwanted scraps.

Unwanted.

Had Sydney felt unwanted when she discovered she was pregnant and alone? After Erica told her about Clint and Jennifer, had Sydney felt a ray of hope? Had she rushed to Fox Island with dreams of telling Clint the truth and hopes he'd declare his love for her?

Sydney arrived at the resort on Friday. Not Wednesday, according to Bess. I picked up the tray. Sydney would have had time to tell Clint.

I needed to talk to Paul.

Crack.

I stopped moving and looked toward the trees surrounding my property. Was it an animal? Maybe my imagination.

The sound of footsteps sent my heart into overdrive. "Hello?"

"Hi, Kate. It looks like I missed the party." Sydney stood in my small yard. "Oh, yeah. Your husband said that I was not invited."

I shrugged. "You know how protective men can be."

"He thought you were in danger from me?" She laughed.

My hands shook so hard, the dishes rattled. "You did pull my hair."

"It happens on school playgrounds all the time. Nothing dangerous." She took a step toward me. "Maybe he thinks you can't handle yourself in dangerous situations."

Her tone creeped me out. "Sydney, I'm sorry, but the party is over. We're cleaning up."

"You're the only one I see." She spread out her arms. "It seems like you're all alone."

"That's not true, and I don't have time to chat." I hurried to the deck stairs. I'd barely taken two steps up when fingers wrapped around my ankle, causing me to trip.

Sydney had stuck her hand between the stairs. Surely, I could outmaneuver her. I struggled to free my leg without losing my balance. I threw the tray into the yard, and the dishes clanked against each other.

With all my might, I grasped the handrail and kicked.

Her grip loosened. Then, a sharp pain pierced my calf.

"Help!" I screamed. Pain ripped up my leg, leaving me lightheaded.

The hand released its grip.

I tried to run up the steps but staggered and fell. My elbow hit first, followed by my ribs, and last was my hip. *Ow.* I turned so my bottom was on the step, and I could face my attacker. I elbowed my way backward up the steps, using my good leg on the torturous journey and dragging my injured leg.

Something rustled, but I couldn't decipher the direction of the sound.

Where was Sydney?

Footsteps pounded on the ground below me.

I reached for my cell phone, but it wasn't in my pocket. Oh, no. It was inside connecting music to the sound system.

Sydney appeared at the bottom of the stairs. "Finally. Revenge will be sweet."

Both of my legs trembled, but I forced myself up another step. "Sydney, Reid will be back any second."

"Hate to burst your bubble, but there's been an accident on Ocean Boulevard. It's going to be a while."

I'd have to save myself, but it wouldn't be easy with my hurt leg. Warm blood trickled down my calf. What had she used to stab me? "Did you murder Clint?"

"Yes. Don't pretend you didn't figure that out." She advanced on me, holding a big, jagged knife. Well, that explained why my leg hurt so much.

"I thought it was Peter for a while. In fact, there were quite a few people on my list of suspects, including Erica. You weren't on my radar. Even after we met, it didn't occur to me to add you to my list. Why did you do it?"

"It's the story as old as time. I loved Clint. He didn't love me." She looked at the sky where stars twinkled.

I continued my backward climb until I reached the top. If I could manage to get across the deck, I'd need to get through the doorway, into the house, and lock her out. But how? My survival would take using my brain more than my body. "I'm sorry to hear that, but it's been close to thirty years since you two were in a relationship. You got married and had a family."

"True love never dies." She stomped up the stairs and loomed over me with the terrifying knife.

So much for brainpower. With my eyes on her, I scrambled away until my back hit the deck railing. I gripped the spindles and pulled myself to a standing position. Warm blood flowed down my leg, but at least I stood taller than Sydney. Too bad, she still had a weapon. "I understand how long true love lasts. Did you come to Fox Island intending to rekindle the feelings you two once had?"

"Yes. Erica told me Jennifer met Clint. She insisted we find a way to end their relationship since he was her biological father. I agreed that they couldn't have an affair."

My pulse thundered in my neck. "Were you jealous of her? She was your biological daughter."

Sydney's eyes widened. "No."

"Oh, my goodness, you were jealous. Didn't you understand? He was her dad."

"You don't realize this, because you didn't know Clint like I did. He didn't have much capacity to care about anybody other than himself. He had a son, an ex-wife, and Diane. There wasn't much more room in his heart, and I couldn't risk he'd choose to squeeze in Jennifer over me."

My brain raced. "If Erica had only told you she'd seen Clint, would you have still come here to declare your love for him?"

She blinked her eyes a few times. "Maybe."

"You should tell the police that it was an accident. You never intended to hurt Clint."

"That's for sure, but they probably won't believe me. You're the only one who suspects what I did."

"That's not true. I'm surprised you were strong enough to strangle Clint with his saxophone strap."

"Obviously, I was strong enough." She lifted her chin.

"What did you do with the strap?"

"It's in my suitcase. It still smells like his cologne, and I couldn't bring myself to throw it away."

She could strangle the man she loved, but couldn't part with the murder weapon. She was one sick woman. "Did you know Diane had been poisoning Clint, hoping he'd get sick and turn to her?"

Her mouth dropped open. "He did seem weak."

If I kept her distracted, it'd buy me time. "Sydney, you did a good job of acting like you only arrived on Wednesday. You could've been an actress."

She smiled, and I wanted to wipe that smile clean off her face. She was proud of what she'd accomplished.

"Wait a minute. You planned to kill him all along."

"No!" She screeched and then looked around. "You're wrong."

I kept a firm grip on the railing. "Why else would you have arrived in secret last Friday?"

Sirens sounded in the distance.

She laughed. "Don't get excited. All of law enforcement will be focused on the accident."

"Where is this accident?" I hoped Reid was safe.

"It's on the main road near the resort. Traffic is blocked in both directions."

Reid was taking Jennifer to the resort. Was he hurt? No, I didn't have the luxury of imagining he was part of the accident. First, I needed to focus on surviving. "How'd you get here?"

"It's low tide, and I rode an electric bike on the beach."

"It appears you've thought of everything." I kept my tone light and hoped frustration wouldn't seep out.

"You might call that my superpower."

"Aren't you worried about your daughter? Reid gave her a ride to the resort."

"A twisted ankle won't kill her."

Whoa. That was harsh. "You knew about her injury?"

"Of course. I've been watching you for hours. I saw you help her get off the beach. You don't seem to be able to stop yourself from interfering in my life. That ends tonight."

My survival was still up to me, and I needed a weapon because it was doubtful I could get inside before Sydney stabbed me again with her knife.

Decorative outdoor lights hung around the deck, giving me better visibility.

There was our all-weather sectional with pillows, a round coffee table, a comfy wicker chair, tall planters, a watering can, and a stainless steel lantern on the ground beside the chair. It was either the lantern or the antique watering can next to one of the plants. I'd take whichever one was easier to reach.

Sydney walked around the deck. "It's too bad there's no hot tub. It'd be easy to drown you, and stage it to look like an accident. Nobody would suspect a thing."

I wasn't positive if killing Clint had been premeditated or not. However, there was no doubt she planned to eliminate me tonight.

Chapter Forty-Five

When Sydney's back was to me, I lunged for the lantern and grabbed the handle, ignoring the pain in my leg.

Sydney turned and thrust the knife at me.

I spun away.

The knife grazed my left arm.

With my right arm, I swung the lantern, aiming for Sydney's shoulder.

Sydney dodged away and bumped into the deck railing.

Missed.

She lunged at me with the knife.

Lady barked. It was a low protective warning. She couldn't protect me from inside the house, but she couldn't get hurt either.

I advanced and swung again. This time, I connected with her head.

My arm shook from the contact.

Sydney slumped to the side and then slithered to the deck floor. She dropped the knife. It hit the deck with a thunk.

Oh, man. Had I killed her?

Her hand twitched.

I kicked the weapon away and hurried to the door as fast as my injured leg allowed. I managed to open the door while keeping Lady in the house. "Good girl."

I turned the lock.

Lady barked.

I looked around the room.

My phone was on the kitchen counter where I'd left it so any of my guests could change the songs playing via Bluetooth over the speakers. I turned off the music and called Reid first.

"Hey, babe, sorry it's taking so long." He sounded happy.

"I know about the crash. Sydney is here, and she attacked me. I think she's unconscious on the back deck. Can you and Paul find a way to get here before she comes to?"

"Are you safe?"

"I think so."

"Are you hurt?"

"A little. She needs to be arrested before she harms anybody else."

"Okay. I'll work on getting to Paul, but you should warn Ethan and the others in case they return."

"Good idea." I double-checked that the doors were locked. After I confirmed they were, I sank onto a kitchen stool and texted Ethan. It's not safe to come home now. Sydney attacked me, and I'm waiting for Paul to come and arrest her.

I'd barely sent the message before my phone rang.

"Mom, what in the world? Are you okay?"

Lady walked in circles around me.

"Kinda. I don't want to worry you, but I'd be mad if you kept a secret from me. She stabbed my calf, and it's bleeding. Reid is trying to find Paul."

"Yeah, we heard there's a major accident. Allie is kinda freaking out. Probably PTSD."

"Ethan, take care of Allie. I'm safe." As long as Sydney didn't make a second run at me, I'd remain okay.

"Love you, Mom."

"I love you too."

My phone vibrated with a text from Reid. **On the way with Paul. Sit tight.**

I sent a heart emoji and waited.

I looked for a weapon to protect myself, although Lady probably wouldn't let Sydney harm me.

The cast-iron skillet.

Perfect.

I grabbed it and watched the back door.

Lady panted at my side.

The things people did in the name of love. Sydney had rationalized her actions, including a plan to do away with me. I shivered and thanked God for sparing my life.

The sound of voices from the back of the house eased the tension that had built from the moment Sydney grabbed my leg.

There was a knock on the back door.

My heart went into overdrive.

"Kate, it's me."

My husband. Oh, my lovely husband was here.

I hobbled to the door and opened it wide.

Lady barked and rubbed her head on Reid's leg.

Reid swept me into his arms and hugged me. "I can't believe I left you alone again."

"Shh. We had no idea Sydney would come after me, and if there hadn't been an accident, you probably would've been home." I stayed in his embrace for a few extra moments. "We need to tell Ethan it's safe to come back."

Reid looked past me. "Too late. He's about to walk in."

"Oh, I locked the door." I started to walk across the great room.

Reid reached for my hand. "Katie, you're bleeding. Bad. You need to sit down.

Between feeling lightheaded and not wanting to risk getting blood on the floor, I sat in a chair at the table.

Reid opened the door for the others. "Your mom is okay. Allie, would you mind looking at her leg? I wouldn't ask except most emergency personnel are at a crash on Ocean Boulevard."

"I'd be happy to look at it. Do you have a first aid kit?"

Ethan gave me a quick hug. "I'll find it."

Reid said, "I'm going to check on Paul."

Kyle walked into my kitchen. "Would anyone like me to fix a pot of decaf?"

"Yes, please." I smiled at Clint's son. "It's very nice of you to offer."

Allie sat in another chair and lifted my leg. "Oh, Kate. You are so lucky she didn't hit your popliteal artery."

"I don't know what that is, but I feel blessed. Definitely blessed." I took a deep breath. "But I feel bad for knocking Sydney out."

Allie looked at me. "Don't. When somebody comes at you with a knife, it's a life-or-death situation. You did the right thing, and I'm proud of you."

I shivered. "Thanks."

She cleaned the wound on my arm and wrapped a bandage around it. "This is temporary. You need stitches in both places. When was your last tetanus shot?"

"It's up to date."

"Good. That's one less concern." She met my gaze. "You may have cracked your ribs. Can you take a full breath?"

I inhaled. There was a tinge of pain, but I managed to breathe. "It's okay."

"Keep an eye on it. You'll probably have bruises." She pointed to my elbow. "There's already one right here. From what you told me, your hip is probably bruised. If the pain lasts or gets worse, you'll need X-rays."

"Yes, ma'am. You know what? If I can physically fight off a woman intent on killing me, I must not be too old."

"Kate, you're not old. If you think getting glasses makes you old, you're wrong. I've worn contacts most of my life. It's a thing, but it's not age-related."

I smiled and didn't argue. I was getting older, but I wasn't old. Until then, I'd handle each phase of life with grace like Reid's mother. No more whining about life's changes. I was grateful to be alive.

The next few hours were a blur. Allie was able to get her medical kit by taking back roads to her home. She stitched my wound and insisted I drink plenty of fluids. If it hadn't been for the wreck, I would've been in the emergency room.

Sydney was arrested and hauled off to the police station.

The others hung out at our home until the streets were cleared after the accident. At that point, I fell into a deep and restful sleep.

Chapter Forty-Six

Reid and I skipped church and enjoyed a leisurely breakfast of blueberry pancakes with fruit and yogurt parfaits. The peaceful morning was what I'd needed after confronting Diane about poisoning Clint and surviving Sydney's attack on me the night before.

In the early afternoon, Reid's parents arrived.

Joy gave me a strong hug and sat next to me on the couch. "Oh, hon. I cannot believe the fixes you get yourself into. Thank the good Lord that you are safe."

Bess burst through the front door. "Kate."

"I'm over here."

The room grew quiet as my best friend beelined it to me. "Girl, you gave me quite a fright."

"I'm sorry, but we're safe now."

Dwayne entered the house behind Bess and shut the door. "Kate, it's good to see you alive and well."

"Thanks, Dwayne."

Paul was the next to arrive, but he remained standing. "I thought it best to get you up to speed before rumors start flying. Sydney and Diane are both in jail. Peter Rodale, also known as Pete Ellison among other aliases, and Hank Ingram are both being questioned by the GBI. Don't be surprised if agents show up before the end of the day. Each of the men has a history of committing financial crimes. They'll be in prison before you know it. Kate, I might need to check the notes on your investigation related to them."

Reid said, "I'll get them." He headed upstairs.

Soon after Reid turned the journal over to Paul, other people began trickling into my home, including Ethan and Allie. The biggest surprise was when Pastor Tom Cross appeared.

Tom said, "I heard about the attack and wanted to see how you're doing."

I'd been in quite a few conversations about forgiveness the past few days, and after the close call with Sydney, it seemed fitting to forgive Tom for how he'd treated Bess. I smiled at the preacher. "Thanks for coming."

Lady greeted each guest with a happy bark and a tail wag.

When there was a lull in the conversation, Joy walked to the middle of the room. "I believe most of you know Sam and I are engaged to be married. All of you are on the invitation list, and we're wondering if anyone would mind us getting married right now? We have the license."

My family and friends clapped and whooped. To know Joy was to love her, and it was obvious how much this group cared about Reid's mother.

I looked at my husband, sitting beside me.

His posture was relaxed, and he smiled.

Sam joined Joy. "Reid, what do you say?"

Reid said, "We'd be honored for you to get married in our home."

"Thanks, hon." Joy beamed. "And what a happy coincidence our pastor just happens to be here."

I reached over and held Reid's hand in mine.

A flurry of activity hit our house, and I sat back with my leg propped up and enjoyed watching my favorite people jump into action to prepare for a wedding. Lady planted herself beside me.

I called our favorite barbecue restaurant and asked if they could cater this event. They hemmed and hawed until I told them it was for Joy's wedding. They immediately agreed to take care of everything.

When I called the bakery, they couldn't make a wedding cake, but they had a seven-tier cake stand of cannoli they'd prepared for a wedding. The bride had backed out, and the bakery offered it to me at an excellent price.

Reid walked over to me. "I've worked up a sweat moving furniture. Are you okay?"

"Yes. I've ordered food, and instead of a wedding cake, we'll have cannoli."

His eyes widened. "Really? That's my mom's favorite dessert."

"Great. I know this is super casual, but I'd like to wear something a tad nicer."

He held his hand out for me and helped me stand.

"Thanks."

Dwayne breezed past us, carrying a guitar.

Allie ran over to me. "Can you believe Dwayne's going to provide the music? I can't help fangirling over him. Do you want me to help you get ready? Bess is taking care of Joy in your bedroom, and Reid, your dad left to take a shower. Oh, what a day!"

I laughed at her enthusiasm. "Okay, it sounds like I can't go into my room."

Reid said, "I'll grab clothes for you and you can get ready in the guest room."

Tom let loose a loud whistle. "Twenty minutes, people."

Squeals and laughter followed his announcement.

I had doubts about his timeline, but in twenty minutes, we circled around the happy couple and Tom.

Last night, I had feared for my life. Today, Joy and Sam were taking vows to live a new life as husband and wife.

I pushed away any thoughts of sadness related to Clint, Sydney, Diane, Peter, and Hank.

It wouldn't surprise me if part of Joy's motivation to get married here and now was to erase the fear of Sydney's attack. As usual, my mother-in-law enjoyed spreading joy. Nobody fit her name better than she did.

Sam kissed the bride, and there were more cheers and hugs.

Dwayne played *You're Still the One* for Joy and Sam's first dance. When we switched to romantic music over the speakers, Dwayne asked Bess to dance.

I glanced at Tom. He was talking to Ethan, but he appeared to stop mid-sentence when he noticed Bess on the dance floor.

To my surprise, I felt sorry for Tom.

Reid walked from the kitchen to where I stood leaning against the wall. "As much as I'd like to dance with you, it's time for you to sit. In fact, I think you're supposed to have ice on your leg."

"The caterer should arrive at any moment. I'd like to sit on a barstool and oversee them."

"I don't think that'll be a problem."

The rest of the day flew by in a happy haze. Joy and Sam were the first to leave, but soon the others cleared out.

At last, Reid and I sat on the deck with Lady and enjoyed the star-filled sky and peace.

I propped my injured leg on a chair. "What a day."

He laughed. "There was no time to obsess over murder and mayhem."

"Oh, baby, that's for sure. I even wondered if that's why your mom decided on an impromptu wedding. You know, to distract us from morbid thoughts. Not that she didn't want to marry your dad."

"She couldn't wait to marry him, and I understand. When you've dreamed of the one person you want to spend the rest of your life with, and it seems possible, you don't want to wait any longer than necessary."

"True. It's amazing how things worked out so well for the four of us."

Reid rubbed Lady's head. "Are you thinking compared to Sydney?"

"Kinda. She never got over her love for Clint."

"You might say obsession."

I didn't like that word, but it fit the situation. "Yeah. We were able to live normal lives. If you hadn't cared about me when I returned to Fox Island, I might have been disappointed, correction, I would have been disappointed, but your rejection wouldn't have turned me into a murderer."

"Good to know."

"It's hard to believe the lengths Sydney and Erica went to in order to hide the truth from Jennifer."

"Yeah, she was collateral damage."

"I'm glad she met her dad and they bonded. A little time together is better than nothing." I closed my eyes.

Reid said, "It's also a shame about Peter and Hank taking advantage of lonely women to make money off them."

"True. Honestly, I know a lot of successful relationships began with online dating and events like Clint provided. If we hadn't gotten back together, I doubt I'd be brave enough to participate."

"There's one thing we haven't really discussed." He reached for my hand. "I don't know what I would've done if Sydney had succeeded in killing you."

"You have no idea how many if-onlys ran through my mind. I did my best to fight her off, but I'm glad you got here when you did."

"Me, too. Katie, I have too much respect to ask you not to take on any more murder cases."

"But?"

"We need to set up some guidelines when you dive into another murder case. I don't want you to put your life on the line again."

"It's doubtful I'll investigate another murder, but if I do, you can join me every step of the way."

"That's all I wanted to hear. I love you, Katie."

"I love you, too." I didn't believe there'd be a reason to solve another murder, but I'd learned a lot the past week while solving Clint's murder. In the right circumstances, I might try again.

About the Author

Jackie Layton is the author of cozy mysteries with Spunky Southern Sleuths. Her stories are set in Texas, Georgia, and South Carolina. She lives on the coast of South Carolina, where she enjoys walks on the beach and golf cart rides around the marsh. Reading, gardening, and traveling are some of her favorite hobbies. Jackie always keeps a notebook handy to write down ideas for future stories. Many of her ideas come from people watching and watching *Dateline* and *American Greed*.

AUTHOR WEBSITE:
  https://jackielaytoncozyauthor.com/

SOCIAL MEDIA HANDLES:
  Tiktok: https://bit.ly/49zn8xM
  https://www.facebook.com/JackieLaytonAuthor
  https://www.pinterest.com/jackielaytonauthor/
  https://twitter.com/joyfuljel

https://www.instagram.com/jackielaytonauthor.com
Jackie Layton (@jackielaytonauthor) on Threads
Goodreads: https://bit.ly/49XTfpf
Bookbub: https://bit.ly/37RqGQ8
Bluesky: @jackiecozyauthor.bsky.social

Also by Jackie Layton

A Low Country Dog Walker Mystery Series:
Bite the Dust
Dog-Gone Dead
Bag of Bones
Caught and Collared
A Killer Unleashed
A Suspicious Breed

A Texas Flower Farmer Cozy Mystery Series:
Weeding Out Lies
Clover Covered Corpse

An Organized Crime Cozy Mystery Series:
Clutter Free
The Con